THE PAGEANT OF SUMMER

The Pageant of Summer

and other essays by

Richard Jefferies

Selected and Introduced by
Andrew Rossabi

QUARTET BOOKS
LONDON MELBOURNE NEW YORK

Published by Quartet Books Limited 1979
A member of the Namara Group
27 Goodge Street, London W1P 1FD

Frontispiece reproduced by courtesy of The Mansell Collection

ISBN 0 7043 3289 2

Printed in Great Britain by litho at The Anchor Press Ltd
and bound by Wm Brendon & Son Ltd
both of Tiptree, Essex

FOR JAN

'Love is a continual dawn'

Contents

Introduction

Richard Jefferies was born at Coate Farm near Swindon in North Wiltshire on 6 November 1848. His father, James Luckett Jefferies, was a small farmer, an original and somewhat eccentric man, Tory yet radical in his views, good with his hands, and with a passion for planting trees, but unsuccessful in the practical business of running a farm. 'There are no wolves,' Jefferies wrote, 'like those debt sends against a house.' The farm went to the bad, and Jefferies' father ended his days as a gardener in Bath. Of his mother less is known. She was a town-bred woman not happy living in the country, and used to scold and berate her husband with a fine flow of invective for his lack of business acumen. She came from the Gydes, a London family of book-binders, printers and engravers, and Jefferies may have inherited his artistic sense and love of books from her. There is an amusing and often heart-rending picture of the domestic altercations between the parents in Jefferies' last and finest novel *Amaryllis at the Fair*, memorable for the portrait of his father, called Iden in the novel. Iden is a philosopher like Bacon, a man of orchard and garden who gathers his ideas from the fields, 'a great mind working under the most unhappy conditions'.

Yet in the beginning these were halcyon years at Coate Farm. The greenfinches sang sweetly in the hawthorns, the nightingale sang in the musical April nights, the June rose came – is there anything lovelier than the June rose? – and the stars shone above the trees in the orchard and fields. Jefferies knew them all, and faithfully observed their risings and settings, charting thereby the progress of the seasons, and so drawing a line between the distant star and the opening of the flower at his feet. The massive shoulder of Orion heaving up through the trees in the frosty nights of winter, his faithful servant Sirius 'flared like a night-sun', Aldebaran the Bull's red eye, lucent Vega, the purest star in the heavens, shining at the zenith of the pale blue dome during the nights of midsummer, the cluster of the Pleiades, Capella, noble Arcturus, Cassiopeia, the Lady in the Chair, Antares the harvest star, the wide cross of Cygnus the Swan, and the Great Bear swinging round the Pole Star 'like a stone in a sling'. Jefferies lived out to the stars, as he lived and felt out to the far-away hills and the sea beyond. 'Just as when you walk in a wood the trees are all about you, on a plane with you, so he felt the constellations and the sun on a plane with him, and that he was moving among them as the earth rolled on, like them, with them, in the stream of space . . . It was living, not thinking. He lived it, never thinking, as the finches live their sunny life in the happy days of June. There was magic in everything, blades of grass and stars, the sun and the stones upon the ground.'

Bevis, the book by which Jefferies is best remembered today, tells the story of a country boyhood and the growth of a poetic mind, as if *Huckleberry Finn* had been fertilized by the early chapters of *The Prelude*. Bevis and his friend Mark make a raft from old packing-cases, sail on the nearby reservoir, maroon themselves on the island of New Formosa, organize a mock battle of Pharsalia, learn to shoot and swim, set snares, hunt and fish. There was another side to the young Jefferies, when he became dreamy and still as a tree, and was lost in the larger consciousness of the heavens. He had a passion for alchemical signs and strange alphabets. 'The Arabic took his fancy as the most mysterious – the sweeping curves, the quivering lines, the blots where the reed pen thickened, there was no knowing what such writing might mean.'

Here was the seed of his later enchantment with the secret language of nature which, like the oracle at Delphi, neither revealed nor concealed her meaning but conveyed it by a sign. The spot-markings on birds' eggs, the sides of a trout, the leaves of the early purple orchis, 'the histories, the stories, the library of knowledge contained in those signs! . . . The language in which they are written has no alphabet and cannot be reduced to order. It can only be understood by the heart and spirit. Look down into this foxglove bell and you will know that: look long and lovingly at this blue butterfly's underwing, and a feeling will rise to your consciousness.'

Yet matters were not well at home. The farm was not prospering. Jefferies had by now left school, where he had been a good but in no way brilliant pupil, and spent most of his time lounging about with a gun. He did no farm work worth speaking of, and gained a reputation as an idler that embittered him against the residents of Coate until his dying day. He hissed his contempt of them in one of his very last essays, *My Old Village*, dictated to his wife when he was too ill to hold a pen. But tongues were wagging: 'That young Jefferies is not the sort of fellow you want hanging about in your covers.' Even his father turned against him and pointed with disgust to 'our Dick poking about in them hedges'. Jefferies' eye, while still that of the sportsman, was in the throes of changing into something else. 'With his finger on the trigger, he hesitated, dropped the barrel, and watched the beautiful bird.' The watching so often stayed the shot that at last it grew to be a habit. However, the shooting instinct died hard. He shot kingfisher and heron, and the redwing as it sang 'to make quite sure of it'. 'I dare say,' comments Edward Thomas in his biography of the author, 'the eagle which he once saw going over was lucky in being at a great height.'

In 1866, at the age of seventeen, Jefferies began work as a reporter on the *North Wilts Herald*, a new Conservative newspaper based at Swindon. This was also the year, he tells us in his autobiography, in which he began to resort to the hills about Coate in search of a higher inspiration, when his heart had grown dusty 'parched for want of the rain of deep feeling'. Liddington Hill was a favourite haven. 'Moving up the sweet short turf, at every step my heart seemed to obtain a wider horizon of feeling; with every inhalation of rich pure air, a deeper desire. The very light of the sun was whiter and more brilliant here. By the time I had reached the summit I had entirely forgotten the petty circumstances and annoyances of existence. I felt myself, myself.' He was also becoming something of an antiquary and local historian, interested in the Roman and early British remains in the vicinity, the old coins, arrowheads, tumuli, barrows, camps and stone circles. But though full of plans, in a ferment of ideas, he was living (and walking) largely on his nerves. In 1867 he was very ill. To walk thirty yards now cost him as much effort as thirty miles previously. 'My head when I got to bed seemed to swell big enough to fill the room.' The following year he was better, and wrote in a letter to Mrs Harrild, an aunt in whom he confided to a degree he never could with his mother at home: 'But when I come to think it over calmly, I can almost thank God that I have been ill, for it has made me pause and think, and I can now see what a wrong and even wicked course I have been secretly pursuing for a long time, and I hope I shall take warning. God has been very merciful to me this time.' The mood of contrition was foreign to Jefferies' proud and wilful nature, and did not last long. Jefferies disliked the Church, abhorred the cold stone walls which shut out the sunlight. Light was life to Jefferies, and the church he regarded as a tomb, grey, dark and cold. 'I am a pagan and think the heart and soul above crowns.' However, he wrote a poignant piece about the local parish church at Chisledon and although he was an irregular church-goer (who used to enter by the Devil's Door), there is no mistaking the vein of piety and intense religious aspiration that runs through his writing, particularly the later essays like *Nature and Eternity*, close to the devout spirit of his contemporary, the poet and priest Gerard Manley Hopkins. But the Christian faith with its tenets and taboos could not contain Jefferies' mystical longing, his sensuous delight in the beauties of creation, his animism which saw life in everything from the sun and stars to the dew-laden grass, flashing emerald and ruby. *The Odyssey* was one of Jefferies' favourite books and he was closer to the world of the Greeks, who saw magic in every flower, heard the voice of a god singing in the music of a brook, the whisper of immortality in the wind through the grass on the hill. ' "There never was a yesterday," whispered the wind presently, "and there never will be tomorrow. It is all one long today." ' (*Wood Magic*) The sky he describes above the front of the British Museum might be the chaste calm blue over the pediments of a Greek temple, the pigeons resting in the cornices doves of peace. 'They have not laboured in mental searching as we have; they have not wasted their time looking among empty straw for the grain that is not there. They have been in the sunlight. Since the days of ancient Greece the doves have remained in the sunshine; we who have laboured have found nothing. In the sunshine, by the shady verge of woods, by the sweet waters where the wild dove sips, there alone will thought be found.' Air and light, the light of the sun, these were Jefferies' gods and it is for the sky that he reserves some of his greatest effects. The clear blue of the sky, his heart could never have enough of it, 'for there is no saint like the sky, sunlight shining from its face'. Where the heart leads, the body must follow, 'toiling up the long and shadowless hill in the burning sunshine' towards 'the rich blue of the unattainable flower of the sky'. Blue chalkhill flowers adorn his pages, speedwell, sheepsbit, harebell, meadow's cranesbill, cornflower, with the force of a symbol akin to the Blue Flower beloved of the German romantics. Blue butterflies flutter over the thyme. He compared the dome of the sky to a bell-flower 'drooping down over us and the magical essence of it filling all the room of the earth'. Such were the visions that came to Jefferies alone with the wind on the hills, drinking inspiration from the downland air. 'The air in the valleys immediately beneath them is pure and pleasant; but the least climb, even a hundred feet, puts you on a plane with the atmosphere itself, uninterrupted by so much as the tree-tops. It is air without admixture. If it comes from the south, the waves refine it; if inland, the wheat and flowers and grass distil it.'

Jefferies often dreamed of the sea on the hills round Coate. 'The eye sometimes expects it,' says Edward Thomas. 'There is something oceanic in their magnitude, their ease, their solitude – above all, in their liquid forms, that combine apparent mobility with placidity, and in the vast playground which they provide for the shadows of the clouds. They are never abrupt, but, flowing on and on, make a type of infinity.' Jefferies planned to visit Cornwall and hear the legends of King Arthur. The north coast of the county, the magnificent stretch of cliffs between Tintagel and Bude – that wild and tragic coast as Hardy called it, the region of dream and mystery, like the twilight of a night-vision – would have been much to his taste, but Jefferies did not go.

In November 1872 he wrote three letters to *The Times* on the subject of the life and working conditions of the Wiltshire labourer. The Agricultural Labourers' Union had recently been formed and farm-workers throughout the country were striking for more pay. Jefferies' letters argued the case of the yeoman farmer class to which he belonged. According to him wages were good, cottages infinitely better than they were, and the only thing wrong with the labourer was his ingratitude. He also praised the clergy for their work with allotments. The letters sparked off a lively correspondence. Support came from Lord Shaftesbury, while 'The Son of a Wiltshire Labourer' was quick to reply to Jefferies' accusations. His letters, let it be said, were grossly misleading and leagues from the author's later views on the labour question. In fact, the Wiltshire labourer was among the worst paid in the country, lived in the most squalid conditions, and worked long hours for a pittance with the spectre of the workhouse beckoning him towards old age. The truth was told by Jefferies himself in other pieces he wrote during this period (later collected under the title *The Toilers of the Field*; the book includes the original trio of letters to *The Times*) and in papers like *One of the New Voters*, the story of a reaper who works fourteen hours in the August sun, fuelled by a gallon of harvest beer, 'probably the vilest drink in the world', where Jefferies exposes the reality behind the scenes of rural life, the life of degradation and hardship behind the veil of arcadian idyll lurking in the imagination of most town-dwellers. 'The wheat is beautiful, but human life is labour.' But whatever his motives in writing the letters, whether he wrote them out of loyalty to his father, whom he had watched work hard all his life for little reward – 'What a fallacy it is that hard work is the making of money; I could show you plenty of men who have worked the whole of their lives as hard as ever could possibly be, and who are still as far off independence as when they began. In fact, that is the rule: the winning of independence is rarely the result of work, else nine out of ten would be well-to-do.' (*Amaryllis at the Fair*) – or to please the conservative readership of *The Times*, their success convinced Jefferies that there was room for a 'natural' writer on rural and agricultural topics. He became a regular contributor to various periodicals of the day, notably

Fraser's Magazine, the *Standard* and the *Pall Mall Gazette*. In 1877 he moved to Surbiton, to be closer to London and his contacts in the publishing world. He was now married (to Miss Jessie Baden, the daughter of a neighbouring farmer at Coate) and the father of a small boy, and had to support himself and his family by what he could earn with his pen.

London at once repelled and fascinated him. He felt the magnetism of the great city, 'stronger than that of the rock which drew the nails from Sinbad's ship', and had a countryman's boyish enthusiasm for the spectacle of the hurrying crowds, the shops, the traffic, the vast concentration of life pulsing and throbbing in the streets. 'The inevitable end of every footpath round about London is London. All paths go thither.' Yet he hated the smoke and grit, the noise and rude jostling, and missed the absolute peace which he had known in the country. Even in the suburbs, twelve miles from London, the proximity of the immense city made its influence felt, inducing a nerve-restlessness. He visited Kew – 'a great green book, whose broad pages are illuminated with flowers, lies open at the feet of Londoners' – and found there some of the stillness his heart craved. He visited the East End and the docks; the sight of the yards and masts of the great clippers rising above the roof-tops stirred his sense of romance and adventure, his migratory instinct, his dream of travel to unknown parts. 'Masts are always dreamy to look at,' he wrote, 'they speak a romance of the sea, of unknown lands, of distant forests aglow with tropical colours and abounding with strange forms of life. In the hearts of most of us there is always a desire for something beyond experience. Hardly any of us but have thought, Some day I will go on a long voyage; but the years go by, and still we have not sailed.' He watched the sunset from Westminster Bridge, 'big with presage, gloom, tragedy', and looked up one evening as he was walking down the Haymarket and found calm from the stars shining overhead. He deplored the introduction of foreign shrubs and trees to suburban gardens, the rhododendrons, laurels, acacias, cedars and planes which were beginning to oust the native species. 'If as many beeches as cedar deodaras and laurels and planes were planted in these grounds, in due course of time the tap of the woodpecker would be heard – a sound truly worth ten thousand laurels.' (*Trees About Town*) But he was astonished and delighted by the richness and variety of bird-life to be found. Never had he heard so many nightingales; there were herons, magpies, jays, sparrow-hawks, kestrels and woodpeckers, and his favourite greenfinches, 'which never cease love-making in the elms'. He was the first to point out that the wild flowers sought sanctuary from the scythe on the sides of railway cuttings and embankments, where they flourished undisturbed, 'bordering the line like a continuous garden'. He kept up his habit of walking, although the scenery of north Surrey could not compare with his native downs. One day, as he was standing under some aspens by the Hogsmill brook, his keen eye discerned the form of a trout by the tail of the arch of a bridge. Henceforward the spot became the site of an almost daily pilgrimage. He watched the trout for weeks, months, years, four seasons in all, and took great pains to prevent anyone discovering its presence, for anglers often came to fish the pool the other side of the bridge. If anyone approached, he would strike the parapet with his stick so as to alarm the fish and send it back under the arch, or take off his hat and wave it, as one heated. It was his trout, he alone knew about it, and the spot under the aspens seemed bleaker, colder, and less hospitable when it was gone.

Meanwhile his writing career was prospering. Drawing on his rich store of country knowledge, he poured it forth in papers and articles which were later collected and published in book form: *The Gamekeeper at Home, The Amateur Poacher, Wild Life in a Southern County* and *Round About a Great Estate*, which the critic Q. D. Leavis has called 'one of the most delightful books in the language'. These books and others, like

Hodge and His Masters, were received with applause by both critics and public and established Jefferies as the foremost country writer of his day. 'There had been unlettered men who knew much that he knew; there had been greater naturalists and more experienced sportsmen, more magical painters – at least, in verse – of country things; but no one English writer before had had such a wide knowledge of labourers, farmers, gamekeepers, poachers, of the fields, and woods, and waters . . . When he wrote these books – *The Amateur Poacher* and its companions – he had no rival, nor have they since been equalled in purity, abundance, and rusticity.' (Edward Thomas)

In 1883 there followed a new collection of essays, *Nature near London*, in which Jefferies forsook his memories of Wiltshire and Coate Farm to describe the wild life to be found in the vicinity of the metropolis. It was a theme he never tired of repeating, that it was not necessary to go far into the country to find nature, it was all about us, had we but eyes to see. 'I have noticed that people are never so astonished as when some fact of natural history is unexpectedly pointed out to them, where it must have been for a long time under their very eyes. There are people who have never seen a humble bee drill a hole in the nectary of a snap-dragon, and yet have whole gardens full of flowers.' Londoners may heed his words today, when kestrels and herons are common, warblers ubiquitous in spring and summer, yellowhammers and flycatchers occasionally to be sighted, alongside the tribe of finches, nuthatches, treecreepers, wagtails, woodpeckers, magpies and jays resident in the woods and parks, where there is often an abundance of wild flowers growing in unsuspected places, wood sorrel, speedwell, comfrey, dog violets, storksbill and many others, down to the tiny flowers of the humble pellitory growing in the crevices in the mortar of old walls. Everyone will make their own discoveries, but it was Jefferies who first opened the eyes of Londoners to the wealth of wild life about them.

A new strain of observation is apparent in these essays, a more delicate eye that is not afraid to linger on fleeting effects of form and colour, a vision more subtle, loving, tragic and intense. In 1881 Jefferies had again been ill. The disease was tubercular in origin. In 1882 he underwent the series of operations then used to abate the disease. The pain was excruciating, 'like lightning through the brain'. At the end of the year he moved to West Brighton to convalesce. The sight of the waters, the sea air, the breeze, the smells of fish, tar, brine and seaweed, the maritime light, clear and pure as that of the Mediterranean, the boats drawn up on the shingle, the whine of rigging, pennants snapping, the holiday crowds and the rich finery of their dress, all were champagne to his senses, already sharpened by illness. Once again he was within reach of the downs. 'There is always hope in the hills;' he wrote, 'hope dwells there, somewhere mayhap in the breeze, in the sward or the pale cups of the harebells'; and elsewhere he speaks of 'the hills that purify those who walk on them'. He was soon familiar with the South Downs, visiting Ditchling Beacon, Firle, Rottingdean, Chanctonbury Ring, the Duke of Norfolk's estate near Arundel, Plumpton, Wolstanbury; and in *The Breeze on Beachy Head* he conjoins all the elements which gave him his highest inspiration, sea, sky and down. 'There is an infinite possibility about the sea,' he wrote. 'It may do what it is not recorded to have done. It is not to be ordered, it may overleap the bounds human observation has fixed for it. It has a potency unfathomable. There is still something in it not quite grasped and understood – something still to be discovered – a mystery.' He was intoxicated and his body revivified. 'This is the land of health,' he wrote. The sea, the air on the hills, the sunshine were 'nature's medicines, that by degrees strengthen not only the body, but the unquiet mind'. It was by the sea, in 1880, while staying at Pevensey, that he had made the seminal notes for a book about which, as he wrote to his publisher, Mr C. J. Longman, he had been meditating for seventeen years. It was called *The Story of My Heart: My Autobiography*.

The Story of My Heart is the cornerstone of Jefferies' work. In it he poured out his soul in a passion. The mystical communion with nature, with him since childhood and gaining in intensity under the stress of illness, was, in Edward Thomas' words, 'as a deep pool that slowly fills with an element so clear that it is unnoticed until it overflows'. The overflowing of the dream into real life, as another poet, Gérard de Nerval, observed, is a symptom of madness and *The Story of My Heart* hovers just this side of sanity, restrained by the lucidity of its thought and the purity of its aspiration. In the analysis he wrote for his publisher Jefferies stated that it might have been called an Autobiography of a Soul, or of Thought. The book's general aim was 'to free thought from every trammel, with the view of its entering upon another and larger series of ideas than those which have occupied the brain of man so many centuries'. The author believed that there was 'a whole world of ideas outside and beyond those which now exercise us'. His was not an autobiography of the petty events of life. 'The soul is the man, and not the clothes he wears.'

The Story of My Heart is unique in English literature, a mixture of prayer, confession and sermon that moves beyond the concept of deity towards something higher, a world of pure ideality. The nearest parallel is Nietzsche, or Walt Whitman, whom Jefferies read and admired. When considering Jefferies' work as a whole, it is wise not to place too much weight on *The Story of My Heart*. After the magnificent opening chapter in which Jefferies describes his long climb up the hill in the burning sunshine, and the prayer he makes at the summit, lying on the grass of an ancient entrenchment with a view out 'over a broad plain, beautiful with wheat, and inclosed by a perfect amphitheatre of green hills', the intensity is unrelieved. Many readers, even D. H. Lawrence, have felt uneasy before the trembling, palpitating nakedness of this heart laid bare. Perhaps it will always be one of those books which remain a little above the head of the ordinary reader, a work of solitude stretched to breaking-point, where it is necessary to have experienced the revelation in order to understand it. The current of glassy isolation, the occasional false note like that issued by the blackbird in the midst of his fluting, as of a cork being wrenched clear of a bottle, the voice sometimes verging on paranoia, these grate on the nerves and do not make for comfortable reading. It is best read aloud, to give some human body to it, as in the radio broadcast of extracts read by Paul Scofield. Passages of exquisitely rarefied feeling mingle with cries of primitive bloodlust. There are hints that Jefferies himself was not satisfied; his notebooks mention a plan for a longer version. Yet whatever its faults, *The Story of My Heart* gives us the whole man. Jefferies' life would have been incomplete without it, this puzzling, marvellous book in which he let his psyche fly unrestrained, like the lark ascending.

> His rash-fresh re-winded new-skeinèd score
> In crisps of curl off wild winch whirl, and pour
> And pelt music, till none's to spill nor spend.
> (*The Sea and the Skylark*, G. M. Hopkins)

These eagle heights were balanced by the abyss into which his illness plunged him. His sense of colour became more acute. In 1884 he took his folding-stool out into a cabbage-field near Eltham, where he was now living, to look at the poppies 'because every spot of colour is a sort of food to me'. In 1885 his health finally broke down. The wasting of his body was extreme, he was starved and half-delirious. In September he moved to Crowborough, and thence in 1886 to Sea View House, Sea Lane, Goring-on-Sea, where he died on 14 August 1887, aged thirty-eight. His body was buried in Broadwater Cemetery, near Worthing. There is a bust in Salisbury Cathedral, and a memorial tablet on Liddington Hill.

The last years of his life, passed in the shadow of his illness, produced Jefferies' finest work. Not only the mature essays like *Wild Flowers, The Pageant of Summer, Meadow Thoughts, Nature and Books, Hours of Spring* and *Walks in the Wheat-fields*, many of which were published posthumously by his widow, but the novels *The Dewy Morn, After London* and *Amaryllis at the Fair*, and two children's stories which have become classics, the well-known *Bevis* and the equally bewitching *Wood Magic*, a fable about a battle between the birds. Jefferies' novels deserve to be better known. The best parts are better and more mature than the best parts of most of Hardy's, in the opinion of Q. D. Leavis, and besides *Amaryllis* at least three other novels by Jefferies merit republication, *Greene Ferne Farm, The Dewy Morn*, and *After London*. Fittingly, one of the last pieces Jefferies wrote was a preface for the Scott Library edition of White's *Natural History of Selborne*.

Despite Q. D. Leavis' eulogy in *Scrutiny* forty years ago, and the magnificent biography by Edward Thomas, a true labour of love, the fact remains that Jefferies has never occupied an easy position in English literature. In recent years he has been allowed to sink into virtual oblivion. The bulk of his work, including the very best, is out of print. He has been neglected even by the naturalists, to whom the stream of impassioned feeling that flows through Jefferies' writing is alien, although Jefferies wrote several pieces of close scientific observation as in *Mind under Water*, on the intelligence of fishes, and in *The Hovering of the Kestrel* and *Birds Climbing the Air*, both about the mechanics of flight, a subject of absorbing interest to Jefferies, whose notebooks are full of pencil sketches and diagrams to illustrate his thesis, that aerial navigation was possible and would soon become commonplace. The paper on *The Hovering of the Kestrel* may usefully be read in conjunction with Hopkins' noble poem *The Windhover* (an old country name for the kestrel) and should help to clear up several of the difficulties in interpretation of the poem which have troubled commentators. The modern naturalist is nothing if not cold, clinical and precise. He believes emotion is best served by its suppression. Poor Jefferies! It is as true now as it was in his own day. 'So many, many books and such a very, very little bit of nature in them!' Perhaps the finest tribute that can be paid to his qualities as a writer is that he gives the lie to one of his own aphorisms – 'the sheaf you may take home with you, but the wind that was among it stays without'. The following passage exhibits his qualities of imagination combined with sustained powers of observation. It comes at the beginning of *Wild Life in a Southern County*. Jefferies is describing the sky over the hills during a drought.

> The breeze comes up from the south, bringing with it white clouds sailing at an immense height, with openings between like azure lakes or aerial Mediterraneans landlocked by banks of vapour.
>
> These, if you watch them from the rampart, slowly dissolve; fragments break away from the mass as the edges of the polar glaciers slip off the ice cliff into the sea, only these are noiseless. The fragment detached grows visibly thinner and more translucent, its margin stretching out in an uneven fringe: the process is almost exactly like the unravelling of a spotless garment, the threads wavering and twisting as they are carried along by the current, diminishing till they fade and are lost in the ocean of blue. This breaking of the clouds is commonly seen in weather that promises to be fine. From the brow here you may note a solitary cloud just risen above the horizon; it floats slowly toward us; presently it divides into several parts; these, again, fall away in jagged, irregular pieces like flecks of foam. By the time it has reached the zenith these flecks have lengthened out, and shortly afterwards the cloud has entirely melted and is gone. The delicate hue,

> the contrast of the fleecy white with the deepest azure, the ever-changing form, the light shining through the gauzy texture, the gentle dreamy motion, lend these clouds an exquisite beauty.

Passages like this (they are the rule rather than the exception) make one wonder how Jefferies could ever have been neglected. Yet there are signs that the tide is turning and that Jefferies may at last be coming into his own. Copies of his books are scarce and eagerly sought, and second-hand booksellers will tell you that there is an inexhaustible demand for them, they go out as fast as they come in. There are signs, too, that people are returning to a taste for plain English prose. None wrote it better than Jefferies. There is no straining after effect, no ornate imagery, no long or complicated periods, no making of fine phrases. Edward Thomas, as usual, puts it best: 'The words call no attention to themselves. There is not an uncommon word, nor a word in an uncommon sense, all through Jefferies' books. There are styles which are noticeable for their very lucidity and naturalness; Jefferies' is not noticeable even to this extent. There are styles more majestic, more persuasive, more bewildering, but none which so rapidly convinces the reader of its source in the heart of one of the sincerest of men.'

Of the man himself we know little: he spent as much as he could of his life outdoors, alone on the hills and in the fields. He was shy and solitary by nature and did not make friends easily, but was happy with his family, a man of simple tastes and regular habits. Thomas tells us that 'he was not a talker, but talked with ease and vigour on his own subjects, most eagerly on the labour question'. He commanded silence in the house, as his father had done, and was a tall, thin, bearded, slightly stooping figure, with a soft mouth and prominent blue eyes, an expression 'silent and aware'.

Perhaps in conclusion I may say a word about the joy and pleasure Jefferies' writings have given me over the years. I have made this selection in the hope of introducing his genius to a new audience, the younger generation of readers who, likely as not, are unfamiliar with his name. This is a pity, for in their ideals and aspirations they have much in common with Jefferies. The basis of the selection has been simple: to present as varied and comprehensive a picture of a many-sided genius as possible within the limitations of space. I have concentrated on the essays, but there is also an extract from the novel *Amaryllis at the Fair*.

The most fitting epitaph to a forward-looking writer who was so wholeheartedly on the side of life, truth and beauty is to be found in his own words. They concern the education of children, and come from *The Dewy Morn*.

> All of you with little children and who have no need to count expense, or even if you had such need, take them somehow into the country among green grass and yellow wheat – among trees – by hills and streams, if you wish their highest education, that of the heart and the soul, to be completed.
>
> Therein shall they find a Secret, a knowledge not to be written, not to be found in books. They shall know the sun and the wind, the running water, and the breast of the broad earth. Under the green spray, among the hazel boughs where the nightingale sings, they shall find a Secret, a feeling, a sense that fills the heart with an emotion never to be forgotten. They will forget their books – they will never forget the grassy fields.
>
> If you wish your children to think deep things – to know the holiest emotions – take them to the woods and hills, and give them the freedom of the meadows.

Sources

'Wild Flowers', 'Red Roofs of London', 'The Modern Thames', 'Sunny Brighton' and 'One of the New Voters' are taken from the collection of papers entitled *The Open Air* (Chatto & Windus, 1885); 'The Pageant of Summer' and 'The Pigeons at the British Museum' from *The Life of the Fields* (Chatto & Windus, 1884); 'Nature and Books', 'Hours of Spring' and 'My Old Village' from *Field and Hedgerow* (Longmans, Green & Co., 1889); 'Village Churches' and 'Nature and Eternity' from *The Hills and the Vale* (Duckworth & Co., 1909). 'A London Trout' is a condensed version of two papers 'A Brook' and 'A London Trout' which, together with 'Trees About Town' and 'The Breeze on Beachy Head', are taken from *Nature near London* (Chatto & Windus, 1883). The extract from *Amaryllis at the Fair* (Sampson Low & Co., 1886) consists of the first five chapters of the novel, the last book published by Jefferies during his lifetime.

1 Wild Flowers

A fir-tree is not a flower, and yet it is associated in my mind with primroses. There was a narrow lane leading into a wood, where I used to go almost every day in the early months of the year, and at one corner it was overlooked by three spruce firs. The rugged lane there began to ascend the hill, and I paused a moment to look back. Immediately the high fir-trees guided the eye upwards, and from their tops to the deep azure of the March sky over, but a step from the tree to the heavens. So it has ever been to me, by day or by night, summer or winter, beneath trees the heart feels nearer to that depth of life the far sky means. The rest of spirit found only in beauty, ideal and pure, comes there because the distance seems within touch of thought. To the heaven thought can reach lifted by the strong arms of the oak, carried up by the ascent of the flame-shaped fir. Round the spruce top the blue was deepened, concentrated by the fixed point; the memory of that spot, as it were, of the sky is still fresh – I can see it distinctly – still beautiful and full of meaning. It is painted in bright colour in my mind, colour thrice laid, and indelible; as one passes a shrine and bows the head to the Madonna, so I recall the picture and stoop in spirit to the aspiration it yet arouses. For there is no saint like the sky, sunlight shining from its face.

The fir-tree flowered thus before the primroses – the first of all to give me a bloom, beyond reach but visible, while even the hawthorn buds hesitated to open. Primroses were late there, a high district and thin soil; you could read of them as found elsewhere in January; they rarely came much before March, and but sparingly then. On the warm red sand (red, at least, to look at, but green by geological courtesy, I think) of Sussex, round about Hurst of the Pierrepoints, primroses are seen soon after the year has turned. In the lanes about that curious old mansion, with its windows reaching from floor to roof, that stands at the base of Wolstanbury Hill, they grow early, and ferns linger in sheltered overhung banks. The South Down range, like a great wall, shuts off the sea, and has a different climate on either hand; south by the sea – hard, harsh, flowerless, almost grassless, bitter, and cold; on the north side, just over the hill – warm, soft, with primroses and fern, willows budding and birds already busy. It is a double England there, two countries side by side.

On a summer's day Wolstanbury Hill is an island in sunshine; you may lie on the grassy rampart, high up in the most delicate air – Grecian air, pellucid – alone, among the butterflies and humming bees at the thyme, alone and isolated; endless masses of hills on three sides, endless weald or valley on the fourth; all warmly lit with sunshine, deep under liquid sunshine like the sands under the liquid sea, no harshness of man-made sound to break the insulation amid nature, on an island in a far Pacific of sunshine. Some people would hesitate to walk down the staircase cut in the turf to the beech trees beneath; the woods look so small beneath, so far down and steep, and no handrail. Many go to the Dyke, but none to Wolstanbury Hill. To come over the range reminds one of what travellers say of coming over the Alps into Italy; from harsh sea-slopes, made dry with salt as they sow salt on razed cities that naught may grow, to warm plains rich in all things, and with great hills as pictures hung on a wall to gaze at. Where there are beech trees the land is always beautiful; beech trees at the foot of this hill, beech trees at Arundel in that lovely park which the Duke of Norfolk, to his glory, leaves open to all the world, and where the anenomes flourish in unusual size and number; beech trees in Marlborough Forest; beech trees at the summit to which the lane leads that was spoken of just now. Beech and beautiful scenery go together.

But the primroses by that lane did not appear till late; they covered the banks under the thousand thousand ash-poles, foxes slipped along there frequently, whose friends in scarlet coats could not endure the pale flowers, for they might chink their spurs homewards. In one meadow near primroses were thicker than the grass, with gorse interspersed, and the rabbits that came out fed among flowers. The primroses last on to the celandines and cowslips, through the time of the bluebells, past the violets – one dies but passes on the life to another, one sets light to the next, till the ruddy oaks and singing cuckoos call up the tall mowing-grass to fringe summer.

Before I had any conscious thought it was a delight to me to find wild flowers, just to see them. It was a pleasure to gather them and to take them home; a pleasure to show them to others – to keep them as long as they would live, to decorate the room with them, to arrange them carelessly with grasses, green sprays, tree-bloom – large branches of chestnut snapped off, and set by a picture perhaps. Without conscious thought of seasons and the advancing hours to light on the white wild violet, the meadow orchis, the blue veronica, the blue meadow cranesbill; feeling the warmth and delight of the increasing sun-rays, but not recognizing whence or why it was joy. All the world is young to a boy, and thought has not entered into it; even the old men with grey hair do not seem old; different but not aged, the idea of age has not been mastered. A boy has to frown and study, and then does not grasp what long years mean. The various hues of the petals pleased without any knowledge of colour-contrasts, no note even of colour except that it was bright, and the mind was made happy without consideration of those ideals and hopes afterwards associated with the azure sky above the fir tree. A fresh footpath, a fresh flower, a fresh delight. The reeds, the grasses, the rushes – unknown and new things at every step – something always to find; no barren spot anywhere, or sameness. Every day the grass painted anew, and its green seen for the first time; not the old green, but a novel hue and spectacle, like the first view of the sea.

If we had never before looked upon the earth, but suddenly came to it man or woman grown, set down in the midst of a summer mead, would it not seem to us a radiant vision? The hues, the shapes, the song and life of birds, above all the sunlight, the breath of heaven, resting on it; the mind would be filled with its glory, unable to grasp it, hardly believing that such things could be mere matter and no more. Like a dream of some spirit-land it would appear, scarce fit to be touched lest it should fall to pieces, too beautiful to be long watched lest it should fade away. So it seemed to me as a boy, sweet and new like this each morning; and even now, after the years that have passed, and the lines they have worn in the forehead, the summer mead shines as bright and fresh as when my foot first touched the grass. It has another meaning now; the sunshine and the flowers speak differently, for a heart that has once known sorrow reads behind the page, and sees sadness in joy. But the freshness is still there, the dew washes the colours before dawn. Unconscious happiness in finding wild flowers – unconscious and unquestioning, and therefore unbounded.

I used to stand by the mower and follow the scythe sweeping down thousands of the broad-flowered daisies, the knotted knapweeds, the blue scabious, the yellow rattles, sweeping so close and true that nothing escaped; and yet, although I had seen so many hundreds of each, although I had lifted armfuls day after day, still they were fresh. They never lost their newness, and even now each time I gather a wild flower it feels a new thing. The greenfinches came to the fallen swathe so near to us they seemed to have no fear; but I remember the yellowhammers most, whose colour, like that of the wild flowers and the sky, has never faded from my memory. The greenfinches sank into the fallen swathe, the loose grass gave under their weight and let them bathe in flowers.

One yellowhammer sat on a branch of ash the livelong morning, still singing in the sun; his bright head, his clean bright yellow, gaudy as Spain, was drawn like a brush charged heavily with colour across the retina, painting it deeply, for there on the eye's memory it endures, though that was boyhood and this is manhood, still unchanged. The field – Stewart's Mash – the very tree, young ash timber, the branch projecting over the sward, I could make a map of them. Sometimes I think sun-painted colours are brighter to me than to many, and more strongly affect the nerves of the eye. Straw going by the road on a dusky winter's day seems so pleasantly golden, the sheaves lying aslant at the top, and these bundles of yellow tubes thrown up against the dark ivy on the opposite wall. Tiles, red burned, or orange coated, the sea sometimes cleanly definite, the shadows of trees in a thin wood where there is room for shadows to form and fall; some such shadows are sharper than light, and have a faint blue tint. Not only in summer but in cold winter, and not only romantic things but plain matter-of-fact things, as a waggon freshly painted red beside the wright's shop, stand out as if wet with colour and delicately pencilled at the edges. It must be out of doors; nothing indoors looks like this.

Pictures are very dull and gloomy to it, and very contrasted colours like those the French use are necessary to fix the attention. Their dashes of pink and scarlet bring the faint shadow of the sun into the room. As for our painters, their works are hung behind a curtain, and we have to peer patiently through the dusk of evening to see what they mean. Out-of-door colours do not need to be gaudy – a mere dull stake of wood thrust in the ground often stands out sharper than the pink flashes of the French studio; a faggot; the outline of a leaf; low tints without reflecting power strike the eye as a bell the ear. To me they are intensely clear, and the clearer the greater the pleasure. It is often too great, for it takes me away from solid pursuits merely to receive the impression, as water is still to reflect the trees. To me it is very painful when illness blots the definition of outdoor things, so wearisome not to see them rightly, and more oppressive than actual pain. I feel as if I was struggling to wake up with dim, half-opened lids and heavy mind. This one yellowhammer still sits on the ash branch in Stewart's Mash over the sward, singing in the sun, his feathers freshly wet with colour, the same sun-song, and will sing to me so long as the heart shall beat.

The first conscious thought about wild flowers was to find out their names – the first conscious pleasure – and then I began to see so many that I had not previously noticed. Once you wish to identify them there is nothing escapes, down to the little white chickweed of the path and the moss of the wall. I put my hand on the bridge across the brook to lean over and look down into the water. Are there any fish? The bricks of the pier are covered with green, like a wall-painting to the surface of the stream, mosses along the lines of the mortar, and among the moss little plants – what are these? In the dry sunlit lane I look up to the top of the great wall about some domain, where the green figs look over upright on their stalks; there are dry plants on the coping – what are these? Some growing thus, high in the air, on stone, and in the chinks of the tower, suspended in dry air and sunshine; some low down under the arch of the bridge over the brook, out of sight utterly, unless you stoop by the brink of the water and project yourself forward to examine under.

The kingfisher sees them as he shoots through the barrel of the culvert. There the sun direct never shines upon them, but the sunlight thrown up by the ripples runs all day in bright bars along the vault of the arch, playing on them. The stream arranges the sand in the shallow in bars, minute fixed undulations; the stream arranges the sunshine in successive flashes, undulating as if the sun, drowsy in the heat, were idly closing and unclosing his eyelids for sleep. Plants everywhere, hiding behind every tree, under the leaves, in the shady places, beside the dry furrows of the field; they are only just behind something, hidden openly. The instant you look for them they multiply a hundred-fold; if you sit on the beach and begin to count the pebbles by you, their number instantly increases to infinity by virtue of that conscious act.

The bird's-foot lotus was the first. The boy must have seen it, must have trodden on it in the bare woodland pastures, certainly run about on it, with wet naked feet from the bathing; but the boy was not conscious of it. This was the first, when the desire came to identify and to know, fixing upon it by means of a pale and feeble picture. In the largest pasture there were different soils and climates; it was so large it seemed a little country of itself then – the more so because the ground rose and fell, making a ridge to divide the view and enlarge by uncertainty. The high sandy soil on the ridge where the rabbits had their warren; the rocky soil of the quarry; the long grass by the elms where the rooks built, under whose nests there were vast unpalatable mushrooms – the true mushrooms with salmon gills grew nearer the warren; the slope towards the nut-tree hedge and spring. Several climates in one field: the wintry ridge over which leaves were always driving in all four seasons of the year; the level sunny plain and fallen cromlech still tall enough for a gnomon and to cast its shadow in the treeless drought; the moist, warm, grassy depression; the lotus-grown slope, warm and dry.

If you have been living in one house in the country for some time, and then go on a visit to another, though hardly half a mile distant, you will find a change in the air, the feeling, and tone of the place. It is close by, but it is not the same. To discover these minute differences, which make one locality healthy and home happy, and the next adjoining unhealthy, the Chinese have invented the science of Feng-shui, spying about with cabalistic mystery, casting the horoscope of an acre. There is something in all superstitions; they are often the foundation of science. Superstition having made the discovery, science composes a lecture on the reason why, and claims the credit. Bird's-foot lotus means a fortunate spot, dry, warm – so far as soil is concerned. If you were going to live out of doors, you might safely build your kibitka where you found it. Wandering with the pictured flower-book, just purchased, over the windy ridge where last year's skeleton leaves, blown out from the alder copse below, came on with grasshopper motion – lifted and laid down by the wind, lifted and laid down – I sat on the sward of the sheltered slope, and instantly recognized the orange-red claws of the flower beside me. That was the first; and this very morning, I dread to consider how many years afterwards, I found a plant on a wall which I do not know. I shall have to trace out its genealogy and emblazon its shield. So many years and still only at the beginning – the beginning, too, of the beginning – for as yet I have not thought of the garden or conservatory flowers (which are wild flowers somewhere), or of the tropics, or the prairies.

The great stone of the fallen cromlech, crouching down afar off in the plain behind me, cast its shadow in the sunny morn as it had done, so many summers, for centuries – for thousands of years: worn white by the endless sunbeams – the ceaseless flood of light – the sunbeams of centuries, the impalpable beams polishing and grinding like rushing water: silent, yet witnessing of the Past; shadowing the Present on the dial of the field: a mere dull stone; but what is it the mind will not employ to express to itself its own thoughts?

There was a hollow near in which hundreds of skeleton leaves had settled, a stage on their journey from the alder copse, so thick as to cover the thin grass, and at the side of the hollow a wasp's nest had been torn out by a badger. On the soft and spreading sand thrown out from his burrow the print of his foot looked as large as an elephant might make. The wild animals of our fields are so small that the badger's foot seemed foreign in its size, calling up the thought of the great game of distant forests. He was a bold badger to make his burrow there in the open warren, unprotected by park walls or preserve laws, where every one might see who chose. I never saw him by daylight: that they do get about in daytime is, however, certain, for one was shot in Surrey recently by sportsmen; they say he weighed forty pounds.

In the mind all things are written in pictures – there is no alphabetical combination of letters and words; all things are pictures and symbols. The bird's-foot lotus is the picture to me of sunshine and summer, and of that summer in the heart which is known only in youth, and then not alone. No words could write that feeling: the bird's-foot lotus writes it.

When the efforts to photograph began, the difficulty was to fix the scene thrown by the lens upon the plate. There the view appeared perfect to the least of details, worked out by the sun, and made as complete in miniature as that he shone upon in nature. But it faded like the shadows as the summer sun declines. Have you watched them in the fields among the flowers? – the deep strong mark of the noonday shadow of a tree such as the pen makes drawn heavily on the paper; gradually it loses its darkness and becomes paler and thinner at the edges as it lengthens and spreads, till shadow and grass mingle together. Image after image faded from the plates, no more to be fixed than the reflection in water of the trees by the shore. Memory, like the sun, paints to me bright pictures of the golden summer time of lotus; I can see them, but how shall I fix them for you? By no process can that be accomplished. It is like a story that cannot be told because he who knows it is tongue-tied and dumb. Motions of hands, wavings and gestures, rudely convey the framework, but the finish is not there.

To-day, and day after day, fresh pictures are coloured instantaneously in the retina as bright and perfect in detail and hue. This very power is often, I think, the cause of pain to me. To see so clearly is to value so highly and to feel too deeply. The smallest of the pencilled branches of the bare ash tree drawn distinctly against the winter sky, waving lines one within the other, yet following and partly parallel, reproducing in the curve of the twig the curve of the great trunk; is it not a pleasure to trace each to its ending? The raindrops as they slide from leaf to leaf in June, the balmy shower that reperfumes each wild flower and green thing, drops lit with the sun, and falling to the chorus of the refreshed birds; is not this beautiful to see? On the grasses tall and heavy the purplish blue pollen, a shimmering dust, sown broadcast over the ripening meadow from July's warm hand – the bluish pollen, the lilac pollen of the grasses, a delicate mist of blue floating on the surface, has always been an especial delight to me. Finches shake it from the stalks as they rise. No day, no hour of summer, no step but brings new mazes – there is no word to express design without plan, and these designs of flower and leaf and colours of the sun cannot be reduced to set order. The eye is for ever drawn onward and finds no end. To see these always so sharply, wet and fresh, is almost too much sometimes for the wearied yet insatiate eye. I am obliged to turn away – to shut my eyes and say I *will* not see, I will concentrate my mind on my own little path of life, and steadily gaze downwards. In vain. Who can do so? who can care alone for his or her petty trifles of existence, that has once entered amongst the wild flowers? How shall I shut out the sun? Shall I deny the constellations of the night? They are there;

the Mystery is for ever about us – the question, the hope, the aspiration cannot be put out. So that it is almost a pain not to be able to cease observing and tracing the untraceable maze of beauty.

Blue veronica was the next identified, sometimes called germander speedwell, sometimes bird's-eye, whose leaves are so plain and petals so blue. Many names increase the trouble of identification, and confusion is made certain by the use of various systems of classification. The flower itself I knew, its name I could not be sure of – not even from the illustration, which was incorrectly coloured; the central white spot of the flower was reddish in the plate. This incorrect colouring spoils much of the flower-picturing done; pictures of flowers and birds are rarely accurate unless hand-painted. Any one else, however, would have been quite satisfied that the identification was right. I was too desirous to be correct, too conscientious, and thus a summer went by with little progress. If you really wish to identify with certainty, and have no botanist friend and no *magnum opus* of Sowerby to refer to, it is very difficult indeed to be quite sure. There was no Sowerby, no Bentham, no botanist friend – no one even to give the common country names; for it is a curious fact that the country people of the time rarely know the names put down as the vernacular for flowers in the books.

No one there could tell me the name of the marsh-marigold which grew thickly in the water-meadows – 'A sort of big buttercup', that was all they knew. Commonest of common plants is the 'sauce alone' – in every hedge, on every bank, the whitish-green leaf is found – yet I could not make certain of it. If some one tells you a plant, you know it at once and never forget it, but to learn it from a book is another matter; it does not at once take root in the mind, it has to be seen several times before you are satisfied – you waver in your convictions. The leaves were described as large and heart-shaped, and to remain green (at the ground) through the winter; but the colour of the flower was omitted, though it was stated that the petals of the hedge-mustard were yellow. The plant that seemed to me to be probably 'sauce alone' had leaves somewhat heart-shaped, but so confusing is *partial* description that I began to think I had hit on 'ramsons' instead of 'sauce alone', especially as ramsons was said to be a very common plant. So it is in some counties, but, as I afterwards found, there was not a plant of ramsons, or garlic, throughout the whole of that district. When, some years afterwards, I saw a white-flowered plant with leaves like the lily of the valley, smelling of garlic, in the woods of Somerset, I recognized it immediately. The plants that are really common – common everywhere – are not numerous, and if you are studying you must be careful to understand that word locally. My 'sauce alone' identification was right; to be right and not certain is still unsatisfactory.

There shone on the banks white stars among the grass. Petals delicately white in a whorl of rays – light that had started radiating from a centre and become fixed – shining among the flowerless green. The slender stem had grown so fast it had drawn its own root partly out of the ground, and when I tried to gather it, flower, stem and root came away together. The wheat was springing, the soft air full of the growth and moisture, blackbirds whistling, wood-pigeons nesting, young oak-leaves out; a sense of swelling, sunny fulness in the atmosphere. The plain road was made beautiful by the advanced boughs that overhung and cast their shadows on the dust – boughs of ash-green, shadows that lay still, listening to the nightingale. A place of enchantment in the mornings, where was felt the power of some subtle influence working behind bough and grass and bird-song. The orange-golden dandelion in the sward was deeply laden with colour brought to it anew again and again by the ships of the flowers, the humble-bees – to their quays they come, unlading priceless essences of sweet odours brought from the East over the green seas of wheat, unlading priceless colours on the broad dandelion discs, bartering these things for honey and pollen. Slowly tacking aslant, the pollen ship hums in the south wind. The little brown wren finds her way through the great thicket of hawthorn. How does she know her path, hidden by a thousand thousand leaves? Tangled and crushed together by their own growth, a crown of thorns hangs over the thrush's nest; thorns for the mother, hope for the young. Is there a crown of thorns over your heart? A spike has gone deep enough into mine. The stile looks farther away because boughs have pushed forward and made it smaller. The willow scarce holds the sap that tightens the bark and would burst it if it did not enlarge to the pressure.

Two things can go through the solid oak; the lightning of the clouds that rends the iron timber, the lightning of the spring – the electricity of the sunbeams forcing him to stretch forth and lengthen his arms with joy. Bathed in buttercups to the dewlap, the roan cows standing in the golden lake watched the hours with calm frontlet; watched the light descending, the meadows filling, with knowledge of long months of succulent clover. On their broad brows the year falls gently; their great, beautiful eyes, which need but a tear or a smile to make them human – without these, such eyes, so large and full, seem above human life, eyes of the immortals enduring without passion, – in these eyes, as a mirror, nature is reflected.

I came every day to walk slowly up and down the plain road, by the starry flowers under the ash-green boughs; ash is the coolest, softest green. The bees went drifting over by my head; as they cleared the hedges they passed by my ears, the wind singing in their shrill wings. White tent-walls of cloud – a warm white, being full to overflowing of sunshine – stretched across from ash-top to ash-top, a cloud-canvas roof, a tent-palace of the delicious air. For of all things there is none so sweet as sweet air – one great flower it is, drawn round about, over, and enclosing, like Aphrodite's arms; as if the dome of the sky were a bell-flower drooping down over us, and the magical essence of it filling all the room of the earth. Sweetest of all things is wild-flower air. Full of their ideal the starry flowers strained upwards on the bank, striving to keep above the rude grasses that pushed by them; genius has ever had such a struggle. The plain road was made beautiful by the many thoughts it gave. I came every morning to stay by the star-lit bank.

A friend said, 'Why do you go the same road every day? Why not have a change and walk somewhere else sometimes? Why keep on up and down the same place?' I could not answer; till then it had not occurred to me that I did always go one way; as for the reason of it I could not tell; I continued in my old mind while the summers went away. Not till years afterwards was I able to see why I went the same round and did not care for change. I do not want change: I want the same old and loved things, the same wild flowers, the same trees and soft ash-green; the turtle-doves, the blackbirds, the coloured yellowhammer sing, sing, singing so long as there is light to cast a shadow on the dial, for such is the measure of his song, and I want them in the same place. Let me find them morning after morning, the starry-white petals radiating, striving upwards to their ideal. Let me see the idle shadows resting on the white dust; let me hear the humble-bees, and stay to look down on the rich dandelion disc. Let me see the very thistles opening their great crowns – I should miss the thistles; the reed-grasses hiding the moorhen; the bryony bine, at first crudely ambitious and lifted by force of youthful sap straight above the hedgerow to sink of its own weight presently and progress with crafty tendrils; swifts shot through the air with outstretched wings like crescent-headed shaftless arrows darted from the clouds; the chaffinch with a feather in her bill; all the living staircase of the spring, step by step, upwards to the great gallery of the summer – let me watch the same succession year by year.

Why, I knew the very dates of them all – the reddening elm, the arum, the hawthorn leaf, the celandine, the may; the yellow iris of the waters, the heath of the hillside. The time of the nightingale – the place to hear the first note; onwards to the drooping fern and the time of the redwing – the place of *his* first note, so welcome to the sportsman as the acorn ripens and the pheasant, come to the age of manhood, feeds himself; onwards to the shadowless days – the long shadowless winter, for in winter it is the shadows we miss as much as the light. They lie over the summer sward, design upon design, dark lace on green and gold; they glorify the sunlight; they repose on the distant hills like gods upon Olympus; without shadow what even is the sun? At the foot of the great cliffs by the sea you may know this, it is dry glare; mighty ocean is dearer as the shadows of the clouds sweep over as they sweep over the green corn. Past the shadowless winter, when it is all shade, and therefore no shadow; onwards to the first coltsfoot and on to the seedtime again; I knew the dates of all of them. I did not want change; I wanted the same flowers to return on the same day, the titlark to rise soaring from the same oak to fetch down love with a song from heaven to his mate on the nest beneath. No change, no new thing; if I found a fresh wild flower in a fresh place, still it wove at once into the old garland. In vain, the very next year was different even in the same place – *that* had been a year of rain, and the flag flowers were wonderful to see; *this* was a dry year, and the flags not half the height, the gold of the flower not so deep; next year the fatal billhook came and swept away a slow-grown hedge that had given me crab-blossom in cuckoo-time and hazelnuts in harvest. Never again the same, even in the same place.

A little feather droops downwards to the ground – a swallow's feather fuller of miracle than the Pentateuch – how shall that feather be placed again in the breast where it grew? Nothing twice. Time changes the places that knew us, and if we go back in after years, still even then it is not the old spot; the gate swings differently, new thatch has been put on the old gables, the road has been widened, and the sward the driven sheep lingered on is gone. Who dares to think then? For faces fade as flowers, and there is no consolation. So now I am sure I was right in always walking the same way by the starry flowers striving upwards on a slender ancestry of stem; I would follow the plain old road to-day if I could. Let change be far from me; that irresistible change must come is bitter indeed. Give me the old road, the same flowers – they were only stitchwort – the old succession of days and garland, ever weaving into it fresh wild flowers from far and near. Fetch them from distant mountains, discover them on decaying walls, in unsuspected corners; though never seen before, still they are the same: there has been a place in the heart waiting for them.

2 Village Churches

The black rooks are busy in the old oak trees, carrying away the brown acorns one by one in their strong beaks to some open place where, undisturbed, they can feast upon the fruit. The nuts have fallen from the boughs, and the mice garner them out of the ditches; but the blue-black sloes cling tight to the thorn-branch still. The first frost has withered up the weak sap left in the leaves, and they whirl away in yellow clouds before the gusts of wind. It is the season, the hour of half-sorrowful, half-mystic thought, when the past becomes a reality and the present a dream, and unbidden memories of sunny days and sunny faces, seen when life was spring, float around.

Dim dream-like forms! your shadowy train
Around me gathers once again;
The same as in life's morning hour,
Before my troubled gaze you passed.

Forms known in happy days you bring,
And much-loved shades amid you spring,
Like a tradition, half expired,
Worn out with many a passing year.

In so busy a land as ours there is no place where the mind can, as it were, turn in upon itself so fully as in the silence and solitude of a village church.

There is no ponderous vastness, no oppressive weight of gloomy roof, no weird cavernous crypts, as in the cathedral; only a *visible* silence, 'still as the hour-glass', which at once isolates the soul, separates it from external present influences, and compels it, in falling back upon itself, to recognize its own depth and powers. In daily life we sit as in a vast library filled with tomes, hurriedly writing frivolous letters upon 'vexatious nothings', snatching our food and slumber, for ever rushing forward with beating pulse, never able to turn our gaze away from the goal to examine the great storehouse, the library around us. Upon the infinitely delicate organization of the brain innumerable pictures are hourly painted; these, too, we hurry by, ignoring them, pushing them back into oblivion. But here, in silence, they pass again before the gaze. Let no man know for what real purpose we come here; tell the aged clerk our business is with brass and inscriptions, press half a crown into his hand, and let him pass to his potato-digging. There is one advantage at least in the closing of the church on week-days, so much complained of – to those who do visit it there is a certainty that their thoughts will not be disturbed. And the sense of man's presence has departed from the walls and oaken seats; the dust here is not the dust of the highway, of the quick footsteps; it is the dust of the past. The ancient heavy key creaks in the cumbrous lock, and the iron latch-ring has worn a deep groove in the solid stone. The narrow-nail-studded door of black oak yields slowly to the push – it is not easy to enter, not easy to quit the present – but once close it, and the living world is gone. The very style of ornament upon the door, the broadheaded nails, has come down from the remotest antiquity. After the battle, says the rude bard in the Saxon chronicle,

> The Northmen departed
> In their nailed barks,

and, earlier still, the treacherous troop that seized the sleeping magician in iron, Wayland the Smith, were clad in 'nailed armour', in both instances meaning ornamented with nails. Incidentally, it may be noted that, until very recently, at least one village church in England had part of the skin of a Dane nailed to the door – a stern reminder of the days when the 'pagans' harried the land. This narrow window, deep in the thick wall, has no painted magnificence to boast of; but as you sit beside it in the square, high-sided pew, it possesses a human interest which even art cannot supply.

The tall grass growing rank on the graves without rustles as it waves to and fro in the wind against the small diamond panes, yellow and green with age – rustles with a melancholy sound; for we know that this window was once far above the ground, but the earth has risen till nearly on the level – risen from the accumulation of human remains. Yet, but a day or two before, on the Sunday morning, in this pew, bright, restless children smiled at each other, exchanging guilty pushes, while the sunbeams from the arrow-slit above shone upon their golden hair. Let us not think of this further, but dimly through the window, as through a 'glass darkly', see the green yew with its red berries, and afar the elms and beeches, brown and yellow. The steep down rises over them, and the moving grey patch is a flock of sheep. The white wall is cold and damp, and the beams of the roof overhead, though the varnish is gone from them, are dark with slow decay.

In the recess lies the figure of a knight in armour, rudely carved, beside his lady, still more rudely rendered in her stiff robes, and of him an ill-spelt inscription proudly recalls that he 'builded ye greate howse at' – no matter where; but history records that cruel war wrapped in flames before half a generation was gone, so that the boast of his building great houses reads as bitter mockery. There stands opposite a grander monument to a mighty earl, and over it hangs a breastplate and gauntlets of steel.

The villagers will tell that in yonder deep shady 'coombe' or valley, in the thick hazel-bushes, when 'the beetle with his drowsy hum' rises through the night air, there comes the wicked old earl, wearing this very breastplate, these iron gloves, to expiate one evil deed of yore. And if we sit in this pew long enough, till the mind is magnetized with the spirit of the past, till the early evening sends its shadowy troops to fill the distant corners of the silent church, then, perhaps, there may come to us forms gliding noiselessly over the stone pavement of the aisles – forms not repelling or ghastly, but filling us with an eager curiosity. Then through the slit made for that very purpose centuries since, when the pew was in a family chapel – through the slit in the pillar, we may see cowled monks assemble at the altar, muttering as magicians might over vessels of gold. The clank of scabbard upon the stones is stilled, the rustle of gowns is silent; if there is a sound, it is of subdued sobs, as the aged monk blesses the troop on the eve of their march. Not even yet has the stern idol of war ceased to demand its victims; even yet brave hearts and noble minds must perish, and leave sterile the hopes of the elders and the love of woman. There is still light enough left to read the few simple lines on the plain marble slab, telling how 'Lieutenant —' at Inkerman, at Lucknow, or, later still, at Coomassie, fell doing his duty. And these plain slabs are dearer to us far than all the sculptured grandeur, and the titles and pomp of belted earl and knight; their simple words go straighter to our hearts than all the quaint curt Latin of the olden time.

The belfry door is ajar – those winding stairs are not easy of access. The edges are worn away and the steps strewn with small sticks of wood; sticks once used by the jackdaws in building their nests in the tower. It is needful to take much care, lest the foot should stumble in the semi-darkness. Listen! there is now a slight sound: it is the dull ticking of the old, old clock above. It is the only thing with motion here; all else is still, and even its motion is not life. A strange old clock, a study in itself; all the works open and visible, simple, but ingenious. For a hundred years it has carried round the one hour-hand upon the square-faced dial without, marking every second of time for a century with its pendulum. Here, too, are the bells, and one, the chief bell, is a noble tenor, a mighty maker of sound. Its curves are full and beautiful, its colour clear; its tone, if you do but tap it, sonorous, yet not harsh. It is an artistic bell. Round the rim runs a rhyme in the monkish tongue, which has a chime in the words, recording the donor, and breathing a prayer for his soul. In the day when this bell was made men put their souls into their works. Their one great object was not to turn out 100,000 all alike, it was rarely they made two alike. Their one great object was to construct a work which should carry their very spirit in it, which should excel all similar works, and cause men in after-times to inquire with wonder for the maker's name, whether it was such a common thing as a knife-handle, or a bell, or a ship. Longfellow has caught the spirit well in the saga of the 'Long Serpent', where the builder of the vessel listens to axe and hammer:

> All this tumult heard the master,
>   It was music to his ear;
> Fancy whispered all the faster,
> 'Men shall hear of Thorberg Skafting
>   For a hundred year!'

Would that there were more of this spirit in the workshops of our day! They did not, when such a work was finished, hasten to blaze it abroad with trumpet and shouting. They were contented with the result of their labour, and cared little where it was placed, or who saw it; and so it is that some of the finest-toned bells in the world are at this moment to be found in village churches, and for so local a fame the maker worked as truly, and in as careful a manner, as if he had known his bell was to be hung in St Peter's at Rome. This was the true spirit of art.

Even the 'old grey turret' shows more signs of decay than the bell, for it is strengthened with iron clamps and rods to bind its feeble walls together. Of the pavements, whose flagstones are monuments, the dates and names worn by footsteps; of the vaults beneath, with their grim and ghastly traditions of coffins moved out of place, as was supposed, by supernatural agency, but, as explained, by water; of the thick walls, in which, in at least one village church, the trembling victim of priestly cruelty was immured alive – of these and a thousand other matters that suggest themselves there is no time to speak.

But just a word must be spared to notice one lovely spot where two village churches stand not a hundred yards apart, separated by a stream, both in the hands of one vicar, whose 'cure' is, nevertheless, so scant of souls that service in the morning in one and in the evening in the other is amply sufficient. And where is there a place where spring-time possesses such a tender yet melancholy interest to the heart as in a village churchyard, where the budding leaves and flowers in the grass may naturally be taken as symbolical of a still more beautiful springtime yet in store for the soul?

3 Nature and Books

What is the colour of the dandelion? There are many dandelions: that which I mean flowers in May, when the meadow-grass has started and the hares are busy by daylight. That which flowers very early in the year has a thickness of hue, and is not interesting; in autumn the dandelions quite change their colour and are pale. The right dandelion for this question is the one that comes about May with a very broad disc, and in such quantities as often to cover a whole meadow. I used to admire them very much in the fields of Surbiton (strong clay soil), and also on the towing-path of the Thames where the sward is very broad, opposite Long Ditton; indeed, I have often walked up that towing path on a beautiful sunny morning, when all was quiet except the nightingales in the Palace hedge, on purpose to admire them. I dare say they are all gone now for evermore; still, it is a pleasure to look back on anything beautiful. What colour is this dandelion? It is not yellow, nor orange, nor gold; put a sovereign on it and see the difference. They say the gipsies call it the Queen's great hairy dog-flower – a number of words to one stalk; and so, to get a colour to it, you may call it the yellow-gold-orange plant. In the winter, on the black mud under a dark, dripping tree, I found a piece of orange peel, lately dropped – a bright red orange speck in the middle of the blackness. It looked very beautiful, and instantly recalled to my mind the great dandelion discs in the sunshine of summer. Yet certainly they are not red-orange. Perhaps, if ten people answered this question, they would each give different answers. Again, a bright day or a cloudy, the presence of a slight haze, or the juxtaposition of other colours, alters it very much; for the dandelion is not a glazed colour, like the buttercup, but sensitive. It is like a sponge, and adds to its own hue that which is passing, sucking it up.

The shadows of the trees in the wood, why are they blue? Ought they not to be dark? Is it really blue, or an illusion? And what is their colour when you see the shadow of a tall trunk aslant in the air like a leaning pillar? The fallen brown leaves wet with dew have a different brown from those that are dry, and the upper surface of the green growing leaf is different from the under surface. The yellow butterfly, if you meet one in October, has so toned down his spring yellow that you might fancy him a pale green leaf floating along the road. There is a shining, quivering, gleaming; there is a changing, fluttering, shifting; there is a mixing, weaving – varnished wings, translucent wings, wings with dots and veins, all playing over the purple heath; a very tangle of many-toned lights and hues. Then come the apples: if you look upon them from an upper window, so as to glance along the level plane of the fruit, delicate streaks of scarlet, like those that lie parallel to the eastern horizon before sunrise; golden tints under bronze, and apple-green, and some that the wasps have hollowed, more glowingly beautiful than the rest; sober leaves and black and white swallows: to see it you must be high up, as if the apples were strewn on a sward of foliage. So have I gone in three steps from May dandelion to September apple; an immense space measured by things beautiful, so filled that ten folio volumes could not hold the description of them, and I have left out the meadows, the brooks, and hills. Often in writing about these things I have felt very earnestly my own incompetence to give the least idea of their brilliancy and many-sided colours. My gamut was so very limited in its terms, and would not give a note to one in a thousand of those I saw. At last I said, I will have more words; I will have more terms; I will have a book on colour; and I will find and use the right technical name for each one of these lovely tints. I was told that the very best book was by Chevreul, which had tinted illustrations, chromatic scales, and all that could be desired.

Quite true, all of it; but for me it contained nothing. There was a good deal about assorted wools, but nothing about leaves; nothing by which I could tell you the difference between the light scarlet of one poppy and the deep purple-scarlet of another species. The dandelion remained unexplained; as for the innumerable other flowers, and wings, and sky-colours, they were not even approached. The book, in short, dealt with the artificial and not with nature. Next I went to science – works on optics, such a mass of them. Some I had read in old time, and turned to again; some I read for the first time, some translated from the German, and so on. It appeared that, experimenting with physical colour, tangible paint, they had found out that red, yellow, and blue were the three primary colours; and then, experimenting with light itself, with colours not tangible, they found out that red, green, and violet were the three primary colours; but neither of these would do for the dandelion. Once upon a time I had taken an interest in spectrum analysis, and the theory of the polarization of light was fairly familiar; any number of books, but not what I wanted to know. Next the idea occurred to me of buying all the colours used in painting, and tinting as many pieces of paper a separate hue, and so comparing these with petals, and wings, and grass, and trifolium. This did not answer at all; my unskilful hands made a very poor wash, and the yellow paper set by a yellow petal did not agree, the scientific reason of which I cannot enter into now. Secondly, the names attached to many of these paints are unfamiliar to general readers; it is doubtful if bistre, Leitch's blue, oxide of chromium, and so on, would convey an idea. They might as well be Greek symbols: no use to attempt to describe hues of heath or hill in that way. These, too, are only distinct colours. What was to be done with all the shades and tones? Still there remained the language of the studio; without doubt a master of painting could be found who would quickly supply the technical term of anything I liked to show him; but again no use, because it would be technical. And a still more insurmountable difficulty occurs: in so far as I have looked at pictures, it seems as if the artists had met with the same obstacle in paints as I have in words – that is to say, a deficiency. Either painting is incompetent to express the extreme beauty of nature, or in some way the canons of art forbid the attempt. Therefore I had to turn back, throw down my books with a bang, and get me to a bit of fallen timber in the open air to meditate.

Would it be possible to build up a fresh system of colour language by means of natural objects? Could we say pine-wood green, larch green, spruce green, wasp yellow, humble-bee amber? And there are fungi that have marked tints, but the Latin names of these agarics are not pleasant. Butterfly blue – but there are several varieties; and this plan is interfered with by two things: first, that almost every single item of nature, however minute, has got a distinctly different colour, so that the dictionary of tints would be immense; and next, so very few would know the object itself that the colour attached to it would have no meaning. The power of language has been gradually enlarging for a great length of time, and I venture to say that the English language at the present time can express more, and is more subtle, flexible, and, at the same time, vigorous, than any of which we possess a record. When people talk to me about studying Sanscrit, or Greek, or

Latin, or German, or, still more absurd, French, I feel as if I could fell them with a mallet happily. Study the English, and you will find everything there, I reply. With such a language I fully anticipate, in years to come, a great development in the power of expressing thoughts and feelings which are now thoughts and feelings only. How many have said of the sea, 'It makes me feel something I cannot say'! Hence it is clear there exists in the intellect a layer, if I may so call it, of thought yet dumb – chambers within the mind which require the key of new words to unlock. Whenever that is done a fresh impetus is given to human progress. There are a million books, and yet with all their aid I cannot tell you the colour of the May dandelion. There are three greens at this moment in my mind: that of the leaf of the flower-de-luce, that of the yellow iris leaf, and that of the bayonet-like leaf of the common flag. With admission to a million books, how am I to tell you the difference between these tints? So many, many books, and such a very, very little bit of nature in them! Though we have been so many thousand years upon the earth we do not seem to have done any more as yet than walk along beaten footpaths, and sometimes really it would seem as if there were something in the minds of many men quite artificial, quite distinct from the sun and trees and hills – altogether house people, whose gods must be set in four-cornered buildings. There is nothing in books that touches my dandelion.

It grows, ah yes, it grows! How does it grow? Builds itself up somehow of sugar and starch, and turns mud into bright colour and dead earth into food for bees, and some day perhaps for you, and knows when to shut its petals, and how to construct the brown seeds to float with the wind, and how to please the children, and how to puzzle me. Ingenious dandelion! If you find out that its correct botanical name is *Leontodon taraxacum,* or *Leontodon dens-leonis,* that will bring it into botany; and there is a place called Dandelion Castle in Kent, and a bell with the inscription:

John de Dandelion with his great dog
Brought over this bell on a mill cog –

which is about as relevant as the mere words *Leontodon taraxacum*. Botany is the knowledge of plants according to the accepted definition; naturally, therefore, when I began to think I would like to know a little more of flowers than could be learned by seeing them in the fields, I went to botany. Nothing could be more simple. You buy a book which first of all tells you how to recognize them, how to classify them; next instructs you in their uses, medical or economical; next tells you about the folk-lore and curious associations; next enters into a lucid explanation of the physiology of the plant and its relation to other creatures; and finally, and most important, supplies you with the ethical feeling, the ideal aspiration to be identified with each particular flower. One moderately thick volume would probably suffice for such a modest round as this.

Lo! now the labour of Hercules when he set about bringing up Cerberus from below, and all the work done by Apollo in the years when he ground corn, are but a little matter compared with the attempt to master botany. Great minds have been at it these two thousand years, and yet we are still only nibbling at the edge of the leaf, as the ploughboys bite the young hawthorn in spring. The mere classification – all plant-lore was a vast chaos till there came the man of Sweden, the great Linnaeus, till the sexes were recognized, and everything was ruled out and set in place again. A wonderful man! I think it would be true to say it was Linnaeus who set the world on its present twist of thinking, and levered our mental globe a little more perpendicular to the ecliptic. He actually gathered the dandelion and took it to bits like a scientific child; he touched nature with his fingers instead of sitting looking out of window – perhaps the first man who had ever done so for seventeen hundred years or so, since superstition blighted the progress of pagan Rome. The work he did! But no one reads Linnaeus now; the folios, indeed, might moulder to dust without loss, because his spirit has got into the minds of men, and the text is of little consequence. The best book he wrote to read now is the delightful *Tour in Lapland*, with its quaint pen-and-ink sketches, so realistically vivid, as if the thing sketched had been banged on the paper and so left its impress. I have read it three times, and I still cherish the old yellow pages; it is the best botanical book, written by the greatest of botanists, specially sent on a botanical expedition, and it contains nothing about botany. It tells you about the canoes, and the hard cheese, and the Laplander's warehouse on top of a pole, like a pigeon-house; and the innocent way in which the maiden helped the traveller in his bath, and how the aged men ran so fast that the devil could not catch them; and, best of all, because it gives a smack in the face to modern pseudo-scientific medical cant about hygiene, showing how the Laplanders break every 'law', human and 'divine', ventilation, bath and diet – all the trash – and therefore enjoy the most excellent health, and live to a great old age. Still I have not succeeded in describing the immense labour there was in learning to distinguish plants on the Linnaean system. Then comes in order of time the natural system, the geographical distribution; then there is the geological relationship, so to say, to Pliocene plants, natural selection and evolution. Of that let us say nothing; let sleeping dogs lie, and evolution is a very weary dog. Most charming, however, will be found the later studies of naturalists on the interdependence of flowers and insects; there is another work the dandelion has got to do – endless, endless botany! Where did the plants come from at first? Did they come creeping up out of the sea at the edge of the estuaries, and gradually run their roots into the ground, and so make green the earth? Did Man come out of the sea, as the Greeks thought? There are so many ideas in plants. Flora, with a full lap, scattering knowledge and flowers together; everything good and sweet seems to come out of flowers, up to the very highest thoughts of the soul, and we carry them daily to the very threshold of the other world. Next you may try the microscope and its literature, and find the crystals in the rhubarb.

I remember taking sly glances when I was a very little boy at an old Culpepper's Herbal, heavily bound in leather and curiously illustrated. It was so deliciously wicked to read about the poisons; and I thought perhaps it was a book like that, only in papyrus rolls, that was used by the sorceress who got ready the poisoned mushrooms in old Rome. Youth's ideas are so imaginative, and bring together things that are so widely separated. Conscience told me I had no business to read about poisons; but there was a fearful fascination in hemlock, and I recollect tasting a little bit – it was very nasty. At this day, nevertheless, if any one wishes to begin a pleasant, interesting, unscientific acquaintance with English plants, he would do very well indeed to get a good copy of Culpepper. Grey hairs had insisted in showing themselves in my beard when, all those weary years afterwards, I thought I would like to buy the still older Englishman, Gerard, who had no Linnaeus to guide him, who walked about our English lanes centuries ago. What wonderful scenes he must have viewed when they were all a tangle of wild flowers, and plants that are now scarce were common, and the old ploughs, and the curious customs, and the wild red-deer – it would make a good picture, it really would, Gerard studying English orchids! Such a volume! – hundreds of pages, yellow of course, close type, and marvellously well printed. The minute care they must have taken in those early days of printing to get up such a book – a wonderful volume both in bodily shape and contents. Just then the only copy I could hear of was much damaged. The cunning old bookseller said he could make it up; but I have no fancy for patched books, they are not genuine; I would rather have them deficient; and the price was rather long, and so I went Gerardless. Of folk-lore and medicinal use and history and associations here you have hints. The bottom of the sack is not yet; there are the monographs, years of study expended upon one species of plant growing in one locality, perhaps; some made up into thick books and some into broad quarto pamphlets, with most beautiful plates, that, if you were to see them, would tempt you to cut them out and steal them, all sunk and lost like dead ships under the sand; piles of monographs. There are warehouses in London that are choked to the beams of the roof with them, and every fresh exploration furnishes another shelf-load. The source of the Nile was unknown a very few years ago, and now, I have no doubt, there are dozens of monographs on the flowers that flourish there. Indeed, there is not a thing that grows that may not furnish a monograph. The author spends perhaps twenty years in collecting his material, during which time he must of course come across a great variety of amusing information, and then he spends another ten years writing out a fair copy of his labours. Then he thinks it does not quite do in that form, so he snips a paragraph out of the beginning and puts it at the end; next he shifts some more matter from the middle to the preface; then he thinks it over. It seems to him that it is too big, it wants condensation. The scientific world will say he has made too much of it; it ought to read very slight, and present the facts while concealing the labour. So he sets about removing the superfluous – leaves out all the personal observations, and all the little adventures he has met with in his investigations; and so, having got it down to the dry bones and stones thereof, and omitted all the mortar that stuck them together, he sends for the engraver, and the next three years are occupied in working up the illustrations. About this time some new discovery is made by a foreign observer, which necessitates a complete revision of the subject: and so having shifted the contents of the book about hither and thither till he does not know which is the end and which is the beginning, he pitches the much-mutilated copy into a drawer and turns the key. Farewell, no more of this; his declining days shall be spent in peace. A few months afterwards a work is announced in Leipsic which 'really trenches on my favourite subject, and really after spending a lifetime I can't stand it'. By this time his handwriting has become so shaky he can hardly read it himself, so he sends in despair for a lady who works a typewriter, and with infinite patience she makes a clean manuscript of the muddled mass. To the press at last, and the proofs come rapidly. Such a relief! How joyfully easy a thing is when you set about it! but by-and-by this won't do. Sub-section A ought to be in a footnote, family B is doubtful; and so the corrections grow and run over the margin in a thin treble hand, till they approach the bulk of the original book – a good profit for the printer; and so after about forty years the monograph is published – the work of a life is accomplished. Fifty copies are sent round to as many public libraries and learned societies, and the rest of the impression lies on the shelves till dust and time and spiders' webs have buried it. Splendid work in it too. Looked back upon from to-day with the key of modern thought, these monographs often contain a whole chest of treasure. And still there are the periodicals, a century of magazines and journals and reviews and notices that have been coming out these hundred years and dropping to the ground like dead leaves unnoticed. And then there are the art works – books about shape and colour and ornament, and a naturalist lately has been trying to see how the leaves of one tree look fitted on the boughs of another. Boundless is the wealth of Flora's lap; the ingenuity of man has been weaving wreaths out of it for ages, and still the bottom of the sack is not yet. Nor have we got much news of the dandelion. For I sit on the thrown timber under the trees and meditate, and I want something more: I want the soul of the flowers.

The bee and the butterfly take their pollen and their honey, and the strange moths so curiously coloured, like the curious colouring of the owls, come to them by night, and they turn towards the sun and live their little day, and their petals fall, and where is the soul when the body decays? I want the inner meaning and the understanding of the wild flowers in the meadow. Why are they? What end? What purpose? The plant knows, and sees, and feels; where is its mind when the petal falls? Absorbed in the universal dynamic force, or what? They make no shadow of pretence, these beautiful flowers, of being beautiful for my sake, of bearing honey for me; in short, there does not seem to be any kind of relationship between us, and yet – as I said just now – language does not express the dumb feelings of the mind any more than the flower can speak. I want to know the soul of the flowers, but the word soul does not in the smallest degree convey the meaning of my wish. It is quite inadequate; I must hope that you will grasp the drift of my meaning. All these life-laboured monographs, these classifications, works of Linnaeus, and our own classic Darwin, microscope, physiology, and the flower has not given us its message yet. There are a million books; there are no books: all the books have to be written. What a field! A whole million of books have got to be written. In this sense there are hardly a dozen of them done, and these mere primers. The thoughts of man are like the foraminifera, those minute shells which build up the solid chalk hills and lay the level plain of endless sand; so minute that, save with a powerful lens, you would never imagine the dust on your fingers to be more than dust. The thoughts of man are like these: each to him seems great in his day, but the ages roll, and they shrink till they become triturated dust, and you might, as it were, put a thousand on your thumb-nail. They are not shapeless dust for all that; they are organic, and they build and weld and grow together, till in the passage of time they will make a new earth and a new life. So I think I may say there are no books; the books are yet to be written.

Let us get a little alchemy out of the dandelions. They were not precise, the Arabian sages, with their flowing robes and handwriting; there was a large margin to their manuscripts, much imagination. Therein they failed, judged by the monograph standard, but gave a subtle food for the mind. Some of this I would fain see now inspiring the works and words of our great men of science and thought – a little alchemy. A great change is slowly going forward all over the printing-press world, I mean wherever men print books and papers. The Chinese are perhaps outside that world at present, and the other Asian races; the myriads, too, of the great southern islands and of Africa. The change is steadily, however, proceeding wherever the printing-press is used. Nor Pope, nor Kaiser, nor Czar, nor Sultan, nor fanatic monk, nor muezzin, shouting in vain from his minaret, nor, most fanatic of all, the fanatic shouting in vain in London, can keep it out – all powerless against a bit of printed paper. Bits of printed paper that listen to no command, to which none can say, 'Stand back; thou shalt not enter'. They rise on the summer whirlwinds from the very dust of the road, and float over the highest walls; they fall on the well-kept lawns – monastery, prison, palace – there is no fortress against a bit of printed paper. They penetrate where even Danaë's gold cannot go. Our Darwins, our Lyalls, Herschels, Faradays – all the immense army of those that go down to nature with considering eye – are steadfastly undermining and obliterating the superstitious past, literally burying it under endless loads of accumulated facts; and the printing-presses, like so many Argos, take these facts on their voyage round the world. Over go temples, and minarets, and churches, or rather there they stay, the hollow shells, like the snail shells which thrushes have picked clean; there they stay like Karnac, where there is no more incense, like the stone circles on our own hills, where there are no more human sacrifices. Thus men's minds all over the printing-press world are unlearning the falsehoods that have bound them down so long; they are unlearning, the first step to learn. They are going down to nature and taking up the clods with their own hands, and so coming to have touch of that which is real. As yet we are in the fact stage; by-and-by we shall come to the alchemy, and get the honey for the inner mind and soul. I found, therefore, from the dandelion that there were no books, and it came upon me, believe me, as a great surprise, for I had lived quite certain that I was surrounded with them. It is nothing but unlearning, I find now; five thousand books to unlearn.

Then to unlearn the first ideas of history, of science, of social institutions, to unlearn one's own life and purpose; to unlearn the old mode of thought and way of arriving at things; to take off peel after peel, and so get by degrees slowly towards the truth – thus writing as it were, a sort of floating book in the mind, almost remaking the soul. It seems as if the chief value of books is to give us something to unlearn. Sometimes I feel indignant at the false views that were instilled into me in early days, and then again I see that that very indignation gives me a moral life. I hope in the days to come future thinkers will unlearn us, and find ideas infinitely better. How marvellous it seems that there should be found communities furnished with the printing-press and fully convinced they are more intelligent than ants, and yet deliberately refusing by a solid 'popular' vote to accept free libraries! They look with scorn on the mediaeval times, when volumes were chained in the college library or to the desk at church. Ignorant times those! A good thing it would be if only three books were chained to a desk, open and free in every parish throughout the kingdom now. So might the wish to unlearn be at last started in the inert mind of the mass. Almost the only books left to me to read, and not to unlearn very much, are my first books – the graven classics of Greece and Rome, cut with a stylus so deeply into the tablet they cannot be erased. Little of the monograph or of classification, no bushel baskets full of facts, no minute dissection of nature, no attempt to find the soul under the scalpel. Thoughts which do not exactly deal with nature direct in a mechanical way, as the chemist labels all his gums and spices and earths in small boxes – I wonder if anybody at Athens ever made a collection of the coleoptera? Yet in some way they had got the spirit of the earth and sea, the soul of the sun. This never dies; this I wish not to unlearn; this is ever fresh and beautiful as a summer morning:

Such the golden crocus,
Fair flower of early spring; the gopher white,
And fragrant thyme, and all the unsown beauty
Which in moist grounds the verdant meadows bear;
The ox-eye, the sweet-smelling flower of Jove,
The chalca, and the much-sung hyacinth,
And the low-growing violet, to which
Dark Proserpine a darker hue has given.

They come nearest to our own violets and cowslips – the unsown beauty of our meadows – to the hawthorn leaf and the high pinewood. I can forget all else that I have read, but it is difficult to forget these even when I will. I read them in English. I had the usual Latin and Greek instruction, but I read them in English deliberately. For the inflexion of the vowel I care nothing; I prize the idea. Scholars may regard me with scorn. I reply with equal scorn. I say that a great classic thought is greater to an English mind in English words than in any other form, and therein fits best to this our life and day. I read them in English first, and intend to do so to the end. I do not know what set me on these books, but I began them when about eighteen. The first of all was Diogenes Laertius's *Lives of the Philosophers*. It was a happy choice; my good genius, I suppose, for you see I was already fairly well read in modern science, and these old Greek philosophies set me thinking backwards, unwinding and unlearning, and getting at that eidolon which is not to be found in the mechanical heavens of this age. I still read him. I still find new things, quite new, because they are so very, very old, and quite true; and with his help I seem in a measure to look back upon our thoughts now as if I had projected myself a thousand years forward in space. An imperfect book, say the critics. I do not know about that; his short paragraphs and chapters in their imperfect state convey more freshness to the mind than the thick, laboured volumes in which modern scholarship professes to describe ancient philosophy. I prefer the imperfect original records. Neither can I read the ponderous volumes of modern history, which are nothing but words. I prefer the incomplete and shattered chronicles themselves, where the swords shine and the armour rings, and all is life though but a broken frieze. Next came Plato (it took me a long time to read Plato, and I have had to unlearn much of him) and Xenophon. Socrates' dialectic method taught me how to write, or rather how to put ideas in sequence. Sophocles, too; and last, that wonderful encyclopaedia of curious things, Athenaeus. So that I found, when the idea of the hundred best books came out, that between seventy and eighty of them had been my companions almost from boyhood, those lacking to complete the number being chiefly ecclesiastical or Continental. Indeed, some years before the hundred books were talked of, the idea had occurred to me of making up a catalogue of books that could be bought for ten pounds. In an article in the *Pall Mall Gazette* on 'The Pigeons at the British Museum' I said, 'It seems as if all the books in the world – really books – can be bought for £10. Man's whole thought is purchasable at that small price – for the value of a watch, of a good dog.' The idea of making a £10 catalogue was in my mind – I did make a rough pencil one – and I still think that a £10 library is worth the notice of the publishing world. My rough list did not contain a hundred. These old books of nature and nature's mind ought to be chained up, free for every man to read in every parish. These are the only books I do not wish to unlearn, one item only excepted, which I shall not here discuss. It is curious, too, that the Greek philosophers, in the more rigid sense of science, anticipated most of the drift of modern thought. Two chapters in Aristotle might almost be printed without change as summaries of our present natural science. For the facts of nature, of course, neither one hundred books nor a £10 library would be worth mentioning; say five thousand, and having read those, then go to Kew, and spend a year studying the specimens of wood only stored there, such a little slice after all of the whole. You will then believe what I have advanced, that there are no books as yet; they have got to be written; and if we pursue the idea a little further, and consider that these are all about the crude clods of life – for I often feel what a very crude and clumsy clod I am – only of the earth, a minute speck among one hundred millions of stars, how shall we write what is *there*? It is only to be written by the mind or soul, and that is why I strive so much to find what I have called the alchemy of nature. Let us not be too entirely mechanical, Baconian, and experimental only; let us let the soul hope and dream and float on these oceans of accumulated facts, and feel still greater aspiration than it has ever known since first a flint was chipped before the glaciers. Man's mind is the most important fact with which we are yet acquainted. Let us not turn then against it and deny its existence with too many brazen instruments, but remember these are but a means, and that the vast lens of the Californian refractor is but glass – it is the infinite speck upon which the ray of light will fall that is the one great fact of the universe. By the mind, without instruments, the Greeks anticipated almost all our thoughts; by-and-by, having raised ourselves up upon these huge mounds of facts, we shall begin to see still greater things; to do so we must look not at the mound under foot, but at the starry horizon.

4 The Pageant of Summer

I

Green rushes, long and thick, standing up above the edge of the ditch, told the hour of the year as distinctly as the shadow on the dial the hour of the day. Green and thick and sappy to the touch, they felt like summer, soft and elastic, as if full of life, mere rushes though they were. On the fingers they left a green scent; rushes have a separate scent of green, so, too, have ferns, very different to that of grass or leaves. Rising from brown sheaths, the tall stems enlarged a little in the middle, like classical columns, and heavy with their sap and freshness, leaned against the hawthorn sprays. From the earth they had drawn its moisture, and made the ditch dry; some of the sweetness of the air had entered into their fibres, and the rushes – the common rushes – were full of beautiful summer. The white pollen of early grasses growing on the edge was dusted from them each time the hawthorn boughs were shaken by a thrush. These lower sprays came down in among the grass, and leaves and grass-blades touched. Smooth round stems of angelica, big as a gun-barrel, hollow and strong, stood on the slope of the mound, their tiers of well-balanced branches rising like those of a tree. Such a sturdy growth pushed back the ranks of hedge parsley in full white flower, which blocked every avenue and winding bird's-path of the bank. But the 'gix,' or wild parsnip, reached already high above both, and would rear its fluted stalk, joint on joint, till it could face a man. Trees they were to the lesser birds, not even bending if perched on; but though so stout, the birds did not place their nests on or against them. Something in the odour of these umbelliferous plants, perhaps, is not quite liked; if brushed or bruised they give out a bitter greenish scent. Under their cover, well shaded and hidden, birds build, but not against or on the stems, though they will affix their nests to much less certain supports. With the grasses that overhung the edge, with the rushes in the ditch itself, and these great plants on the mound, the whole hedge was wrapped and thickened. No cunning of glance could see through it; it would have needed a ladder to help anyone look over.

It was between the may and the June roses. The may-bloom had fallen, and among the hawthorn boughs were the little green bunches that would feed the redwings in autumn. High up the briars had climbed, straight and towering while there was a thorn, or an ash sapling, or a yellow-green willow to uphold them, and then curving over towards the meadow. The buds were on them, but not yet open; it was between the may and the rose.

As the wind, wandering over the sea, takes from each wave an invisible portion, and brings to those on shore the ethereal essence of ocean, so the air lingering among the woods and hedges – green waves and billows – became full of fine atoms of summer. Swept from notched hawthorn leaves, broad-topped oak-leaves, narrow ash sprays and oval willows; from vast elm cliffs and sharp-taloned brambles under; brushed from the waving grasses and stiffening corn, the dust of the sunshine was borne along and breathed. Steeped in flower and pollen to the music of bees and birds, the stream of the atmosphere became a living thing. It was life to breathe it, for the air itself was life. The strength of the earth went up through the leaves into the wind. Fed thus on the food of the Immortals, the heart opened to the width and depth of the summer – to the broad horizon afar, down to the minutest creature in the grass, up to the highest swallow. Winter shows us Matter in its dead form, like the Primary rocks, like granite and basalt – clear but cold and frozen crystal. Summer shows us Matter changing into life, sap rising from the earth through a million tubes, the alchemic power of light entering the solid oak: and see! it bursts forth in countless leaves. Living things leap in the grass, living things drift upon the air, living things are coming forth to breathe in every hawthorn bush. No longer does the immense weight of Matter – the dead, the crystallized – press ponderously on the thinking mind. The whole office of Matter is to feed life – to feed the green rushes, and the roses that are about to be; to feed the swallows above, and us that wander beneath them. So much greater is this green and common rush than all the Alps.

Fanning so swiftly, the wasp's wings are but just visible as he passes; did he pause, the light would be apparent through their texture. On the wings of the dragon-fly as he hovers an instant before he darts there is a prismatic gleam. These wing textures are even more delicate than the minute filaments on a swallow's quill, more delicate than the pollen of a flower. They are formed of matter indeed, but how exquisitely it is resolved into the means and organs of life! Though not often consciously recognized, perhaps this is the great pleasure of summer, to watch the earth, the dead particles, resolving themselves into the living case of life, to see the seed-leaf push aside the clod and become by degrees the perfumed flower. From the tiny mottled egg come the wings that by-and-by shall pass the immense sea. It is in this marvellous transformation of clods and cold matter into living things that the joy and the hope of summer reside. Every blade of grass, each leaf, each separate floret and petal, is an inscription speaking of hope. Consider the grasses and the oaks, the swallows, the sweet blue butterfly – they are one and all a sign and token showing before our eyes earth made into life. So that my hope becomes as broad as the horizon afar, reiterated by every leaf, sung on every bough, reflected in the gleam of every flower. There is so much for us yet to come, so much to be gathered, and enjoyed. Not for you and me, now, but for our race, who will ultimately use this magical secret for their happiness. Earth holds secrets enough to give them the life of the fabled Immortals. My heart is fixed firm and stable in the belief that ultimately the sunshine and the summer, the flowers and the azure sky, shall become, as it were, interwoven into man's existence. He shall take from all their beauty and enjoy their glory. Hence it is that a flower is to me so much more than stalk and petals. When I look in the glass I see that every line in my face means pessimism; but in spite of my face – that is my experience – I remain an optimist. Time with an unsteady hand has etched thin crooked lines, and, deepening the hollows, has cast the original expression into shadow. Pain and sorrow flow over us with little ceasing, as the sea-hoofs beat on the beach. Let us not look at ourselves but onwards, and take strength from the leaf and the signs of the field. He is indeed despicable who cannot look onwards to the ideal life of man. Not to do so is to deny our birthright of mind.

The long grass flowing towards the hedge has reared in a wave against it. Along the hedge it is higher and greener, and rustles into the very bushes. There is a mark only now where the footpath was; it passed close to the hedge, but its place is traceable only as a groove in the sorrel and seed-tops. Though it has quite filled the path, the grass there cannot send its tops so high; it has left a winding crease. By the hedge here stands a moss-grown willow, and its slender branches extend over the sward. Beyond it is an oak, just apart from the bushes; then the ground gently rises, and an ancient pollard ash, hollow and black inside, guards an open gateway like a low tower. The different tone of green shows that the hedge is there of nut trees; but one great hawthorn spreads out in a semicircle, roofing the grass which is yet more verdant in the still pool (as it were) under it. Next a corner, more oaks, and a chestnut in bloom. Returning to this spot an old apple tree stands right out in the meadow like an island. There seemed just now the tiniest twinkle of movement by the rushes, but it was lost among the hedge parsley. Among the grey leaves of the willow there is another flit of motion; and visible now against the sky there is a little brown bird not to be distinguished at the moment from the many other little brown birds that are known to be about. He got up into the willow from the hedge parsley somehow, without being seen to climb or fly. Suddenly he crosses to the tops of the hawthorn and immediately flings himself up into the air a yard or two, his wings and ruffled crest making a ragged outline; jerk, jerk, jerk, as if it were with the utmost difficulty he could keep even at that height. He scolds, and twitters, and chirps, and all at once sinks like a stone into the hedge and out of sight as a stone into a pond. It is a whitethroat; his nest is deep in the parsley and nettles. Presently he will go out to the island apple tree and back again in a minute or two; the pair of them are so fond of each other's affectionate company they cannot remain apart.

Watching the line of the hedge, about every two minutes, either near at hand or yonder a bird darts out just at the level of the grass, hovers a second with labouring wings, and returns as swiftly to the cover. Sometimes it is a flycatcher, sometimes a greenfinch, or chaffinch, now and then a robin, in one place a shrike, perhaps another is a redstart. They are fly-fishing all of them, seizing insects from the sorrel tips and grass, as the kingfisher takes a roach from the water. A blackbird slips up into the oak and a dove descends in the corner by the chestnut tree. But these are not visible together, only one at a time and with intervals. The larger part of the life of the hedge is out of sight. All the thrush-fledglings, the young blackbirds, and finches are hidden, most of them on the mound among the ivy, and parsley, and rough grasses, protected too by a roof of brambles. The nests that still have eggs are not, like the nests of the early days of April, easily found; they are deep down in the tangled herbage by the shore of the ditch, or far inside the thorny thickets which then looked mere bushes, and are now so broad. Landrails are running in the grass concealed as a man would be in a wood; they have nests and eggs on the ground for which you may search in vain till the mowers come.

Up in the corner a fragment of white fur and marks of scratching show where a doe has been preparing for a litter. Some well-trodden runs lead from mound to mound; they are sandy near the hedge where the particles have been carried out adhering to the rabbits' feet and fur. A crow rises lazily from the upper end of the field, and perches in the chestnut. His presence, too, was unsuspected. He is there by far too frequently. At this season the crows are always in the mowing-grass, searching about, stalking in winding tracks from furrow to furrow, picking up an egg here and a foolish fledgling that has wandered from the mound yonder. Very likely there may be a moorhen or two slipping about under cover of the long grass; thus hidden, they can leave the shelter of the flags and wander a distance from the brook. So that beneath the surface of the grass and under the screen of the leaves there are ten times more birds than are seen.

Besides the singing and calling, there is a peculiar sound which is only heard in summer. Waiting quietly to discover what birds are about, I become aware of a sound in the very air. It is not the midsummer hum which will soon be heard over the heated hay in the valley and over the cooler hills alike. It is not enough to be called a hum, and does but just tremble at the extreme edge of hearing. If the branches wave and rustle they overbear it; the buzz of a passing bee is so much louder it overcomes all of it that is in the whole field. I cannot define it, except by calling the hours of winter to mind – they are silent; you hear a branch crack or creak as it rubs another in the wood, you hear the hoar-frost crunch on the grass beneath your feet, but the air is without sound in itself. The sound of summer is everywhere – in the passing breeze, in the hedge, in the broad-branching trees, in the grass as it swings; all the myriad particles that together make the summer are in motion. The sap moves in the trees, the pollen is pushed out from grass and flower, and yet again these acres and acres of leaves and square miles of grass blades – for they would cover acres and square miles if reckoned edge to edge – are drawing their strength from the atmosphere. Exceedingly minute as these vibrations must be, their numbers perhaps may give them a volume almost reaching in the aggregate to the power of the ear. Besides the quivering leaf, the swinging grass, the fluttering bird's wing, and the thousand oval membranes which innumerable insects whirl about, a faint resonance seems to come from the very earth itself. The fervour of the sunbeams descending in a tidal flood rings on the strung harp of earth. It is this exquisite undertone, heard and yet unheard, which brings the mind into sweet accordance with the wonderful instrument of nature.

By the apple tree there is a low bank, where the grass is less tall and admits the heat direct to the ground; here there are blue flowers – bluer than the wings of my favourite butterflies – with white centres – the lovely bird's-eyes, or veronica. The violet and cowslip, bluebell and rose, are known to thousands; the veronica is overlooked. The ploughboys know it, and the wayside children, the mower and those who linger in fields, but few else. Brightly blue and surrounded by greenest grass, imbedded in and all the more blue for the shadow of the grass, these growing butterflies' wings draw to themselves the sun. From this island I look down into the depth of the grasses. Red sorrel spires – deep drinkers of reddest sun wine – stand the boldest, and in their numbers threaten the buttercups. To these in the distance they give the gipsy-gold tint – the reflection of fire on plates of the precious metal. It will show even on a ring by firelight; blood in the gold, they say. Gather the open marguerite daisies, and they seem large – so wide a disc, such fingers of rays; but in the grass their size is toned by so much green. Clover heads of honey lurk in the bunches and by the hidden footpath. Like clubs from Polynesia the tips of the grasses are varied in shape: some tend to a point – the foxtails – some are hard and cylindrical; others, avoiding the club shape, put forth the slenderest branches with fruit of seed at the ends, which tremble as the air goes by. Their stalks are ripening and becoming of the colour of hay while yet the long blades remain green.

Each kind is repeated a hundred times, the foxtails are succeeded by foxtails, the narrow blades by narrow blades, but never become monotonous; sorrel stands by sorrel, daisy flowers by daisy. This bed of veronica at the foot of the ancient apple has a whole handful of flowers, and yet they do not weary the eye. Oak follows oak and elm ranks with elm, but the woodlands are pleasant; however many times reduplicated, their beauty only increases. So, too, the summer days; the sun rises on the same grasses and green hedges, there is the same blue sky, but did we ever have enough of them? No, not in a hundred years! There seems always a depth, somewhere, unexplored, a thicket that has not been seen through, a corner full of ferns, a quaint old hollow tree, which may give us something. Bees go by me as I stand under the apple, but they pass on for the most part bound on a long journey, across to the clover fields or up to the thyme lands; only a few go down into the mowing-grass. The hive bees are the most impatient of insects; they cannot bear to entangle their wings beating against grasses or boughs. Not one will enter a hedge. They like an open and level surface, places cropped by sheep, the sward by the roadside, fields of clover, where the flower is not deep under grass.

II

It is the patient humble-bee that goes down into the forest of the mowing-grass. If entangled, the humble-bee climbs up a sorrel stem and takes wing, without any sign of annoyance. His broad back with tawny bar buoyantly glides over the golden buttercups. He hums to himself as he goes, so happy is he. He knows no skep, no cunning work in glass receives his labour, no artificial saccharine aids him when the beams of the sun are cold, there is no step to his house that he may alight in comfort; the way is not made clear for him that he may start straight for the flowers, nor are any sown for him. He has no shelter if the storm descends suddenly; he has no dome of twisted straw well thatched and tiled to retreat to. The butcher-bird, with a beak like a crooked iron nail, drives him to the ground, and leaves him pierced with a thorn; but no hail of shot revenges his tortures. The grass stiffens at nightfall (in autumn), and he must creep where he may, if possibly he may escape the frost. No one cares for the humble-bee. But down to the flowering nettle in the mossy-sided ditch, up into the tall elm, winding in and out and round the branched buttercups, along the banks of the brook, far inside the deepest wood, away he wanders and despises nothing. His nest is under the rough grasses and the mosses of the mound, a mere tunnel beneath the fibres and matted surface. The hawthorn overhangs it, the fern grows by, red mice rustle past.

It thunders, and the great oak trembles; the heavy rain drops through the treble roof of oak and hawthorn and fern. Under the arched branches the lightning plays along, swiftly to and fro, or seems to, like the swish of a whip, a yellowish-red against the green; a boom! a crackle as if a tree fell from the sky.

The thick grasses are bowed, the white florets of the wild parsley are beaten down, the rain hurls itself, and suddenly a fierce blast tears the green oak leaves and whirls them out into the fields; but the humble-bee's home, under moss and matted fibres, remains uninjured. His house at the root of the king of trees, like a cave in the rock, is safe. The storm passes and the sun comes out, the air is the sweeter and the richer for the rain, like verses with a rhyme; there will be more honey in the flowers. Humble he is, but wild; always in the field, the wood; always by the banks and thickets; always wild and humming to his flowers. Therefore I like the humble-bee, being, at heart at least, for ever roaming among the woodlands and the hills and by the brooks. In such quick summer storms the lightning gives the impression of being far more dangerous than the zigzag paths traced on the autumn sky. The electric cloud seems almost level with the ground and the livid flame to rush to and fro beneath the boughs as the little bats do in the evening.

Caught by such a cloud, I have stayed under thick larches at the edge of plantations. They are no shelter, but conceal one perfectly. The wood-pigeons come home to their nest trees; in larches they seem to have permanent nests, almost like rooks. Kestrels, too, come home to the wood. Pheasants crow, but not from fear – from defiance; in fear they scream. The boom startles them, and they instantly defy the sky. The rabbits quietly feed on out in the field between the thistles and rushes that so often grow in woodside pastures, quietly hopping to their favourite places, utterly heedless how heavy the echoes may be in the hollows of the wooded hills. Till the rain comes they take no heed whatever, but then make for shelter. Blackbirds often make a good deal of noise; but the soft turtle-doves coo gently, let the lightning be as savage as it will. Nothing has the least fear. Man alone, more senseless than a pigeon, put a god in vapour; and to this day, though the printing-press has set a foot on every threshold, numbers bow the knee when they hear the roar the timid dove does not heed. So trustful are the doves, the squirrels, the birds of the branches, and the creatures of the field. Under their tuition let us rid ourselves of mental terrors, and face death itself as calmly as they do the livid lightning; so trustful and so content with their fate, resting in themselves and unappalled. If but by reason and will I could reach the godlike calm and courage of what we so thoughtlessly call the timid turtle-dove, I should lead a nearly perfect life.

The bark of the ancient apple tree under which I have been standing is shrunken like iron which has been heated and let cool round the rim of a wheel. For a hundred years the horses have rubbed against it while feeding in the aftermath. The scales of the bark are gone or smoothed down and level, so that insects have no hiding-place. There are no crevices for them, the horsehairs that were caught anywhere have been carried away by birds for their nests. The trunk is smooth and columnar, hard as iron. A hundred times the mowing-grass has grown up around it, the birds have built their nests, the butterflies fluttered by, and the acorns dropped from the oaks. It is a long, long time, counted by artificial hours or by the seasons, but it is longer still in another way. The greenfinch in the hawthorn yonder has been there since I came out, and all the time has been happily talking to his love. He has left the hawthorn indeed, but only for a minute or two, to fetch a few seeds, and comes back each time more full of song-talk than ever. He notes no slow movement of the oak's shadow on the grass; it is nothing to him and his lady dear that the sun, as seen from his nest, is crossing from one great bough of the oak to another. The dew even in the deepest and most tangled grass has long since been dried, and some of the flowers that close at noon will shortly fold their petals. The morning airs, which breathe so sweetly, come less and less frequently as the heat increases. Vanishing from the sky, the last fragments of cloud have left an untarnished azure. Many times the bees have returned to their hives, and thus the index of the day advances. It is nothing to the greenfinches; all their thoughts are in their song-talk. The sunny moment is to them all in all. So deeply are they rapt in it that they do not know whether it is a moment or a year. There is no clock for feeling, for joy, for love.

And with all their motions and stepping from bough to bough, they are not restless; they have so much time, you see. So, too, the whitethroat in the wild parsley; so, too, the thrush that just now peered out and partly fluttered his wings as he stood to look. A butterfly comes and stays on a leaf – a leaf much warmed by the sun – and shuts his wings. In a minute he opens them, shuts them again, half wheels round, and by-and-by – just when he chooses, and not before – floats away. The flowers open, and remain open for hours, to the sun. Hastelessness is the only word one can make up to describe it; there is much rest, but no haste. Each moment, as with the greenfinches, is so full of life that it seems so long and so sufficient in itself. Not only the days, but life itself lengthens in summer. I would spread abroad my arms and gather more of it to me, could I do so.

All the procession of living and growing things passes. The grass stands up taller and still taller, the sheaths open, and the stalk arises, the pollen clings till the breeze sweeps it. The bees rush past, and the resolute wasps; the humble-bees, whose weight swings them along. About the oaks and maples the brown chafers swarm, and the fern-owls at dusk, and the blackbirds and jays by day, cannot reduce their legions while they last. Yellow butterflies, and white, broad red admirals, and sweet blues; think of the kingdom of flowers which is theirs! Heavy moths burring at the edge of the copse; green, and red, and gold flies: gnats, like smoke, around the tree-tops; midges so thick over the brook, as if you could haul a netful; tiny leaping creatures in the grass; bronze beetles across the path; blue dragonflies pondering on cool leaves of water-plantain. Blue jays flitting, a magpie dropping across from elm to elm; young rooks that have escaped the hostile shot blundering up into the branches; missel thrushes leading their fledglings, already strong on the wing, from field to field. An egg here on the sward dropped by a starling; a red ladybird creeping, tortoise-like, up a green fern frond. Finches undulating through the air, shooting themselves with closed wings, and linnets happy with their young.

Golden dandelion discs – gold and orange – of a hue more beautiful, I think, than the higher and more visible buttercup. A blackbird, gleaming, so black is he, splashing in the runlet of water across the gateway. A ruddy kingfisher swiftly drawing himself, as you might draw a stroke with a pencil, over the surface of the yellow buttercups, and away above the hedge. Hart's-tongue fern, thick with green, so green as to be thick with its colour, deep in the ditch under the shady hazel boughs. White meadow-sweet lifting its tiny florets, and black-flowered sedges. You must push through the reed grass to find the sword-flags; the stout willow-herbs will not be trampled down, but resist the foot like underwood. Pink lychnis flowers behind the withy stoles, and little black moorhens swim away, as you gather it, after their mother, who has dived under the water-grass, and broken the smooth surface of the duckweed. Yellow loosestrife is rising, thick comfrey stands at the very edge; the sand-pipers run where the shore is free from bushes. Back by the underwood the prickly and repellent brambles will presently present us with fruit. For the squirrels the nuts are forming, green beechmast is there – green wedges under the spray; up in the oaks the small knots, like bark rolled up in a dot, will be acorns. Purple vetches along the mounds, yellow lotus where the grass is shorter, and orchis succeeds to orchis. As I write them, so these things come – not set in gradation, but like the broadcast flowers in the mowing-grass.

Now follows the gorse, and the pink rest-harrow, and the sweet lady's-bedstraw, set as it were in the midst of a little thorn-bush. The broad repetition of the yellow clover is not to be written; acre upon acre, and not one spot of green, as if all the green had been planed away, leaving only the flowers to which the bees come by the thousand from far and near. But one white campion stands in the midst of the lake of yellow. The field is scented as though a hundred hives of honey had been emptied on it. Along the mound by it the bluebells are seeding, the hedge has been cut and the ground is strewn with twigs. Among those seeding bluebells and dry twigs and mosses I think a titlark has his nest, as he stays all day there and in the oak over. The pale clear yellow of charlock, sharp and clear, promises the finches bushels of seed for their young. Under the scarlet of the poppies the larks run, and then for change of colour soar into the blue. Creamy honeysuckle on the hedge around the cornfield, buds of wild rose everywhere, but no sweet petal yet. Yonder, where the wheat can climb no higher up the slope, are the purple heath-bells, thyme and flitting stonechats.

The lone barn shut off by acres of barley is noisy with sparrows. It is their city, and there is a nest in every crevice, almost under every tile. Sometimes the partridges run between the ricks, and when the bats come out of the roof, leverets play in the waggon-track. At even a fern-owl beats by, passing close to the eaves whence the moths issue. On the narrow waggon-track which descends along a coombe and is worn in chalk, the heat pours down by day as if an invisible lens in the atmosphere focused the sun's rays. Strong woody knapweed endures it, so does toadflax and pale blue scabious, and wild mignonette. The very sun of Spain burns and burns and ripens the wheat on the edge of the coombe, and will only let the spring moisten a yard or two around it; but there a few rushes have sprung, and in the water itself brooklime with blue flowers grows so thickly that nothing but a bird could find space to drink. So down again from this sun of Spain to woody coverts where the wild hops are blocking every avenue, and green-flowered bryony would fain climb to the trees; where grey-flecked ivy winds spirally about the red rugged bark of pines, where burdocks fight for the footpath, and teazle-heads look over the low hedges. Brake-fern rises five feet high: in some way woodpeckers are associated with brake, and there seem more of them where it flourishes. If you count the depth and strength of its roots in the loamy sand, add the thickness of its flattened stem, and the width of its branching fronds, you may say that it comes near to be a little tree. Beneath where the ponds are bushy mare's-tails grow, and on the moist banks jointed pewterwort; some of the broad bronze leaves of waterweeds seem to try and conquer the pond and cover it so firmly that a wagtail may run on them. A white butterfly follows along the waggon-road, the pheasants slip away as quietly as the butterfly flies, but a jay screeches loudly and flutters in high rage to see us. Under an ancient garden wall among matted bines of trumpet convolvulus, there is a hedge-sparrow's nest overhung with ivy on which even now the last black berries cling.

There are minute white flowers on the top of the wall, out of reach, and lichen grows against it dried by the sun till it looks ready to crumble. By the gateway grows a thick bunch of meadow geranium, soon to flower; over the gate is the dusty highway road, quiet but dusty, dotted with the innumerable footmarks of a flock of sheep that has passed. The sound of their bleating still comes back, and the bees driven up by their feet have hardly had time to settle again on the white clover beginning to flower on the short roadside sward. All the hawthorn leaves and briar and bramble, the honeysuckle, too, is gritty with the dust that has been scattered upon it. But see – can it be? Stretch a hand high, quick, and reach it down; the first, the sweetest, the dearest rose of June. Not yet expected, for the time is between the may and the roses, least of all here in the hot and dusty highway; but it is found – the first rose of June.

Straight go the white petals to the heart; straight the mind's glance goes back to how many other pageants of summer in old times! When perchance the sunny days were even more sunny; when the stilly oaks were full of mystery, lurking like the Druid's mistletoe in the midst of their mighty branches. A glamour in the heart came back to it again from every flower; as the sunshine was reflected from them so the feeling in the heart returned tenfold. To the dreamy summer haze love gave a deep enchantment, the colours were fairer, the blue more lovely in the lucid sky. Each leaf finer, and the gross earth enamelled beneath the feet. A sweet breath on the air, a soft warm hand in the touch of the sunshine, a glance in the gleam of the rippled waters, a whisper in the dance of the shadows. The ethereal haze lifted the heavy oaks and they were buoyant on the mead, the rugged bark was chastened and no longer rough, each slender flower beneath them again refined. There was a presence everywhere though unseen, on the open hills, and not shut out under the dark pines. Dear were the June roses then because for another gathered. Yet even dearer now with so many years as it were upon the petals; all the days that have been before, all the heart-throbs, all our hopes lie in this opened bud. Let not the eyes grow dim, look not back but forward; the soul must uphold itself like the sun. Let us labour to make the heart grow larger as we become older, as the spreading oak gives more shelter. That we could but take to the soul some of the greatness and the beauty of the summer!

Still the pageant moves. The song-talk of the finches rises and sinks like the tinkle of a waterfall. The greenfinches have been by me all the while. A bullfinch pipes now and then further up the hedge where the brambles and thorns are thickest. Boldest of birds to look at, he is always in hiding. The shrill tone of a goldfinch came just now from the ash branches, but he has gone on. Every four or five minutes a chaffinch sings close by, and another fills the interval near the gateway. There are linnets somewhere, but I cannot from the old apple tree fix their exact place. Thrushes have sung and ceased; they will begin again in ten minutes. The blackbirds do not cease; the note uttered by a blackbird in the oak yonder before it can drop is taken up by a second near the top of the field, and ere it falls is caught by a third on the left-hand side. From one of the topmost boughs of an elm there fell the song of a willow warbler for awhile; one of the least of birds, he often seeks the highest branches of the highest tree.

A yellowhammer has just flown from a bare branch in the gateway, where he has been perched and singing a full hour. Presently he will commence again, and as the sun declines will sing him to the horizon, and then again sing till nearly dusk. The yellowhammer is almost the longest of all the singers; he sits and sits and has no inclination to move. In the spring he sings, in the summer he sings, and he continues when the last sheaves are being carried from the wheat field. The redstart yonder has given forth a few notes, the whitethroat flings himself into the air at short intervals and chatters, the shrike calls sharp and determined, faint but shrill calls descend from the swifts in the air. These descend, but the twittering notes of the swallows do not reach so far – they are too high to-day. A cuckoo has called by the brook, and now fainter from a greater distance. That the titlarks are singing I know, but not within hearing from here; a dove, though, is audible, and a chiffchaff has twice passed. Afar beyond the oaks at the top of the field dark specks ascend from time to time, and after moving in wide circles for awhile descend again to the corn. These must be larks; but their notes are not powerful enough to reach me, though they would were it not for the song in the hedges, the hum of innumerable insects, and the ceaseless 'crake, crake' of landrails. There are at least two landrails in the mowing-grass; one of them just now seemed coming straight towards the apple tree, and I expected in a minute to see the grass move, when the bird turned aside and entered the tufts and wild parsley by the hedge. Thence the call has come without a moment's pause, 'crake, crake', till the thick hedge seems filled with it. Tits have visited the apple tree over my head, a wren has sung in the willow, or rather on a dead branch projecting lower down than the leafy boughs, and a robin across under the elms in the opposite hedge. Elms are a favourite tree of robins – not the upper branches, but those that grow down the trunk, and are the first to have leaves in spring.

The yellowhammer is the most persistent individually, but I think the blackbirds when listened to are the masters of the fields. Before one can finish another begins, like the summer ripples succeeding behind each other, so that the melodious sound merely changes its position. Now here, now in the corner, then across the field, again in the distant copse, where it seems about to sink, when it rises again almost at hand. Like a great human artist, the blackbird makes no effort, being fully conscious that his liquid tone cannot be matched. He utters a few delicious notes, and carelessly quits the green stage of the oak till it pleases him to sing again. Without the blackbird, in whose throat the sweetness of the green fields dwells, the days would be only partly summer. Without the violet all the bluebells and cowslips could not make a spring, and without the blackbird, even the nightingale would be but half welcome. It is not yet noon, these songs have been ceaseless since dawn; this evening, after the yellowhammer has sung the sun down, when the moon rises and the faint stars appear, still the cuckoo will call, and the grasshopper lark, the landrail's 'crake, crake' will echo from the mound, a warbler or a blackcap will utter his notes, and even at the darkest of the summer night the swallows will hardly sleep in their nests. As the morning sky grows blue, an hour before the sun, up will rise the larks singing and audible now, the cuckoo will recommence, and the swallows will start again on their tireless journey. So that the songs of the summer birds are as ceaseless as the sound of the waterfall which plays day and night.

I cannot leave it; I must stay under the old tree in the midst of the long grass, the luxury of the leaves, and the song in the very air. I seem as if I could feel all the glowing life the sunshine gives and the south wind calls to being. The endless grass, the endless leaves, the immense strength of the oak expanding, the unalloyed joy of finch and blackbird; from all of them I receive a little. Each gives me something of the pure joy they gather for themselves. In the blackbird's melody one note is mine; in the dance of the leaf shadows the formed maze is for me, though the motion is theirs; the flowers with a thousand faces have collected the kisses of the morning. Feeling with them, I receive some, at least, of their fulness of life. Never could I have enough; never stay long enough – whether here or whether lying on the shorter sward under the sweeping and graceful birches, or on the thyme-scented hills. Hour after hour, and still not enough. Or walking the footpath was never long enough, or my strength sufficient to endure till the mind was weary. The exceeding beauty of the earth, in her splendour of life, yields a new thought with every petal. The hours when the mind is absorbed by beauty are the only hours when we really live, so that the longer we can stay among these things so much the more is snatched from inevitable Time. Let the shadow advance upon the dial – I can watch it with equanimity while it is there to be watched. It is only when the shadow is *not* there, when the clouds of winter cover it, that the dial is terrible. The invisible shadow goes on and steals from us. But now, while I can see the shadow of the tree and watch it slowly gliding along the surface of the grass, it is mine. These arc the only hours that are not wasted – these hours that absorb the soul and fill it with beauty. This is real life, and all else is illusion, or mere endurance. Does this reverie of flowers and waterfall and song form an ideal, a human ideal, in the mind? It does; much the same ideal that Phidias sculptured of man and woman filled with a godlike sense of the violet fields of Greece, beautiful beyond thought, calm as my turtledove before the lurid lightning of the unknown. To be beautiful and to be calm, without mental fear, is the ideal of nature. If I cannot achieve it, at least I can think it.

5 A London Trout

Some low wooden rails guarding the approach to a bridge over a brook one day induced me to rest under an aspen, with my back against the tree. Some horse-chestnuts, beeches, and alders grew there, fringing the end of a long plantation of willow stoles which extended in the rear following the stream. In front, southwards, there were open meadows and cornfields over which shadow and sunshine glided in succession as the sweet westerly wind carried the white clouds before it.

The brimming brook, as it wound towards me through the meads, seemed to tremble on the verge of overflowing, as the crown of wine in a glass rises yet does not spill. Level with the green grass, the water gleamed as if polished where it flowed smoothly, crossed with the dark shadows of willows which leaned over it. By the bridge, where the breeze rushed through the arches, a ripple flashed back the golden rays. The surface by the shore slipped towards a side hatch and passed over in a liquid curve, clear and unvarying as if of solid crystal, till shattered on the stones, where the air caught up and played with the sound of the bubbles as they broke.

Beyond the green slope of corn, a thin soft vapour hung on the distant woods, and hid the hills. The pale young leaves of the aspen rustled faintly, not yet with their full sound; the sprays of the horse-chestnut, drooping with the late frosts, could not yet keep out the sunshine with their broad green. A white spot on the footpath yonder was where the bloom had fallen from a blackthorn bush.

The note of the tree pipit came from over the corn – there were some detached oaks away in the midst of the field, and the birds were doubtless flying continually up and down between the wheat and the branches. A willow wren sang plaintively in the plantation behind, and once a cuckoo called in the distance. How beautiful is the sunshine! The very dust of the road at my feet seemed to glow with whiteness, to be lit up by it and to become another thing. This spot henceforward was a place of pilgrimage.

Looking that morning over the parapet of the bridge downstream there was a dead branch at the mouth of the arch; it had caught and got fixed as it floated along. A quantity of aquatic weeds coming down the stream had drifted against the branch and remained entangled in it. Fresh weeds were still coming and adding to the mass, which had attracted a water-rat.

Perched on the branch the little brown creature bent forward over the surface, and with its two forepaws drew towards it the slender thread of a weed exactly as with hands. Holding the thread in the paws it nibbled it, eating the sweet and tender portions, feeding without fear though but a few feet away, and precisely beneath me.

In a minute the surface of the current was disturbed by larger ripples. There had been a ripple caused by the draught under the arch, but this was now increased. Directly afterwards a moorhen swam out, and began to search among the edge of the tangled weeds. So long as I was perfectly still the bird took no heed, but at a slight movement instantly scuttled back under the arch. The water-rat, less timorous, paused, looked round, and continued feeding.

Crossing to the other side of the bridge, upstream, and looking over, the current had scooped away the sand at the bottom by the central pier, exposing the brickwork to some depth – the same undermining process that goes on by the piers of bridges over great rivers. Nearer the shore the sand had silted up, leaving it shallow, where water parsnip and other weeds joined, as it were, the verge of the grass and the stream. The sunshine reflected from the ripples on this, the southern side, continually ran with a swift trembling motion up the arch.

Penetrating the clear water, the light revealed the tiniest stone at the bottom; but there was no fish, no water-rat, no moorhen, on that side. Neither on that nor many succeeding mornings could anything be seen there; the tail of the arch was evidently the favourite spot. Carefully looking over that side again; the moorhen who had been out, rushed back; the water-rat was gone. Were there any fish? In the shadow the water was difficult to see through, and the brown scum of spring that lined the bottom rendered everything uncertain. By gazing steadily at a stone my eyes gradually became accustomed to the peculiar light, the pupils adjusted themselves to it, and the brown tints became more distinctly defined. Then, sweeping by degrees from one stone to another, and from thence to a rotten stick embedded in the sand, I searched the bottom inch by inch. If you look, as it were, at large – at everything at once – you see nothing. If you take some object as a fixed point, gaze all around it, then move to another, nothing can escape. Even the deepest, darkest water (not, of course, muddy) yields after a while to the eye. Half-close the eyelids, and while gazing into it, let your intelligence rather wait upon the corners of the eye than on the glance you cast straight forward. For some reason, while thus gazing, the edge of the eye becomes exceedingly sensitive, and you are conscious of slight motions or of a thickness – not a defined object – which is otherwise quite invisible.

The slow feeling sway of a fish's tail, the edges of which curl over and grasp the water, may, in this manner, be identified without being positively seen, and the dark outline of its body known to exist against the equally dark water or bank. Shift, too, your position according to the fall of the light, just as in looking at a painting. From one point of view the canvas shows little but the presence of paint and blurred colour, from another, at the side, the picture stands out.

Sometimes the water can be seen into best from above, sometimes by lying on the sward, now by standing back a little way or crossing to the opposite shore. A spot where the sunshine sparkles with dazzling gleam is perfectly impenetrable until you get to the other side of the ripple, when the same rays, that just now baffled the glance, light up the bottom as if thrown by a mirror for the purpose. I convinced myself that there was nothing here, nothing visible at present, not so much as a stickleback.

Yet the stream ran clear and sweet, and deep in places. It was too broad for leaping over. Down the current, sedges grew thickly at a curve, up the stream the young flags were rising, it had an *inhabited* look if such a term may be used, and moorhens and water-rats were about but no fish.

A wide furrow came along the meadow and joined the stream from the side. Into this furrow at flood time, the stream overflowed farther up, and irrigated the level sward.

At present it was dry, its course traced by the yellowish and white hue of the grasses in it only recently under water, contrasting with the brilliant green of the sweet turf around.

There was a marsh marigold in it, with stems a quarter of an inch thick, and in the grass, on the verge, but just beyond where the flood reached, grew the lilac-tinted cuckoo flowers, or cardamine.

The side hatch supplied a pond which was only

divided from the brook by a strip of sward not more than twenty yards across. The surface of the pond was dotted with patches of scum that had risen from the bottom. Part at least of it was shallow, for a dead branch blown from an elm, projected above the water, and to it came a sedge reedling for a moment . . . there were fish there, I felt sure as I left the spot and returned along the dusty road, but where were they?

Coming to my seat under the aspen by the bridge, week after week, the burdocks by the wayside gradually spread their leaves, and the procession of flowers went on. The dandelion and lesser celandine, the marsh marigolds, the coltsfoot, all yellow, had already led the van closely, accompanied by the purple ground ivy, the red dead-nettle, and the daisy; this last a latecomer in the neighbourhood. The blackthorn, the horse-chestnut and the hawthorn came, and the meadows were golden with buttercups.

Once only had I noticed any indication of fish in the brook; it was on a warm Saturday afternoon, when there was a labourer a long way up the stream, stooping in a peculiar manner near the edge of the water with a stick in his hand. He was, I felt sure, trying to wire a spawning jack, but he did not succeed. Many weeks had passed, and now there came (as the close season for coarse fish expired) a concourse of anglers to the almost stagnant pool fed by the side hatch.

Well-dressed lads with elegant and finished tackle rode up on their bicycles, with their rods slung on their backs. Hoisting the bicycles over the gate into the meadow, they left them leaning against the elms, fitted their rods and fished in the pond. Poorer boys, with long wands cut from the hedge and ruder lines, trudged up on foot, sat down on the sward, and watched their corks for hours together. Grown men of the artisan class, covered with the dust of many miles tramping, came with their luncheons in a handkerchief, and set about their sport with a quiet earnestness which argued long, if desultory, practice.

In fine weather there were often a dozen youths and

four or five men standing, sitting, or kneeling on the turf along the shore of the pond, all intent on their floats and very nearly silent. People driving along the highway stopped their traps, carts and vans a minute or two, to watch them; passengers on foot leaned over the gate, or sat down and watched expectantly.

Sometimes one of the more venturesome anglers would tuck up his trousers and walk into the shallow water, so as to be able to cast his bait under the opposite bank where the pond was deep. Then an ancient and much-battered punt was discovered aground in a field at some distance and dragged to the pond. One end of the punt had quite rotted away, but by standing at the other so as to depress it there and lift the open end above the surface, two, or even three, could make shift to fish from it.

The silent and motionless eagerness with which these anglers dwelt upon their floats, grave as herons, could not have been exceeded. They were there day after day, always patient and always hopeful. Occasionally a small catch, a mere 'bait' was handed round for inspection; and once a cunning fisherman acquainted with the secrets of his craft, succeeded in drawing forth three perch perhaps a quarter of a pound each and one slender eel. These made quite a show and were greatly admired; but I never saw the same man there again. He was satisfied.

As I sat on the white rail under the aspen, and inhaled the scent of the beans flowering hard by, there was a question which suggested itself to me, and the answer to which I never could supply. The crowd about the pond all stood with their backs to the beautiful flowing brook. They had before them the muddy banks of the stagnant pool, on whose surface patches of scum floated.

Behind them was the delicious stream, clear and limpid, bordered with sedge and yellow flags, and overhung by branches. The strip of sward between the two waters was certainly not more than twenty yards; there was no division, no hedge, or railing, and evidently no preservation, for the mouchers came and washed their watercress in the ditches by the side hatch and no one interfered with them.

There was no keeper or water bailiff, not even a notice board. Policemen, mounted and on foot, passed several times daily, and, like everybody else, paused to see the sport, but said no word. Clearly there was nothing whatever to prevent any of those present from angling in the stream; yet they one and all without exception, fished the pond. This seemed to me a very remarkable fact.

After a while I noticed another circumstance; nobody ever even looked into the stream or under the arches of the bridge. No one spared a moment from his float amid the scum of the pond, just to stroll twenty paces and glance at the swift current. It appeared that this pond had a reputation for fish, and the brook had not. Everybody who had angled in the pond recommended his friends to go and do likewise. There were fish in the pond.

So every fresh-comer went and angled there, and accepted the fact that there were fish . . .

One morning, looking very gently over the parapet of the bridge (downstream) into the shadowy depths beneath, just as my eyes began to see the bottom, something like a short, thick, dark stick drifted out from the arch, somewhat sideways.

Instead of proceedingwith the current, it had hardly cleared the arch when it took up a position parallel to the flowing water and brought up. It was thickest at the end that faced the stream; at the other there was slight motion as if caused by the current against a flexible membrane, as it sways a flag. Gazing down intently into the shadow the colour of the sides of the fish appeared at first not exactly uniform, and presently these indistinct differences resolved themselves into spots. It was a trout, perhaps a pound and a half in weight.

His position was at the side of the arch, out of the rush of the current, and almost behind the pier, but where he could see anything that came floating along under the culvert. Immediately above, but not over him was a mass of weed tangled in the dead branch. Thus in the shadow of the bridge and in the darkness of the weeds he might easily have escaped notice. He was, too, extremely wary. The slightest motion was enough to send him instantly under the arch; his cover was but a foot distant, and a trout shoots twelve inches in a fraction of time.

The summer advanced, the hay was carted, and the wheat ripened. Already, here and there, the reapers had cut portions of the more forward corn. As I sat from time to time under the aspen, within hearing of the murmuring water, the thought did arise occasionally that it was a pity to leave the trout there till someone blundered into the knowledge of its existence.

There were ways and means by which he could be withdrawn without any noise or publicity. But then, what would be the pleasure of securing him, the fleeting pleasure of an hour, compared with the delight of seeing him almost day by day? I watched him for many weeks, taking great precautions that no one should observe how continually I looked over the water there. Sometimes, after a glance, I stood with my back to the wall as if regarding an object on the other side. If anyone was following me, or appeared likely to peer over the parapet, I carelessly struck the top of the wall with my stick in such a manner that it would project, an action sufficient to send the fish under the arch. Or I raised my hat as if heated, and swung it so that it should alarm him.

If the coast was clear when I had looked at him, still I never left without sending him under the arch in order to increase his alertness. It was a relief to know that so many persons who went by wore tall hats, a safeguard against their seeing anything, for if they approached and the shadow of the tall hat reached out beyond the shadow of the parapet it was enough to alarm him before they could look over.

So the summer passed, and, though never free from apprehensions, to my great pleasure without discovery. The sword flags are rusting at their edges, and their sharp points are turned. On the matted and entangled sedges lie the scattered leaves which every rush of the October wind hurries from the boughs. Some fall on the water and float slowly with the current, brown and yellow spots on a dark surface. The grey willows bend to the breeze; soon the osier beds will look reddish as the wands are stripped by the gusts. Alone the thick-polled alders remain green, and in their shadow the brook is still darker. Through the poplars' thin branches the wind sounds as in the rigging of a ship; for the rest, silence.

The thrushes have forgotten the frost of the morning, and will not sing at noon, the summer visitors have flown, and the moorhens feed quietly. The plantation by the brook is silent, for the sedges, though they have drooped, are not too dry and sapless yet to rustle loudly. They will rustle dry enough next spring, when the sedge birds come.

The sharp points of the sword flags are turned, their edges rusty, the forget-me-nots are gone. October winds are too searching for us to linger beside the brook, but still it is pleasant to pass by and remember the summer days. For the year is never gone by; in a moment we can recall the sunshine we enjoyed in May, the roses we gathered in June, the first wheat ear we plucked as the green corn filled. Other events go by and are forgotten, and even the details of our own lives, so immensely important to us at the moment, in time fade from memory till the date we fancied we should never forget has to be sought in a diary. But the year is always with us; the months are familiar always; they have never gone by.

There is a beech in the plantation standing so near the verge of the stream that its boughs droop over. It has a number of twigs around the stem – as a rule the beech bole is clear of boughs, but some which are of rather stunted growth are fringed with them. The leaves on the longer boughs fall off and voyage down the brook, but those on the lesser twigs remain on, dry and brown, all through the winter. Under the shelter of these leaves, and close to the trunk, there grew a plant of flag – the tops of the flags almost reached to the leaves – and all the winter through, despite the frosts which were remarkable, despite the snow and bitter winds which followed, this plant remained fresh and green. From this beech in the morning a shadow stretches to a bridge across the brook, and in that shadow my trout used to lie. The bank under the drooping boughs forms a tiny cliff a foot high covered with moss and here I once observed shrew mice diving and racing about. But only once, though I frequently passed the spot; it is curious that I did not see them afterwards.

Just below the shadow of the beech there is a sandy, oozy shore, where the footprints of moorhens are often traceable. Many of the trees in the plantation stand in water after heavy rain – their leaves drop into it in autumn, and, being away from the influence of the current, stay and soak, and lie several layers thick. Their edges overlap, red, brown, and pale yellow, with the clear water above and shadows athwart it, and dry white grass at the verge. A horse-chestnut drops its fruit in the dusty road; high above its leaves are tinted with scarlet. It was at the tail of one of the arches of the bridge over the brook that my favourite trout used to lie. Sometimes the shadow of the beech came as far as his haunts, that was early in the morning, and for the rest of the day the bridge cast a shadow. The other parapet faces south, and looking down from it the bottom of the brook is generally visible, because the light is so strong. At the bottom a green plant may be seen waving to and fro, in summer, as the current sways it. It is not a weed or flag, but a plant with pale green leaves, and looks as if it had come there by chance; this is the water-parsnip.

By the shore on this, the sunny side of the bridge, a few forget-me-nots grow in their season, water crows-foot flowers, flags lie along the surface and slowly swing from side to side like a boat at anchor. The breeze brings a ripple, and the sunlight sparkles on it, the light reflected dances up the piers of the bridge. Those that pass along the road are naturally drawn to this bright parapet where the brook winds brimming full through green meadows. You can see right to the bottom; you can see where the rush of the water has scooped out a deeper channel under the arches, but look as long as you like there are no fish.

The trout I watched so long, and with such pleasure, was always on the other side, at the tail of the arch, waiting for whatever might come through to him. There in perpetual shadow he lay in wait, a little at the side of the arch, scarcely ever varying his position except to dart a yard up under the bridge to seize anything he fancied, and to drift out again to bring up at his anchorage.

If people looked over the parapet that side they did not see him; they could not see the bottom there for the shadow, or if the summer noonday cast a strong beam, even then it seemed to cover the surface with a film of light which could not be seen through. There are some aspects from which even a picture hung on the rail close at hand cannot be seen. So no one saw the trout; if anyone more curious leant over the parapet he was gone in a moment under the arch.

Folk fished in the pond about the verge of which the sedge-birds chattered, and but a few yards distant; but they never looked under the arch on the northern and shadowy side, where the water flowed beside the beech. For three seasons this continued. For three summers I had the pleasure to see the trout day after day whenever I walked that way, and all that time, with fishermen close at hand, he escaped notice, though the place was not preserved. It is wonderful to think how difficult it is to see anything under one's very eyes, and thousands of people walked actually and physically right over the fish.

However, one morning in the third summer, I

found a fisherman standing in the road and fishing over the parapet in the shadowy water. But he was fishing at the wrong arch, and only with paste, for roach. While the man stood there fishing, along came two navvies; naturally enough they went quietly up to see what the fisherman was doing, and one instantly uttered an exclamation. He had seen the trout! The man who was fishing with paste had stood so still and patiently that the trout, reassured, had come out, and the navvy – trust a navvy to see anything of the kind – caught sight of him. The navvy knew how to see through water. He told the fisherman, and there was a stir of excitement, a changing of hooks and bait. I could not stay to see the result but went on, fearing the worst. But he did not succeed; next day the wary trout was still there, and the next, and the next. Either this particular fisherman was not able to come again, or was discouraged; at any rate he did not try again. The fish escaped, doubtless more wary than ever.

In the spring of the next year the trout was still there, and up to the summer I used to go and glance at him. This was the fourth season, and still he was there; I took friends to look at this wonderful fish, which defied all the loafers and poachers, and above all, surrounded himself not only with shadow over the minds of passers by, so that they never thought of the possibility of such a thing as trout. But one morning something happened. The brook was dammed up on the sunny side of the bridge, and the water let off by a side-hatch, that some accursed main or pipe, or other horror, might be laid across the bed of the stream somewhere far down.

Above the bridge there was a brimming broad brook, below it the flags lay on the mud, the weeds drooped, and the channel was dry. It was dry up to the beech tree. There, under the drooping boughs of the beech, was a small pool of muddy water, perhaps two yards long, and very narrow – a stagnant muddy pool not more than three or four inches deep. In this I saw the trout. In the shallow water, his back came up to the surface (for his fins must have touched the mud sometimes), once it came above the surface, and his spots showed as plain as if you had held him in your hand. He was swimming round to try and find out the reason for this sudden stinting of room. Twice he heaved himself somewhat on to his side over a dead branch that was at the bottom, and exhibited all his beauty to the air and sunshine. Then he went away into another part of the shallow and was hidden by the muddy water. Now, under the arch of the bridge, his favourite arch, close by, there was a deep pool, for, as already mentioned, the scour of the current scooped away the sand and made a hole there. When the stream was shut off by this dam above, this hole remained partly full. Between this pool and the shallow under the beech there was a sufficient connection for the fish to move into it.

My only hope was that he would do so and as some showers fell, temporarily increasing the depth of the narrow canal between the two pools, there seemed every reason to believe that he had got to that under the arch. If now only that accursed pipe or main, or whatever repair it was, could only be finished quickly even now the trout might escape! Every day my anxiety increased, for the intelligence would soon get about that the brook was dammed up, and any pools left in it would be sure to attract attention.

Sunday came, and directly the bells had done ringing, four men attacked the pool under the arch. They took off shoes and stockings and waded in, two at each end of the arch. Stuck in the mud close by was an eel spear. They churned up the mud, wading in, and thickened and darkened it as they groped under. No one could watch these barbarians longer.

Is it possible that he could have escaped? He was a wonderful fish, wary and quick. Is it just possible that they may not even have known that a trout was there at all; but had merely hoped for perch or eels? The pool was deep and the fish quick – they did not bail it, might he have escaped? Might they even, if they did find him, have mercifully taken him and placed him alive in some other water nearer their home? Is it possible that he may have almost miraculously made his way down the stream into other pools?

There was heavy rain one night, which might have given him such a chance. These 'mights' and 'ifs' and 'is it possibles' even now keep alive some little hope that some day I may yet see him again. But that was in the early summer. It is now winter, and the beech has brown spots. Among the limes the sedges are matted and entangled, the sword flags rusty; the rooks are at the acorns, and the plough is at work in the stubble. I have never seen him since. I never failed to glance over the parapet into the shadowy water. Somehow it seemed to look colder, darker, less pleasant than it used to do. The spot was empty, and thc shrill winds whistled through the poplars.

6 Trees About Town

Just outside London there is a circle of fine, large houses, each standing in its own grounds, highly rented, and furnished with every convenience money can supply. If anyone will look at the trees and shrubs growing in the grounds about such a house, chosen at random for an example, and make a list of them, he may then go round the entire circumference of Greater London, mile after mile, many days' journey, and find the list ceaselessly repeated.

There are acacias, sumachs, cedar deodaras, araucarias, laurels, planes, beds of rhododendrons, and so on. There are various other foreign shrubs and trees whose names have not become familiar, and then the next grounds contain exactly the same, somewhat differently arranged. Had they all been planted by Act of Parliament, the result could scarcely have been more uniform.

If, again, search were made in these enclosures for English trees and English shrubs, it would be found that none have been introduced. The English trees, timber trees, that are there, grew before the house was built; for the rest, the products of English woods and hedgerows have been carefully excluded. The law is,

'Plant planes, laurels, and rhododendrons; root up everything natural to this country.'

To those who have any affection for our own woodlands this is a pitiful spectacle, produced, too, by the expenditure of large sums of money. Will no one break through the practice, and try the effect of English trees? There is no lack of them, and they far excel anything yet imported in beauty and grandeur.

Though such suburban grounds mimic the isolation and retirement of ancient country houses surrounded with parks, the distinctive feature of the ancient houses is omitted. There are no massed bodies, as it were, of our own trees to give a substance to the view. Are young oaks ever seen in those grounds so often described as park-like? Some time since it was customary for the builder to carefully cut down every piece of timber on the property before putting in the foundations.

Fortunately, the influence of a better taste now preserves such trees as chance to be growing on the site at the moment it is purchased. These remain, but no others are planted. A young oak is not to be seen. The oaks that are there drop their acorns in vain, for if one takes root it is at once cut off; it would spoil the laurels. It is the same with elms; the old elms are decaying, and no successors are provided.

As for ash, it is doubtful if a young ash is anywhere to be found; if so, it is an accident. The ash is even rarer than the rest. In their places are put more laurels, cedar deodaras, various evergreens, rhododendrons, planes. How tame and insignificant are these compared with the oak! Thrice a year the oaks become beautiful in a different way.

In spring the opening buds give the trees a ruddy hue; in summer the great head of green is not to be surpassed; in autumn, with the falling leaf and acorn, they appear buff and brown. The nobility of the oak casts the pitiful laurel into utter insignificance. With elms it is the same; they are reddish with flower and bud very early in the year, the fresh leaf is a tender green; in autumn they are sometimes one mass of yellow.

Ashes change from almost black to a light green, then a deeper green, and again light green and yellow. Where is the foreign evergreen in the competition? Put side by side, competition is out of the question: you have only to get an artist to paint the oak in its three phases to see this. There is less to be said against the deodara than the rest, as it is a graceful tree; but it is not English in any sense.

The point, however, is that the foreigners oust the English altogether. Let the cedar and the laurel, and the whole host of invading evergreens, be put aside by themselves, in a separate and detached shrubbery, maintained for the purpose of exhibiting strange growths. Let them not crowd the lovely English trees out of the place. Planes are much planted now, with ill effect; the blotches where the bark peels, the leaves which lie on the sward like brown leather, the branches wide apart and giving no shelter to birds – in short, the whole ensemble of the plane is unfit for our country.

It was selected for London plantations, as the Thames Embankment, because its peeling bark was believed to protect it against the deposit of sooty particles, and because it grows quickly. For use in London itself it may be preferable: for semi-country seats, as the modern houses surrounded with their own grounds assume to be, it is unsightly. It has no association. No one has seen a plane in a hedgerow, or a wood, or a copse. There are no fragments of English history clinging to it as there are to the oak.

If trees of the plane class be desirable, sycamores may be planted, as they have in a measure become acclimatized. If trees that grow fast are required, there are limes and horse-chestnuts; the lime will run a race with any tree. The lime, too, has a pale yellow blossom, to which bees resort in numbers, making a pleasant hum, which seems the natural accompaniment of summer sunshine. Its leaves are put forth early.

Horse-chestnuts, too, grow quickly and without any attention, the bloom is familiar, and acknowledged to be fine, and in autumn the large sprays of leaves take orange and even scarlet tints. The plane is not to be mentioned beside either of them. Other trees as well as the plane would have flourished on the Thames Embankment, in consequence of the current of fresh air caused by the river. Imagine the Embankment with double rows of oaks, elms, or beeches; or, if not, even with limes or horse-chestnuts! To these certainly birds would have resorted – possibly rooks, which do not fear cities. On such a site the experiment would have been worth making.

If in the semi-country seats fast-growing trees are needed, there are, as I have observed, the lime and horse-chestnut; and if more variety be desired, add the Spanish chestnut and the walnut. The Spanish chestnut is a very fine tree; the walnut, it is true, grows slowly. If as many beeches as cedar deodaras and laurels and planes were planted in these grounds, in due course of time the tap of the woodpecker would be heard: a sound truly worth ten thousand laurels. At Kew, far closer to town than many of the semi-country seats are now, all our trees flourish in perfection.

Hardy birches, too, will grow in thin soil. Just compare the delicate drooping boughs of birch – they could not have been more delicate if sketched with a pencil – compare these with the gaunt planes!

Of all the foreign shrubs that have been brought to these shores, there is not one that presents us with so beautiful a spectacle as the bloom of the common old English hawthorn in May. The mass of blossom, the pleasant fragrance, its divided and elegant leaf, place it far above any of the importations. Besides which, the traditions and associations of the May give it a human interest.

The hawthorn is a part of natural English life – country life. It stands side by side with the Englishman, as the palm tree is pictured side by side with the

Arab. You cannot pick up an old play, or book of the time when old English life was in the prime, without finding some reference to the hawthorn. There is nothing of this in the laurel, or any shrub whatever that may be thrust in with a ticket to tell you its name; it has a ticket because it has no interest, or else you would know it.

For use there is nothing like hawthorn; it will trim into a thick hedge, defending the enclosure from trespassers, and warding off the bitter winds; or it will grow into a tree. Again, the old hedge-crab – the common, despised crab-apple – in spring is covered with blossom, such a mass of blossom that it may be distinguished a mile. Did any one ever see a plane or a laurel look like that?

How pleasant, too, to see the clear white flower of the blackthorn come out in the midst of the bitter easterly breezes! It is like a white handkerchief beckoning to the sun to come. There will not be much more frost; if the wind is bitter to-day, the sun is rapidly gaining power. Probably, if a blackthorn bush were by any chance discovered in the semi-parks or enclosures alluded to, it would at once be rooted out as an accursed thing. The very brambles are superior; there is the flower, the sweet berry, and afterwards the crimson leaves – three things in succession.

What can the world produce equal to the June rose? The common briar, the commonest of all, offers a flower which, whether in itself, or the moment of its appearance at the juncture of all sweet summer things, or its history and associations, is not to be approached by anything a millionaire could purchase. The labourer casually gathers it as he goes to his work in the field, and yet none of the rich families whose names are synonymous with wealth can get anything to equal it if they ransack the earth.

After these, fill every nook and corner with hazel, and make filbert walks. Up and down such walks men strolled with rapiers by their sides while our admirals were hammering at the Spaniards with culverin and demi-cannon, and looked at the sundial and adjourned for a game at bowls, wishing that they only had a chance to bowl shot instead of peaceful wood. Fill in the corners with nut-trees, then, and make filbert walks. All these are like old story books, and the old stories are always best.

Still, there are others for variety, as the wild guelder rose, which produces heavy bunches of red berries; dogwood, whose leaves when frost-touched take deep colours; barberry, yielding a pleasantly acid fruit; the wayfaring tree; not even forgetting the elder, but putting it at the outside, because, though flowering, the scent is heavy, and because the elder was believed of old time to possess some of the virtue now attributed to the blue gum, and to neutralize malaria by its own odour.

For colour add the wild broom and some furze. Those who have seen broom in full flower, golden to the tip of every slender bough, cannot need any persuasion, surely, to introduce it. Furze is specked with yellow when the skies are dark and storms sweep around, besides its prime display. Let wild clematis climb wherever it will. Then laurels may come after these, put somewhere by themselves, with their thick changeless leaves, unpleasant to the touch; no one ever gathers a spray.

Rhododendrons it is unkind to attack, for in themselves they afford a rich flower. It is not the rhododendron, but the abuse of it, which must be protected against. Whether the soil suits or not – and, for the most part, it does not suit – rhododendrons are thrust in everywhere. Just walk in amongst them – behind the show – and look at the spindly, crooked stems, straggling how they may, and then look at the earth under them, where not a weed even will grow. The rhododendron is admirable in its place, but it is often overdone and a failure, and has no right to exclude those shrubs that are fitter. Most of the foreign shrubs about these semi-country seats look exactly like the stiff and painted little wooden trees that are sold for children's toys, and, like the toys, are the same colour all the year round.

Now, if you enter a copse in spring the eye is delighted with cowslips on the banks where the sunlight comes, with blue-bells, or earlier with anemones and violets, while later the ferns rise. But enter the semi-parks of the semi-country seat, with its affected assumption of countryness, and there is not one of these. The fern is actually purposely eradicated – just think! Purposely! Though indeed they would not grow, one would think, under rhododendrons and laurels, cold-blooded laurels. They will grow under hawthorns, ash, or beside the bramble bushes.

If there chance to be a little pond or 'fountain', there is no such thing as a reed, or a flag, or a rush. How the rushes would be hastily hauled out and hurled away with execrations!

Besides the greater beauty of English trees, shrubs, and plants, they also attract the birds, without which the grandest plantation is a vacancy, and another interest, too, arises from watching the progress of their growth and the advance of the season. Our own trees and shrubs literally keep pace with the stars which shine in our northern skies. An astronomical floral almanack might almost be constructed, showing how, as the constellations marched on by night, the buds and leaves and flowers appeared by day.

The lower that brilliant Sirius sinks in the western sky after ruling the winter heavens, and the higher that red Arcturus rises, so the buds thicken, open, and bloom. When the Pleiades begin to rise in the early evening, the leaves are turning colour, and the seed vessels of the flowers take the place of the petals. The coincidences of floral and bird life, and of these with the movements of the heavens, impart a sense of breadth to their observation.

It is not only the violet or the anemone, there are the birds coming from immense distances to enjoy the summer with us; there are the stars appearing in succession, so that the most distant of objects seems brought into connection with the nearest, and the world is made one. The sharp distinction, the line artificially drawn between things, quite disappears when they are thus associated.

Birds, as just remarked, are attracted by our own trees and shrubs. Oaks are favourites with rooks and wood-pigeons; blackbirds whistle in them in spring; if there is a pheasant about in autumn he is sure to come under the oak; jays visit them. Elms are resorted to by most of the larger birds. Ash plantations attract wood-pigeons and turtledoves. Thrushes are fond of the ash, and sing much on its boughs. The beech is the woodpecker's tree so soon as it grows old – birch one of the missel-thrush's.

In blackthorn the long-tailed tit builds the domed nest everyone admires. Under the cover of brambles white-throats build. Nightingales love hawthorn, and so does every bird. Plant hawthorn, and almost every bird will come to it, from the wood-pigeon down to the wren. Do not clear away the fallen branches and brown leaves, sweeping the plantation as if it were the floor of a ballroom, for it is just the tangle and the wilderness that brings the birds, and they like the disarray.

If evergreens are wanted, there are the yew, the box, and holly – all three well sanctioned by old custom. Thrushes will come for the yew berries, and birds are fond of building in the thick cover of high box hedges. Notwithstanding the prickly leaves, they slip in and out of the holly easily. A few bunches of rushes and sedges, with some weeds and aquatic grasses, allowed to grow about a pond, will presently bring moorhens. Bare stones – perhaps concrete – will bring nothing.

If a bough falls into the water, let it stay; sparrows will perch on it to drink. If a sandy drinking-place can be made for them the number of birds that will come in the course of the day will be surprising.

Kind-hearted people, when winter is approaching, should have two posts sunk in their grounds, with planks across at the top; a raised platform with the edges projecting beyond the posts, so that cats cannot climb up, and of course higher than a cat can spring. The crumbs cast out upon this platform would gather crowds of birds; they will come to feel at home, and in springtime will return to build and sing.

7 Red Roofs of London

Tiles and tile roofs have a curious way of tumbling to pieces in an irregular and eye-pleasing manner. The roof-tree bends, bows a little under the weight, curves in, and yet preserves a sharpness at each end. The Chinese exaggerate this curve of set purpose. Our English curve is softer, being the product of time, which always works in true taste. The mystery of tile-laying is not known to everyone; for to all appearance tiles seem to be put on over a thin bed of hay or hay-like stuff. Lately they have begun to use some sort of tarpaulin or a coarse material of that kind; but the old tiles, I fancy, were comfortably placed on a shake-down of hay. When one slips off, little bits of hay stick up; and to these the sparrows come, removing it bit by bit to line their nests. If they can find a gap they get in, and a fresh couple is started in life. By-and-by a chimney is overthrown during a twist of the wind, and half a dozen tiles are shattered. Time passes; and at last the tiler arrives to mend the mischief. His labour leaves a light red patch on the dark dull red of the breadth about it. After another while the leaks along the ridge need plastering: mortar is laid on to stay the inroad of wet, adding a dull white and forming a rough, uncertain undulation along the general drooping curve. Yellow edgings of straw project under the eaves – the work of the sparrows. A cluster of blue-tinted pigeons gather about the chimneyside; the smoke that comes out of the stack droops and floats sideways, downwards, as if the chimney enjoyed the smother as a man enjoys his pipe. Shattered here and cracked yonder, some missing, some overlapping in curves, the tiles have an aspect of irregular existence. They are not fixed, like slates, as it were for ever: they have a newness, and then a middle-age, and a time of decay like human beings.

One roof is not much; but it is often a study. Put a thousand roofs, say rather thousands of red-tiled roofs, and overlook them – not at a great altitude, but at a pleasant easy angle – and then you have the groundwork of the first view of London over Bermondsey from the railway. I say groundwork, because the roofs seem the level and surface of the earth, while the glimpses of streets are glimpses of catacombs. A city – as something to look at – depends very much on its roofs. If a city have no character in its roofs it stirs neither heart nor thought. These red-tiled roofs of Bermondsey, stretching away mile upon mile, and brought up at the extremity with thin masts rising above the mist – these red-tiled roofs have a distinctiveness, a character; they are something to think about. Nowhere else is there an entrance to a city like this. The roads by which you approach them give you distant aspects – minarets, perhaps, in the East, domes in Italy; but, coming nearer, the highway somehow plunges into houses, confounding you with façades, and the real place is hidden. Here from the railway you see at once the vastness of London. Roof-tree behind roof-tree, ridge behind ridge, is drawn along in succession, line behind line till they become as close together as the test-lines used for microscopes. Under this surface of roofs what a profundity of life there is! Just as the great horses in the waggons of London streets convey the idea of strength, so the endlessness of the view conveys the idea of a mass of life. Life converges from every quarter. The iron way has many ruts: the rails are its ruts; and by each of these a ceaseless stream of men and women pours over the tiled roofs into London. They come from the populous suburbs, from faraway towns and quiet villages, and from over sea.

Glance down as you pass into the excavations, the streets, beneath the red surface: you catch a glimpse of men and women hastening to and fro, of vehicles, of horses struggling with mighty loads, of groups at the corners, and fragments, as it were, of crowds. Busy life everywhere: no stillness, no quiet, no repose. Life crowded and crushed together; life that has hardly room to live. If the train slackens, look in at the open windows of the houses level with the line – they are always open for air, smoke-laden as it is – and see women and children with scarce room to move, the bed and the dining-table in the same apartment. For they dine and sleep and work and play all at the same time. A man works at night and sleeps by day: he lies yonder as calmly as if in a quiet country cottage. The children have no place to play in but the living-room or the street. It is not squalor – it is crowded life. The people are pushed together by the necessities of existence. These people have no dislike to it at all: it is right enough to them, and so long as business is brisk they are happy. The man who lies sleeping so calmly seems to me to indicate the immensity of the life around more than all the rest. He is oblivious of it all; it does not make him nervous or wakeful; he is so used to it, and bred to it, that it seems to him nothing. When he is awake he does not see it; now he sleeps he does not hear it. It is only in great woods that you cannot see the trees. He is like a leaf in a forest – he is not conscious of it. Long hours of work have given him slumber, and as he sleeps he seems to express by contrast the immensity and endlessness of the life around him.

Sometimes a floating haze, now thicker here, and

now lit up yonder by the sunshine, brings out objects more distinctly than a clear atmosphere. Away there tall thin masts stand out, rising straight up above the red roofs. There is a faint colour on them; the yards are dark – being inclined, they do not reflect the light at an angle to reach us. Half-furled canvas droops in folds, now swelling a little as the wind blows, now heavily sinking. One white sail is set and gleams alone among the dusky folds; for the canvas at large is dark with coal-dust, with smoke, with the grime that settles everywhere where men labour with bare arms and chests. Still and quiet as trees the masts rise into the hazy air; who would think, merely to look at them, of the endless labour they mean? The labour to load, and the labour to unload; the labour at sea, and the long hours of ploughing the waves by night; the labour at the warehouses; the labour in the fields, the mines, the mountains; the labour in the factories. Ever and again the sunshine gleams now on this group of masts, now on that; for they stand in groups as trees often grow, a thicket here and a thicket yonder. Labour to obtain the material, labour to bring it hither, labour to force it into shape – work without end. Masts are always dreamy to look at: they speak a romance of the sea; of unknown lands; of distant forests aglow with tropical colours and abounding with strange forms of life. In the hearts of most of us there is always a desire for something beyond experience. Hardly any of us but have thought, Some day I will go on a long voyage; but the years go by, and still we have not sailed.

8 The Modern Thames

I

The wild red deer can never again come down to drink at the Thames in the dusk of the evening as once they did. While modern civilization endures, the larger fauna must necessarily be confined to parks or restrained to well-marked districts; but for that very reason the lesser creatures of the wood, the field, and the river should receive the more protection. If this applies to the secluded country, far from the stir of cities, still more does it apply to the neighbourhood of London. From a sportsman's point of view, or from that of a naturalist, the state of the river is one of chaos. There is no order. The Thames appears free even from the usual rules which are in force upon every highway. A man may not fire a gun within a certain distance of a road under a penalty – a law enacted for the safety of passengers, who were formerly endangered by persons shooting small birds along the hedges bordering roads. Nor may he shoot at all, not so much as fire off a pistol (as recently publicly proclaimed by the Metropolitan police to restrain the use of revolvers), without a licence. But on the river people do as they choose, and there does not seem to be any law at all – or at least there is no authority to enforce it, if it exists. Shooting from boats and from the towing-path is carried on in utter defiance of the licensing law, of the game law (as applicable to wild fowl), and of the safety of persons who may be passing. The moorhens are shot, the kingfishers have been nearly exterminated or driven away from some parts, the once common black-headed bunting is comparatively scarce in the more frequented reaches, and if there is nothing else to shoot at, then the swallows are slaughtered. Some have even taken to shooting at the rooks in the trees or fields by the river with small-bore rifles – a most dangerous thing to do. The result is that the osier-beds on the eyots and by the backwaters – the copses of the river – are almost devoid of life. A few moorhens creep under the aquatic grasses and conceal themselves beneath the bushes, water-voles hide among the flags, but the once extensive host of water-fowl and river life has been reduced to the smallest limits. Water-fowl cannot breed because they are shot on the nest, or their eggs taken. As for rarer birds, of course they have not the slightest chance.

The fish have fared better because they have received the benefit of close seasons, enforced with more or less vigilance all along the river. They are also protected by regulations making it illegal to capture them except in a sportsmanlike manner; snatching, for instance, is unlawful. Riverside proprietors preserve some reaches, piscatorial societies preserve others, and the complaint indeed is that the rights of the public have been encroached upon. The too exclusive preservation of fish is in a measure responsible for the destruction of water-fowl, which are cleared off preserved places in order that they may not help themselves to fry or spawn. On the other hand, the societies may claim to have saved parts of the river from being entirely deprived of fish, for it is not long since it appeared as if the stream would be quite cleared out. Large quantities of fish have also been placed in the river, taken from ponds and bodily transported to the Thames. So that upon the whole the fish have been well looked after of recent years.

The most striking of the aquatic plants – such as white water-lilies – have been much diminished in quantity by the constant plucking, and injury is said to have been done by careless navigation. In things of this kind a few persons can do a great deal of damage. Two or three men with guns, and indifferent to the interests of sport or natural history, at work every day, can clear a long stretch of river of water-fowl, by scaring if not by actually killing them. Imagine three or four such gentry allowed to wander at will in a large game preserve – in a week they would totally destroy it as a preserve. The river, after all, is but a narrow band as it were, and is easily commanded by a gun. So, too, with fish poachers; a very few men with nets can quickly empty a good piece of water: and flowers like water-lilies, which grow only in certain spots, are soon pulled or spoiled. This aspect of the matter – the immense mischief which can be effected by a very few persons – should be carefully borne in mind in framing any regulations. For the mischief done on the river is really the work of a small number, a mere fraction of the thousands of all classes who frequent it. Not one in a thousand probably perpetrates any intentional damage to fish, fowl, or flowers.

As the river above all things is, and ought to be, a place of recreation, care must be particularly taken that in restraining these practices the enjoyment of the many be not interfered with. The rational pleasure of 999 people ought not to be checked because the last of the thousand acts as a blackguard. This point, too, bears upon the question of steam-launches. A launch can pass as softly and quietly as a skiff floating with the stream. And there is a good deal to be said on the other side, for the puntsmen stick themselves very often in the way of everyone else; and if you analyse fishing for minnows from a punt you will not find it a noble sport. A river like the Thames, belonging as it does –

or as it ought – to a city like London, should be managed from the very broadest standpoint. There should be pleasure for all, and there certainly is no real difficulty in arranging matters to that end. The Thames should be like a great aquarium, in which a certain balance of life has to be kept up. When aquaria first came into favour such things as snails and weeds were excluded as eyesores and injurious. But it was soon discovered that the despised snails and weeds were absolutely necessary; an aquarium could not be maintained in health without them, and now the most perfect aquarium is the one in which the natural state is most completely copied. On the same principle it is evident that too exclusive preservation must be injurious to the true interests of the river. Fish enthusiasts, for instance, desire the extinction of water-fowl – there is not a single aquatic bird which they do not accuse of damage to fry, spawn, or full-grown fish; no, not one, from the heron down to the tiny grebe. They are nearly as bitter against animals; the poor water-vole (or water-rat) even is denounced and shot. Any one who chooses may watch the water-rat feeding on aquatic vegetation; never mind, shoot him because he's there. There is no other reason. Bitterest, harshest, most envenomed of all is the outcry and hunt directed against the otter. It is as if the otter were a wolf – as if he were as injurious as the mighty boar whom Meleager and his companions chased in the days of dim antiquity. What, then, has the otter done? Has he ravaged the fields? does he threaten the homesteads? is he at Temple Bar? are we to run, as the old song says, from the Dragon? The fact is, the ravages attributed to the otter are of a local character. They are chiefly committed in those places where fish are more or less confined. If you keep sheep close together in a pen the wolf who leaps the hurdles can kill the flock if he chooses. In narrow waters, and where fish are maintained in quantities out of proportion to extent, an otter can work doleful woe. That is to say, those who want too many fish are those who give the otter his opportunity.

In a great river like the Thames a few otters cannot do much or lasting injury except in particular places. The truth is, that the otter is an ornament of the river, and more worthy of preservation than any other creature. He is the last and largest of the wild creatures who once roamed so freely in the forests which enclosed Londinium, that fort in the woods and marshes – marshes which to this day, though drained and built over, enwrap the nineteenth-century city in thick mists. The red deer are gone, the boar is gone, the wolf necessarily destroyed – the red deer can never again drink at the Thames in the dusk of the evening while our civilization endures. The otter alone remains – the wildest, the most thoroughly self-supporting of all living things left – a living link going back to the days of Cassivelaunus. London ought to take the greatest interest in the otters of its river. The shameless way in which every otter that dares to show itself is shot, trapped, beaten to death, and literally battered out of existence, should rouse the indignation of every sportsman and every lover of nature. The late Rev. John Russell, who, it will be admitted, was a true sportsman, walked three thousand miles to see an otter. That was a different spirit, was it not?

That is the spirit in which the otter in the Thames should be regarded. Those who offer money rewards for killing Thames otters ought to be looked on as those who would offer rewards for poisoning foxes in Leicestershire. I suppose we shall not see the ospreys again; but I should like to. Again, on the other side of the boundary, in the tidal waters, the same sort of ravenous destruction is carried on against everything that ventures up. A short time ago a porpoise came up to Mortlake; now, just think, a porpoise up from the great sea – that sea to which Londoners rush with such joy – past Gravesend, past Greenwich, past the Tower, under London Bridge, past Westminster and the Houses of Parliament, right up to Mortlake. It is really a wonderful thing that a denizen of the sea, so large and interesting as a porpoise, should come right through the vast City of London. In an aquarium, people would go to see it and admire it, and take their children to see it. What happened? Some one hastened out in a boat, armed with a gun or a rifle, and occupied himself with shooting at it. He did not succeed in killing it, but it was wounded. Some difference here to the spirit of John Russell. If I may be permitted to express an opinion, I think that there is not a single creature, from the sand-marten and the black-headed bunting to the broad-winged heron, from the water-vole to the otter, from the minnow on one side of the tidal boundary to the porpoise on the other – big and little, beasts and birds (of prey or not) – that should not be encouraged and protected on this beautiful river, morally the property of the greatest city in the world.

II

I looked forward to living by the river with delight, anticipating the long rows I should have past the green eyots and the old houses red-tiled among the trees. I should pause below the weir and listen to the pleasant roar, and watch the fisherman cast again and again with the 'transcendent patience' of genius by which alone the Thames trout is captured. Twisting the end of a willow bough round my wrist I could moor myself and rest at ease, though the current roared under the skiff, fresh from the waterfall. A thousand thousand bubbles rising to the surface would whiten the stream – a thousand thousand succeeded by another thousand thousand – and still flowing, no multiple could express the endless number. That which flows continuously by some sympathy is acceptable to the mind, as if thereby it realized its own existence without an end. Swallows would skim the water to and fro as yachts tack, the sandpiper would run along the strand, a black-headed bunting would perch upon the willow; perhaps, as the man of genius fishing and myself made no noise, a kingfisher might come, and we might see him take his prey.

Or I might quit hold of the osier and, entering a shallow backwater, disturb shoals of roach playing where the water was transparent to the bottom, after their wont. Winding in and out like an Indian in his canoe, perhaps traces of an otter might be found – his kitchen mödding – and in the sedges moorhens and wildfowl would hide from me. From its banks I should gather many a flower and notice many a plant, there would be, too, the beautiful water-lily. Or I should row on up the great stream by meadows full of golden buttercups, past fields crimson with trifolium or green with young wheat. Handsome sailing-craft would come down spanking before the breeze, laden with bright girls – laughter on board, and love the golden fleece of their argosy.

I should converse with the ancient men of the ferries, and listen to their river lore; they would show me the mark to which the stream rose in the famous year of floods. On again to the cool hostelry whose sign was reflected in the water, where there would be a draught of fine ale for the heated and thirsty sculler. On again till steeple or tower rising over the trces marked my journey's end for the day, some old town where, after rest and refreshment, there would be a ruin or a timbered house to look at, where I should meet folk full of former days and quaint tales of yore. Thus to journey on from place to place would be the great charm of the river – travelling by water, not merely sculling to and fro, but really travelling. Upon a lake I could but row across and back again, and however lovely the scenery might be, still it would always be the same. But the Thames, upon the river I could really travel, day after day, from Teddington Lock upwards to Windsor, to Oxford, on to quiet Lechlade, or even farther deep into the meadows by Cricklade. Every hour there would be something interesting, all the freshwater life to study, the very barges would amuse me, and at last there would be the delicious ease of floating home carried by the stream, repassing all that had pleased before.

The time came. I lived by the river, not far from its widest reaches, before the stream meets its tide. I went down to the eyot for a boat, and my difficulties began. The crowd of boats lashed to each other in strings ready for the hirer disconcerted me. There were so many I could not choose; the whole together looked like a broad raft. Others were hauled on the shore. Over on the eyot, a little island, there were more boats, boats launched, boats being launched, boats being carried by gentlemen in coloured flannels as carefully as mothers handle their youngest infants, boats covered in canvas mummy-cases, and dim boats under roofs, their sharp prows projecting like crocodiles' snouts. Tricksy outriggers, ready to upset on narrow keel, were held firmly for the sculler to step daintily into his place. A strong eight shot by up the stream, the men all pulling together as if they had been one animal. A strong sculler shot by down the stream, his giant arms bare and the muscles visible as they rose, knotting and unknotting with the stroke. Every one on the bank and eyot stopped to watch him – they knew him, he was training. How could an amateur venture out and make an exhibition of himself after such splendid rowing! Still it was noticeable that plenty of amateurs did venture out, till the waterway was almost concealed – boated over instead of bridged – and how they managed to escape locking their oars together, I could not understand.

I looked again at the boats. Some were outriggers. I could not get into an outrigger after seeing the great sculler. The rest were one and all after the same pattern, i.e. with the stern cushioned and prepared for a lady. Some were larger, and could carry three or four ladies, but they were all intended for the same purpose. If the sculler went out in such a boat by himself he must either sit too forward and so depress the stem and dig himself, as it were, into the water at each stroke, or he must sit too much to the rear and depress the stern, and row with the stem lifted up, sniffing the air. The whole crowd of boats on hire were exactly the same; in short, they were built for woman and not for man, for lovely woman to recline, parasol in one hand and tiller ropes in the other, while man – inferior man – pulled and pulled and pulled as an ox yoked to the plough. They could only be balanced by man and woman, that was the only way they could be trimmed on an even keel; they were like scales, in which the weight on one side must be counterpoised by a weight on the other. They were dead against bachelors. They belonged to woman, and she was absolute mistress of the river.

As I looked, the boats ground together a little, chafing, laughing at me, making game of me, asking distinctly what business a man had there without at least one companion in petticoats? My courage ebbed, and it was in a feeble voice that I inquired whether there was no such thing as a little skiff a fellow might paddle about in? No, nothing of the kind; would a canoe do? Somehow a canoe would not do. I never took kindly to canoes, excepting always the Canadian birch-bark pattern; evidently there was no boat for me. There was no place on the great river for an indolent, dreamy particle like myself, apt to drift up into nooks, and to spend much time absorbing those pleasures which enter by the exquisite sensitiveness of the eye – colour, and shade, and form, and the cadence of glittering ripple and moving leaf. You must be prepared to pull and push, and struggle for your existence on the river, as in the vast city hard by men push and crush for money. You must assert yourself, and insist upon having your share of the waterway; you must be perfectly convinced that yours is the very best style of rowing to be seen; everyone ought to get out of your way. You must consult your own convenience only, and drive right into other people's boats, forcing them up into the willows, or against the islands. Never slip along the shore, or into quiet backwaters; always select the more frequented parts, not because you want to go there, but to make your presence known, and go amongst the crowd; and if a few sculls get broken, it only proves how very inferior and how very clumsy other people are. If you see another boat coming downstream in the centre of the river with a broad space on either side for others to pass, at once head your own boat straight at her, and take possession of the way. Or, better still, never look ahead, but pull straight on, and let things happen as they may. Annoy everybody, and you are sure to be right, and to be respected; splash the ladies as you pass with a dexterous flip of the scull, and soak their summer costumes; it is capital sport, and they look so sulky – or is it contemptuous?

There was no such thing as a skiff in which one could quietly paddle about, or gently make way – mile after mile – up the beautiful stream. The boating throng grew thicker, and my courage less and less, till I desperately resorted to the ferry – at all events, I could be rowed over in the ferry-boat, that would be something; I should be on the water, after a fashion – and the ferryman would know a good deal. The burly ferryman cared nothing at all about the river, and merely answered 'Yes', or 'No'; he was full of the Derby and Sandown; didn't know about the fishing; supposed there were fish; didn't see 'em, nor eat 'em; want a punt? No. So he landed me, desolate and hopeless, on the opposite bank, and I began to understand how the souls felt after Charon had got them over. They could not have been more unhappy than I was on the towing-path, as the ferry-boat receded and left me watching the continuous succession of boats passing up and down the river.

By-and-by an immense black hulk came drifting round the bend – an empty barge – almost broadside across the stream, for the current at the curve naturally carried it out from the shore. This huge helpless monster occupied the whole river, and had no idea where it was going, for it had no fins or sweeps to guide its course, and the rudder could only induce it to submit itself lengthways to the stream after the lapse of some time. The fairway of the river was entirely taken up by this irresponsible Frankenstein of the Thames, which someone had started, but which now did as it liked. Some of the small craft got up into the willows and waited; some seemed to narrowly escape being crushed against a wall on the opposite bank. The bright white sails of a yacht shook and quivered as its steersman tried all he knew to coax his vessel an inch more into the wind out of the monster's path. In vain! He had to drop down the stream, and lose what it had taken him half an hour's skill to gain. What a pleasing monster to meet in the narrow arches of a bridge! The man in charge leaned on the tiller, and placidly gazed at the wild efforts of some unskilful oarsmen to escape collision. In fact, the monster had charge of the man, and did as it liked with him.

Down the river they drifted together, Frankenstein swinging round and thrusting his blunt nose first this way and then that; down the river, blocking up the narrow passage by the eyot; stopping the traffic at the lock; out at last into the tidal stream, there to begin a fresh life of annoyance, and finally to endanger the good speed of many a fine three-master and ocean steamer off the docks. The Thames barge knows no law. No judge, no jury, no Palace of Justice, no Chancery, no appeal to the Lords has any terror for the monster barge. It drifts by the Houses of Parliament with no more respect than it shows for the lodge of the lock-keeper. It drifts by Royal Windsor, and cares not. The guns of the Tower are of no account. There is nothing in the world so utterly free as this monster.

Often have I asked myself if the bargee at the tiller, now sucking at his short black pipe, now munching onions and cheese (the little onions he pitches on the lawns by the riverside, there to take root and flourish) – if this amiable man has any notion of his own incomparable position. Just some inkling of the irony of the situation must, I fancy, now and then dimly dawn within his grimy brow. To see all these gentlemen shoved on one side; to be lying in the way of a splendid

Australian clipper; to stop an incoming vessel, impatient for her berth; to swing, and sway, and roll as he goes; to bump the big ships, and force the little ones aside; to slip, and slide, and glide with the tide, ripples dancing under the prow, and be master of the world-famed Thames from source to mouth, is not this a joy for ever? Liberty is beyond price; now no one is really free unless he can crush his neighbour's interest underfoot, like a horse-roller going over a daisy. Bargee is free, and the ashes of his pipe are worth a king's ransom.

Imagine a great van loaded at the East-end of London with the heaviest merchandise, with bags of iron nails, shot, leaden sheets in rolls, and pig iron; imagine four strong horses – dray-horses – harnessed thereto. Then let the waggoner mount behind in a seat comfortably contrived for him facing the rear, and settle himself down happily among his sacks, light his pipe, and fold his hands untroubled with any worry of reins. Away they go through the crowded city, by the Bank of England, and across into Cheapside, cabs darting this way, carriages that, omnibuses forced up into side-streets, foot traffic suspended till the monster has passed; up Fleet Street, clearing the road in front of them – right through the stream of lawyers always rushing to and fro the Temple and the New Law Courts, along the Strand, and finally in triumph into Rotten Row at five o'clock on a June afternoon. See how they scatter! see how they run! The Row is swept clear from end to end – beauty, fashion, rank, – what are such trifles of an hour? The monster van grinds them all to powder. What such a waggoner might do on land, bargee does on the river.

Of olden time the silver Thames was the chosen mode of travel of Royalty – the highest in the land were rowed from palace to city, or city to palace, between its sunlit banks. Noblemen had their special oarsmen, and were in like manner conveyed, and could any other mode of journeying be equally pleasant? The coal-barge has bumped them all out of the way.

No man dares send forth the commonest cart unless in proper charge, and if the horse is not under control a fine is promptly administered. The coal-barge rolls and turns and drifts as chance and the varying current please. How huge must be the rent in the meshes of the law to let so large a fish go through! But in truth there is no law about it, and to this day no man can confidently affirm that he knows to whom the river belongs. These curious anomalies are part and parcel of our political system, and as I watched the black monster slowly go by with the stream it occurred to me that grimy bargee, with his short pipe and his onions, was really the guardian of the British Constitution.

Hardly had he gone past than a loud Pant! pant! pant! began some way down the river; it came from a tug, whose short puffs of steam produced a giant echo against the walls and quays and houses on the bank. These angry pants sounded high above the splash of oars and laughter, and the chorus of singers in a boat; they conquered all other sounds and noises, and domineered the place. It was impossible to shut the ears to them, or to persuade the mind not to heed. The swallows dipped their breasts; how gracefully they drank on the wing! Pant! pant! pant! The sunlight gleamed on the wake of a four-oar. Pant! pant! pant! The soft wind blew among the trees and over the hawthorn hedge. Pant! pant! pant! Neither the eye nor ear could attend to aught but this hideous uproar. The tug was weak, the stream strong, the barges behind heavy, broad, and deeply laden, so that each puff and pant and turn of the screw barely advanced the mass a foot. There are many feet in a mile, and for all that weary time – Pant! pant! pant! This dreadful uproar, like that which Don Quixote and Sancho Panza heard proceeding from the fulling mill, must be endured. Could not philosophy by stoic firmness shut out the sound? Can philosophy shut out anything that is real? A long black streak of smoke hung over the water, fouling the gleaming surface. A noise of Dante –

hideous, uncompromising as the rusty hinge of the gate which forbids hope. Pant! pant! pant!

Once upon a time a Queen of England was rowed adown the silver Thames to the sweet low sound of the flute.

At last the noise grew fainter in the distance, and the black hulls disappeared round the bend. I walked on up the towing-path. Accidentally lifting my hand to shade my eyes, I was hailed by a ferryman on the watch. He conveyed me over without much volition on my part, and set me ashore by the inn of my imagination. The rooms almost overhung the water: so far my vision was fulfilled. Within there was an odour of spirits and spilled ale, a rustle of sporting papers, talk of racings, and the click of billiard-balls. Without there were two or three loafers, half boatmen, half vagabonds, waiting to pick up stray sixpences – a sort of leprosy of rascal and sneak in their faces and the lounge of their bodies. These Thames-side 'beach-combers' are a sorry lot, a special Pariah class of themselves. Some of them have been men once: perhaps one retains his sculling skill, and is occasionally engaged by a gentleman to give him lessons. They regarded me eagerly – they 'spotted' a Thames freshman who might be made to yield silver; but I walked away down the road into the village. The spire of the church interested me, being of shingles – i.e. of wooden slates – as the houses are roofed in America, as houses were roofed in Elizabethan England; for Young America reproduces Old England even in roofs. Some of the houses so closely approached the churchyard that the pantry windows on a level with the ground were partly blocked up by the green mounds of graves. Borage grew thickly all over the yard, dropping its blue flowers on the dead. The sharp note of a bugle rang in the air: they were changing guard, I suppose, in Wolsey's Palace.

III

In time I did discover a skiff moored in a little-visited creek, which the boatman got out for me. The sculls were rough and shapeless – it is a remarkable fact that sculls always are, unless you have them made and keep them for your own use. I paddled up the river; I paused by an osier-grown islet; I slipped past the barges, and avoided an unskilful party; it was the morning, and none of the uproarious as yet were about. Certainly, it was very pleasant. The sunshine gleamed on the water, broad shadows of trees fell across; swans floated in the by-channels. A peacefulness which peculiarly belongs to water hovered above the river. A house-boat was moored near the willow-grown shore, and it was evidently inhabited, for there was a fire smouldering on the bank, and some linen that had been washed spread on the bushes to bleach. All the windows of this gipsy-van of the river were wide open, and the air and light entered freely into every part of the dwelling-house under which flowed the stream. A lady was dressing herself before one of these open windows, twining up large braids of dark hair, her large arms bare to the shoulder, and somewhat farther. I immediately steered out into the channel to avoid intrusion; but I felt that she was regarding me with all a matron's contempt for an unknown man – a mere member of the opposite sex, not introduced, or of her 'set'. I was merely a man – no more than a horse on the bank, – and had she been in her smock she would have been just as indifferent.

Certainly it was a lovely morning; the old red palace of the Cardinal seemed to slumber amid its trees, as if the passage of the centuries had stroked and soothed it into indolent peace. The meadows rested; even the swallows, the restless swallows, glided in an effortless way through the busy air. I could see this, and yet I did not quite enjoy it; something drew me away from perfect contentment, and gradually it dawned upon me that it was the current causing an unsuspected amount of labour in sculling. The forceless particles of water, so yielding to the touch, which slipped aside at the motion of the oar, in their countless myriads ceaselessly flowing grew to be almost a solid obstruction to the boat. I had not noticed it for a mile or so; now the pressure of the stream was becoming evident. I persuaded myself that it was nothing. I held on by the boathook to a root and rested, and so went on again. Another mile or more; another rest: decidedly sculling against a swift current is work – downright work. You have no energy to spare over and above that needed for the labour of rowing, not enough even to look round and admire the green loveliness of the shore. I began to think that I should not get as far as Oxford after all.

By-and-by, I began to question if rowing on a river is as pleasant as rowing on a lake, where you can rest on your oars without losing ground, where no current opposes progress, and after the stroke the boat skips ahead some distance of its own impetus. On the river the boat only travels as far as you actually pull it at each stroke; there is no life in it after the scull is lifted, the impetus dies, and the craft first pauses and then drifts backward. I crept along the shore, so near that one scull occasionally grounded, to avoid the main force of the water, which is in the middle of the river. I slipped behind eyots and tried all I knew. In vain, the river was stronger than I, and my arms could not for many hours contend with the Thames. So faded another part of my dream. The idea of rowing from one town to another – of expeditions and travelling across the country, so pleasant to think of – in practice became impossible. An athlete bent on nothing but athleticism – a canoeist thinking of nothing but his canoe – could accomplish it, setting himself daily so much work to do, and resolutely performing it. A dreamer, who wanted to enjoy his passing moment, and not to keep regular time with his strokes, who wanted to gather flowers, and indulge his luxurious eyes with effects of light and shadow and colour, could not succeed. The river is for the man of might.

With a weary back at last I gave up the struggle at the foot of a weir, almost in the splash of the cascade. My best friend, the boathook, kept me stationary without effort, and in time rest restored the strained muscles to physical equanimity. The roar of the river falling over the dam soothed the mind – the sense of an immense power at hand, working with all its might while you are at ease, has a strangely soothing influence. It makes me sleepy to see the vast beam of an engine regularly rise and fall in ponderous irresistible labour. Now at last some fragment of my fancy was realized – a myriad myriad rushing bubbles whitening the stream burst, and were instantly succeeded by myriads more; the boat faintly vibrated as the wild waters shot beneath it; the green cascade, smooth at its first curve, dashed itself into the depth beneath, broken to a million million particles; the eddies whirled, and sucked, and sent tiny whirlpools rotating along the surface; the roar rose or lessened in intensity as the velocity of the wind varied; sunlight sparkled – the warmth inclined the senses to a drowsy idleness. Yonder was the trout fisherman, just as I had imagined him, casting and casting again with that transcendental patience which is genius; his line and the top of his rod formed momentary curves pleasant to look at. The kingfisher did not come – no doubt he had been shot – but a reed-sparrow did, in velvet black cap and dainty brown, pottering about the willow near me. This was really like the beautiful river I had dreamed of. If only we could persuade ourselves to remain quiescent when we are happy! If only we would remain still in the armchair as the last curl of vapour rises from a cigar that has been enjoyed! If only we would sit still in the shadow and not go indoors to write that letter! Let happiness alone. Stir not an inch; speak not a word: happiness is a coy maiden – hold her hand and be still.

In an evil moment I spied the corner of a newspaper projecting from the pocket of my coat in the stern-sheets. Folly led me to open the newspaper, and in it I saw and read a ghastly paragraph. Two ladies and a gentleman while boating had been carried by the current against the piles of a weir. The boat upset; the ladies were rescued, but the unfortunate gentleman was borne over the fall and drowned. His body had not been recovered; men were watching the pool day and night till some chance eddy should bring it to the surface. So perished my dream, and the coy-maiden happiness left me because I could not be content to be silent and still. The accident had not happened at this weir, but it made no difference; I could see all as plainly. A white face, blurred and indistinct, seemed to rise up from beneath the rushing bubbles till, just as it was about to jump to the surface, as things do that come up, down it was drawn again by that terrible underpull which had been fatal to so many good swimmers.

Who can keep afloat with a force underneath dragging at the feet? Who can swim when the water – all bubbles, that is air – gives no resistance to the hands? Hands and feet slip through the bubbles. You might as well spring from the parapet of a house and think to float by striking out as to swim in such a medium. Sinking under, a hundred tons of water drive the body to the bottom; there it rotates, it rises, it is forced down again, a hundred tons of water beat upon it; the foot, perhaps, catches among stones or woodwork, and what was once a living being is imprisoned in death. Enough of this. I unloosed the boathook, and drifted down with the stream, anxious to get away from the horrible weir.

These accidents, which are entirely preventable, happen year after year with lamentable monotony. Each weir is a little Niagara, and a boat once within its influence is certain to be driven to destruction. The current carries it against the piles, where it is either broken or upset, the natural and reasonable alarm of the occupants increasing the risk. In descending the river every boat must approach the weir, and must pass within a few yards of the dangerous current. If there is a press of boats one is often forced out of the proper course into the rapid part of the stream without any negligence on the part of those in it. There is nothing to prevent this – no fence, or boom; no mark, even, between what is dangerous and what is not; no division whatever. Persons ignorant of the river may just as likely as not row right into danger. A vague caution on a notice-board may or may not be seen; in either case it gives no directions, and is certainly no protection. Let the matter be argued from whatever point of view, the fact remains that these accidents occur from the want of an efficient division between the dangerous and the safe part of the approach to a weir. A boom or some kind of fence is required, and how extraordinary it seems that nothing of the kind is done! It is not done because there is no authority, no control, no one responsible. Two or three gentlemen acquainted with aquatics could manage the river from end to end, to the safety and satisfaction of all, if they were entrusted with discretionary powers. Stiff rules and rigid control are not needed; what is wanted is a rational power freely using its discretion. I do not mean a Board with its attendant follies; I mean a small committee, unfettered, untrammelled by 'legal advisers' and so forth, merely using their own good sense.

I drifted away from the weir – now grown hideous – and out of hearing of its wailing dirge for the unfortunate. I drifted past more barges coming up, and more steam-tugs; past river lawns, where gay parties were now sipping claret-cup or playing tennis. By-and-by, I began to meet pleasure-boats and to admire their manner of progress. First there came a gentleman in white flannels, walking on the tow-path, with a rope round his waist, towing a boat in which two ladies were comfortably seated. In a while came two more gentlemen in striped flannels, one streaked with gold the other with scarlet, striding side by side and towing a boat in which sat one lady. They were very earnestly at work, pacing in step, their bodies slightly leaning forwards, and every now and then they mopped their faces with handkerchiefs which they carried in their girdles. Something in their slightly-bowed attitude reminded me of the captives depicted on Egyptian monuments, with cords about their necks. How curious is that instinct which makes each sex, in different ways, the willing slave of the other! These human steam-tugs paced and pulled, and drew the varnished craft swiftly against the stream, evidently determined to do a certain distance by a certain hour. As I drifted by without labour, I admired them very much. An interval, and still more gentlemen in flannel, labouring like galley-slaves at the tow-rope, hot, perspiring, and happy after their kind, and ladies under parasols, comfortably seated, cool, and happy after their kind.

Considering upon these things, I began to discern the true and only manner in which the modern Thames is to be enjoyed. Above all things – nothing heroic. Don't scull – don't row – don't haul at tow-ropes – don't swim – don't flourish a fishing-rod. Set your mind at ease. Make friends with two or more athletes, thorough good fellows, good-natured, delighting in their thews and sinews. Explain to them that somehow, don't you see, nature did not bless you with such superabundant muscularity, although there is nothing under the sun you admire so much. Forthwith these good fellows will pet you, and your Thames fortune is made. You take your place in the stern-sheets, happily protected on either side by feminine human nature, and the parasols meeting above shield you from the sun. The tow-rope is adjusted, and the tugs start. The gliding motion soothes the soul. Feminine boating nature has no antipathy to the cigarette. A delicious odour, soft as new-mown hay, a hint of spices and distant flowers – sunshine dried and preserved, sunshine you can handle – rises from the smouldering fibres. This is smoking summer itself. Yonder in the fore part of the craft I espy certain vessels of glass on which is the label of Epernay. And of such is peace.

Drifting ever downwards, I approached the creek where my skiff had to be left; but before I reached it a 'beach-comber', with a coil of cord over his shoulder, asked me if he should tow me 'up to 'Ampton'. I shook my head, whereupon he abused me in such choice terms that I listened abashed at my ignorance. It had never occurred to me that swearing could be done like that. It is true we have been swearing now, generation after generation, these eight thousand years for certain, and language expands with use. It is also true that we are all educated now. Shakespeare is credited with knowing everything, past or future, but I doubt if he knew how a Thames 'beach-comber' can curse in these days.

The Thames is swearing free. You must moderate your curses on the Queen's highway; you must not be even profane in the streets, lest you be taken before the magistrates; but on the Thames you may swear as the wind blows – howsoever you list. You may begin at the mouth, off the Nore, and curse your way up to Cricklade. A hundred miles for swearing is a fine preserve. It is one of the marvels of our civilization.

Aided by scarce a touch of the sculls the stream drifted me up into the creek, and the boatman took charge of his skiff. 'Shall I keep her handy for you, sir?' he said, thinking to get me down every day as a new-comer. I begged him not to put himself to any trouble, still he repeated that he would keep her ready. But in the road I shook off the dust of my feet against the river, and earnestly resolved never, never again to have anything to do with it (in the heroic way) lower down than Henley.

9 Sunny Brighton

Some of the old streets opening out of the King's Road look very pleasant on a sunny day. They run to the north, so that the sun over the sea shines nearly straight up them, and at the farther end, where the houses close in on higher ground, the deep blue sky descends to the rooftrees. The old red tiles, the red chimneys, the green jalousies, give some colour; and beneath there are shadowy corners and archways. They are not too wide to whisper across, for it is curious that to be interesting a street must be narrow, and the pavements are but two or three bricks broad. These pavements are not for the advantage of foot passengers; they are merely to prevent cart-wheels from grating against the houses. There is nothing ancient or carved in these streets, they are but moderately old, yet turning from the illuminated sea it is pleasant to glance up them as you pass, in their stillness and shadow, lying outside the inconsiderate throng walking to and fro, and contrasting in their irregularity with the set façades of the front. Opposite, across the King's Road, the mastheads of the fishing-boats on the beach just rise above the rails of the cliff, tipped with fluttering pennants, or fish-shaped vanes changing to the wind. They have a pulley at the end of a curved piece of iron for hauling up the lantern to the top of the mast when trawling; this thin curve, with a dot at the extremity surmounting the straight and rigid mast, suits the artist's pencil. The gold-plate shop – there is a bust of Psyche in the doorway – often attracts the eye in passing; gold and silver plate in large masses is striking, and it is a very good place to stand a minute and watch the passers-by.

It is a Piccadilly crowd by the sea – exactly the same style of people you meet in Piccadilly, but freer in dress, and particularly in hats. All fashionable Brighton parades the King's Road twice a day, morning and afternoon, always on the side of the shops. The route is up and down the King's Road as far as Preston Street, back again and up East Street. Riding and driving Brighton extends its Rotten Row sometimes to Third Avenue, Hove. These well-dressed and leading people never look at the sea. Watching by the gold-plate shop you will not observe a single glance in the direction of the sea, beautiful as it is, gleaming under the sunlight. They do not take the slightest interest in sea, or sun, or sky, or the fresh breeze calling white horses from the deep. Their pursuits are purely 'social', and neither ladies nor gentlemen ever go on the beach or lie where the surge comes to the feet. The beach is ignored; it is almost, perhaps quite vulgar; or rather it is entirely outside the pale. No one rows, very few sail; the sea is not 'the thing' in Brighton, which is the least nautical of seaside places. There is more talk of horses.

The wind coming up the cliff seems to bring with it whole armfuls of sunshine, and to throw the warmth and light against you as you linger. The walls and glass reflect the light and push back the wind in puffs and eddies; the awning flutters; light and wind spring upwards from the pavement; the sky is richly blue against the parapets overhead; there are houses on one side, but on the other open space and sea, and dim clouds in the extreme distance. The atmosphere is full of light, and gives a sense of liveliness; every atom of it is in motion. How delicate are the fore-legs of these thoroughbred horses passing! Small and slender, the hoof, as the limb rises, seems to hang by a thread, yet there is strength and speed in those sinews. Strength is often associated with size, with the mighty flank, the round barrel, the great shoulder. But I marvel more at the manner in which that strength is conveyed through these slender sinews; the huge brawn and breadth of flesh all depend upon these little cords. It is at these junctions that the wonder of life is most evident. The succession of well-shaped horses, overtaking and passing, crossing, meeting, their high-raised heads and action increase the impression of pleasant movement. Quick wheels, sometimes a tandem, or a painted coach, towering over the line, – so rolls the procession of busy pleasure. There is colour in hat and bonnet, feathers, flowers, and mantles, not brilliant but rapidly changing, and in that sense bright. Faces on which the sun shines and the wind blows whether cared for or not, and lit up thereby; faces seen for a moment and immediately followed by others as interesting; a flowing gallery of portraits; all life, life! Waiting unobserved under the awning, occasionally, too, I hear voices as the throng goes by on the pavement – pleasant tones of people chatting and the human sunshine of laughter. The atmosphere is full of movement, full of light, and life streams to and fro.

Yonder, over the road, a row of fishermen lean against the rails of the cliff, some with their backs to the sea, some facing it. 'The cliff' is rather a misnomer, it is more like a sea-wall in height. This row of stout men in blue jerseys, or copper-hued tan frocks, seems to be always there, always waiting for the tide – or nothing. Each has his particular position; one, shorter than the rest, leans with his elbows backwards on the low rail; another hangs over and looks down at the site of the fish market; an older man stands upright, and from long habit looks steadily out to sea. They have their hands in their pockets; they appear fat and jolly, as round as the curves of their smacks drawn up on the beach beneath them. They are of such that 'sleep o' nights'; no anxious ambition disturbs their placidity. No man in this world knows how to absolutely do – nothing, like a fisherman. Sometimes he turns round, sometimes he does not, that is all. The sun shines, the breeze comes up the cliff, far away a French fishing lugger is busy enough. The boats on the beach are idle, and swarms of boys are climbing over them, swinging on a rope from the bowsprit, or playing at marbles under the cliff. Bigger boys collect under the lee of a smack, and do nothing cheerfully. The fashionable throng hastens to and fro, but the row leaning against the railings do not stir.

Doleful tales they have to tell anyone who inquires about the fishing. There have been 'no herrings' these two years. One man went out with his smack, and after working for hours returned with *one sole.* I can never get this one sole out of my mind when I see the row by the rails. While the fisherman was telling me this woeful story, I fancied I heard voices from a crowd of the bigger boys collected under a smack, voices that said, 'Ho! ho! Go on! you're kidding the man!' Is there much 'kidding' in this business of fish? Another man told me (but he was not a smack proprietor) that £50, £70, or £80 was a common night's catch. Some people say that the smacks never put to sea until the men have spent every shilling they have got, and are obliged to sail. If truth lies at the bottom of a well, it is the well of a fishing-boat, for there is nothing so hard to get at as the truth about fish. At the time when society was pluming itself on the capital results attained by the Fisheries Exhibition in London, and gentlemen described in the papers how they had been to market and purchased cod at sixpence a pound, one shilling and eightpence a pound was the price in the Brighton fishmongers' shops, close to the sea. Not the least effect was produced in Brighton; fish remains at precisely the same price as before all this ridiculous trumpeting. But while the fishmongers charge twopence each for fresh herrings, the old women bring them to the door at sixteen a shilling. The poor who live in the old part of Brighton, near the markets, use great quantities of the smaller and cheaper fish, and their children weary of the taste to such a degree that when the girls go out to service they ask to be excused from eating it.

The fishermen say they can often find a better market by sending their fish to Paris; much of the fish caught off Brighton goes there. It is fifty miles to London, and 250 to Paris; how then can this be? Fish somehow slip through ordinary rules, being slimy of surface; the maxims of the writers on demand and supply are quite ignored, and there is no groping to the bottom of this well of truth.

Just at the corner of some of the old streets that come down to the King's Road one or two old fishermen often stand. The front one props himself against the very edge of the buildings, and peers round into the broad sunlit thoroughfare; his brown copper frock makes a distinct patch of colour at the edge of the house. There is nothing in common between him and the moving throng: he is quite separate and belongs to another race; he has come down from the shadow of the old street, and his copper-hued frock might have come out of the last century.

The fishing-boats and the fishing, the nets, and all the fishing work are a great ornament to Brighton. They are real; there is something about them that forms a link with the facts of the sea, with the forces of the tides and winds, and the sunlight gleaming on the white crests of the waves. They speak to thoughts lurking in the mind; they float between life and death as with a billow on either hand; their anchors go down to the roots of existence. This is real work, real labour of man, to draw forth food from the deep as the plough draws it from the earth. It is in utter contrast to the artificial work – the feathers, the jewellery, the writing at desks of the town. The writings of a thousand clerks, the busy factory work, the trimmings and feathers, and counter-attendance do not touch the real. They are all artificial. For food you must still go to the earth and to the sea, as in primeval days. Where would your thousand clerks, your trimmers, and counter-salesmen be without a loaf of bread, without meat, without fish? The old brown sails and the nets, the anchors and tarry ropes, go straight to nature. You do not care for nature now? Well! all I can say is, you will have to go to nature one day – when you die: you will find nature very real then. I rede you to recognize the sunlight and the sea, the flowers and woods *now*.

I like to go down on the beach among the fishing-boats, and to recline on the shingle by a smack when the wind comes gently from the west, and the low wave breaks but a few yards from my feet. I like the occasional passing scent of pitch: they are melting it close by. I confess I like tar: one's hands smell nice after touching ropes. It is more like home down on the beach here; the men are doing something real, sometimes there is the clink of a hammer; behind me there is a screen of brown net, in which rents are being repaired; a big rope yonder stretches as the horse goes round, and the heavy smack is drawn slowly up over the pebbles. The full curves of the rounded bows beside me are pleasant to the eye, as any curve is that recalls those of woman. Mastheads stand up against the sky, and a loose rope swings as the breeze strikes it; a veer of the wind brings a puff of smoke from the funnel of a cabin, where some one is cooking, but it is not disagreeable, like smoke from a house chimney-pot; another veer carries it away again, – depend upon it the simplest thing cooked there is nice. Shingle rattles as it is shovelled up for ballast – the sound of labour makes me more comfortably lazy. They are not in a hurry, nor 'chivy' over their work either; the tides rise and fall slowly, and they work in correspondence. No infernal fidget and fuss. Wonder how long it would take me to pitch a pebble so as to lodge on the top of that large brown pebble there? I try, once now and then.

Far out over the sea there is a peculiar bank of clouds. I was always fond of watching clouds; these do not move much. In my pocket-book I see I have several notes about these peculiar sea-clouds. They form a band not far above the horizon, not very thick but elongated laterally. The upper edge is curled or wavy, not so heavily as what is called mountainous, not in the least threatening; this edge is white. The body of the vapour is a little darker, either because thicker, or because the light is reflected at a different angle. But it is the lower edge which is singular: in direct contrast with the curled or wavy edge above, the under edge is perfectly straight and parallel to the line of the horizon. It looks as if the level of the sea made this under line. This bank moves very slowly – scarcely perceptibly – but in course of hours rises, and as it rises spreads, when the extremities break off in detached pieces, and these gradually vanish. Sometimes when travelling I have pointed out the direction of the sea, feeling sure it was there, and not far off, though invisible, on account of the appearance of the clouds, whose under edge was cut across so straight. When this peculiar bank appears at Brighton it is an almost certain sign of continued fine weather, and I have noticed the same thing elsewhere; once particularly it remained fine after this appearance despite every threat the sky could offer of a storm. All the threats came to nothing for three weeks, not even thunder and lightning could break it up, – 'deceitful flashes', as the Arabs say; for, like the sons of the desert, just then the farmers longed for rain on their parched fields. To me, while on the beach among the boats, the value of these clouds lies in their slowness of movement, and consequent effect in soothing the mind. Outside the hurry and drive of life a rest comes through the calm of nature. As the swell of the sea carries up the pebbles, and arranges the largest farthest inland, where they accumulate and stay unmoved, so the drifting of the clouds, and the touch of the wind, the sound of the surge, arrange the molecules of the mind in still layers. It is then that a dream fills it, and a dream is sometimes better than the best reality. Laugh at the idea of dreaming where there is an odour of tar if you like, but you see it is outside intolerable civilization. It is a hundred miles from the King's Road, though but just under it.

There is a scheme on foot for planking over the ocean, beginning at the bottom of West Street. An immense central pier is proposed, which would occupy the only available site for beaching the smacks. If carried out, the whole fishing industry must leave Brighton, – to the fishermen the injury would be beyond compensation, and the aspect of Brighton itself would be destroyed. Brighton ought to rise in revolt against it.

All Brighton chimney-pots are put on with giant cement, in order to bear the strain of the tremendous winds rushing up from the sea. Heavy as the gales are, they seldom do much mischief to the roofs, such as are recorded inland. On the King's Road a plate-glass window is now and then blown in, so that on hurricane days the shutters are generally half shut. It is said that the wind gets between the iron shutters and the plate glass and shakes the windows loose. The heaviest waves roll in by the West Pier, and at the bottom of East Street. Both sides of the West Pier are washed by larger waves than can be seen all along the coast from the Quarter Deck. Great rollers come in at the concrete groyne at the foot of East Street. Exposed as the coast is, the waves do not convey so intense an idea of wildness, confusion, and power as they do at Dover. To see waves in their full vigour go to the Admiralty Pier and watch the seas broken by the granite wall. Windy Brighton has not an inch of shelter anywhere in a gale, and the salt rain driven by the wind penetrates the thickest coat. The windiest spot is at the corner of Second Avenue, Hove; the wind just there is almost enough to choke those who face it. Double windows – Russian fashion – are common all along the sea-front, and are needed.

After a gale, when the wind changes, as it usually does, it is pleasant to see the ships work in to the verge of the shore. The sea is turbid and yellow with sand beaten up by the recent billows, – this yellowness extends outwards to a certain line, and is there succeeded by the green of clearer water. Beyond this again the surface looks dark, as if still half angry, and clouds hang over it, loth to retire from the strife. As bees come out of their hives when the rain ceases and the sun shines, so the vessels which have been lying-to in harbour, or under shelter of promontories, are now eagerly making their way down Channel, and, in order to get as long a tack and as much advantage as possible, they are brought to the edge of the shallow water. Sometimes fifteen or twenty or more stand in; all sizes from the ketch to the three-master. The wind is not strong, but that peculiar drawing breeze which seems to pull a ship along as if with a tow-rope. The brig stands straight for the beach, with all sail set; she heels a little, not much; she scarcely heaves to the swell, and is not checked by meeting waves; she comes almost to the yellow line of turbid water, when round she goes, and you can see the sails shiver as the breeze touches them on both surfaces for a moment. Then again she shows her stern and away she glides, while another approaches: and all day long they pass. There is always something shadowy, not exactly unreal, but shadowy about a ship; it seems to carry a romance, and the imagination fashions a story to the swelling sails.

The bright light of Brighton brings all things into clear relief, giving them an edge and outline; as steel burns with a flame like wood in oxygen, so the minute particles of iron in the atmosphere seem to burn and glow in the sunbeams, and a twofold illumination fills the air. Coming back to the place after a journey this brilliant light is very striking, and most new visitors notice it. Even a room with a northern aspect is full of light, too strong for some eyes, till accustomed to it. I am a great believer in light – sunlight – and of my free will never let it be shut out with curtains. Light is essential to life, like air; life is thought; light is as fresh air to the mind. Brilliant sunshine is reflected from the houses and fills the streets. The walls of the houses are clean and less discoloured by the deposit of carbon than usual in most towns, so that the reflection is stronger from these white surfaces. Shadow there is none in summer, for the shadows are lit up by diffusion. Something in the atmosphere throws light down into shaded places as if from a mirror. Waves beat ceaselessly on the beach, and the undulations of light flow continuously forwards into the remotest corners. Pure air, free from suspended matter, lets the light pass freely, and perhaps this absence of suspended material is the reason that the heat is not so oppressive as would be supposed considering the glare. Certainly it is not so hot as London; on going up to town on a July or August day it seems much hotter there, so much so that one pants for air. Conversely in winter, London appears much colder, the thick dark atmosphere seems to increase the bitterness of the easterly winds, and returning to Brighton is entering a warmer because clearer air. Many complain of the brilliance of the light; they say the glare is overpowering, but the eyes soon become acclimatized. This glare is one of the great recommendations of Brighton; the strong light is evidently one of the causes of its healthfulness to those who need change. There is no such glowing light elsewhere along the south coast; these things are very local.

A demand has been made for trees, to plant the streets and turn them into boulevards for shade, than which nothing could be more foolish. It is the dryness of the place that gives it its character. After a storm, after heavy rain for days, in an hour the pavements are not only dry but clean; no dirt, sticky and greasy, remains. The only dirt in Brighton, for three-fourths of the year, is that made by the water-carts. Too much water is used, and a good clean road covered with mud an inch thick in August; but this is not the fault of Brighton – it is the lack of observation on the part of the Cadi who ought to have noticed the wretched condition of ladies' boots when compelled to cross these miry promenades. Trees are not wanted in Brighton; it is the peculiar glory of Brighton to be treeless. Trees are the cause of damp, they suck down moisture, and fill a circle round them with humidity. Places full of trees are very trying in spring and autumn even to robust people, much more so to convalescents and delicate persons. Have nothing to do with trees, if Brighton is to retain its value. Glowing light, dry, clear, and clean air, general dryness – these are the qualities that rendered Brighton a sanatorium; light and glow without oppressive, moist heat; in winter a clear cold. Most terrible of all to bear is cold when the atmosphere is saturated with water. If any reply that trees have no leaves in winter and so do not condense moisture, I at once deny the conclusion; they have no leaves, but they condense moisture nevertheless. This is effected by the minute twigs, thousands of twigs and little branches, on which the mists condense, and distil in drops. Under a large tree, in winter, there is often a perfect shower, enough to require an umbrella, and it lasts for hours. Eastbourne is a pleasant place, but visit Eastbourne, which is proud of its trees, in October, and feel the damp fallen leaves under your feet, and you would prefer no trees.

Let nothing check the descent of those glorious beams of sunlight which fall at Brighton. Watch the pebbles on the beach; the foam runs up and wets them, almost before it can slip back the sunshine has dried them again. So they are alternately wetted and dried. Bitter sea and glowing light, bright clear air, dry as dry – that describes the place. Spain is the country of sunlight, burning sunlight; Brighton is a Spanish town in England, a Seville. Very bright colours can be worn in summer because of this powerful light; the brightest are scarcely noticed, for they seem to be in concert with the sunshine. Is it difficult to paint in so strong a light? Pictures in summer look dull and out of tune when this Seville sun is shining. Artificial colours of the palette cannot live in it. As a race we do not seem to care much for colour or art – I mean in the common things of daily life – else a great deal of colour might be effectively used in Brighton in decorating houses and woodwork. Much more colour might be put in the windows, brighter flowers and curtains; more, too, inside the rooms; the sober hues of London furniture and carpets are not in accord with Brighton light. Gold and ruby and blue, the blue of transparent glass, or purple, might be introduced, and the romance of colour freely indulged. At high tide of summer Spanish mantillas, Spanish fans, would not be out of place in the open air. No tint is too bright – scarlet, cardinal, anything the imagination fancies; the brightest parasol is a mattter of course. Stand, for instance, by the West Pier, on the Esplanade, looking east on a full-lit August day. The sea is blue, streaked with green, and is stilled with heat; the low undulations can scarcely rise and fall for somnolence. The distant cliffs are white; the houses yellowish-white; the sky blue, more blue than fabled Italy. Light pours down, and the bitter salt sea wets the pebbles; to look at them makes the mouth dry, in the unconscious recollection of the saltness and bitterness. The flags droop, the sails of the fishing-boats hang idle; the land and the sea are conquered by the great light of the sun.

Some people become famous by being always in one attitude. Meet them when you will, they have invariably got an arm – the same arm – crossed over the breast, and the hand thrust in between the buttons of the coat to support it. Morning, noon, or evening, in the street, the carriage, sitting, reading the paper, always the same attitude; thus they achieve social distinction; it takes the place of a medal or the red ribbon. What is a general or a famous orator compared to a man always. in the same attitude? Simply nobody, nobody knows him, everybody knows the mono-attitude man. Some people make their mark by invariably wearing the same short pilot coat. Doubtless it has been many times renewed, still it is the same coat In winter it is thick, in summer thin, but identical in cut and colour. Some people sit at the same window of the reading-room at the same hour every day, all the year round. This is the way to become marked and famous;

winning a battle is nothing to it. When it was arranged that a military band should play on the Brunswick Lawns, it became the fashion to stop carriages in the road and listen to it. Frequently there were carriages four deep, while the gale blew the music out to sea and no one heard a note. Still they sat content.

There are more handsome women in Brighton than anywhere else in the world. They are so common that gradually the standard of taste in the mind rises, and good-looking women who would be admired in other places pass by without notice. Where all the flowers are roses, you do not see a rose. They are all plump, not to say fat, which would be rude; very plump, and have the glow and bloom of youth upon the cheeks. They do not suffer from 'pernicious anaemia', that evil bloodlessness which London physicians are not unfrequently called upon to cure, when the cheeks are white as paper and have to be rosied with minute doses of arsenic. They extract their arsenic from the air. The way they step and the carriage of the form show how full they are of life and spirits. Sarah Bernhardt will not come to Brighton if she can help it, lest she should lose that high art angularity and slipperiness of shape which suits her rôle. Dresses seem always to fit well, because people somehow expand to them. It is pleasant to see the girls walk, because the limbs do not drag, the feet are lifted gaily and with ease. Horse-exercise adds a deeper glow to the face; they ride up on the Downs first, out of pure cunning, for the air there is certain to impart a freshness to the features like dew on a flower, and then return and walk their horses to and fro the King's Road, certain of admiration. However often these tricks are played, they are always successful. Those philanthropic folk who want to reform women's dress, and call upon the world to observe how the present style contracts the chest, and forces the organs of the body out of place (what a queer expression it seems, 'organs'!), have not a chance in Brighton. Girls lace tight and 'go in' for the tip of the fashion, yet they bloom and flourish as green bay trees, and do not find their skirts any obstacle in walking or tennis. The horse-riding that goes on is a thing to be chronicled; they are always on horseback, and you may depend upon it that it is better for them than all the gymnastic exercises ever invented. The liability to strain, and even serious internal injury, which is incurred in gymnastic exercises, ought to induce sensible people to be extremely careful how they permit their daughters to sacrifice themselves on this scientific altar. Buy them horses to ride, if you want them to enjoy good health and sound constitutions. Nothing like horses for women. Send the professors to Suakim, and put the girls on horseback. Whether Brighton grows handsome girls, or whether they flock there drawn by instinct, or become lovely by staying there, is an inquiry too difficult to pursue.

There they are, one at least in every group, and you have to walk, as the Spaniards say, with your beard over your shoulder, continually looking back at those who have passed. The only antidote known is to get married before you visit the place, and doubts have been expressed as to its efficacy. In the south-coast Seville there is nothing done but heart-breaking; it is so common it is like hammering flints for road-mending; nobody cares if your heart is in pieces. They break hearts on horseback, and while walking, playing tennis, shopping – actually at shopping, not to mention parties of every kind. No one knows where the next danger will be encountered – at the very next corner perhaps. Feminine garments have an irresistible flutter in the sea-breeze; feathers have a beckoning motion. No one can be altogether good in Brighton, and that is the great charm of it. The language of the eyes is cultivated to a marvellous degree; as we say of dogs, they quite talk with their eyes. Even when you do not chance to meet an exceptional beauty, still the plainer women are not plain like the plain women in other places. The average is higher among them, and they are not so irredeemably uninteresting. The flash of an eye, the shape of a shoulder, the colour of the hair

– something or other pleases. Women without a single good feature are often good-looking in New Seville because of an indescribable style or manner. They catch the charm of the good-looking by living among them, so that if any young lady desires to acquire the art of attraction she has only to take train and join them. Delighted with our protectorate of Paphos, Venus has lately decided to reside on these shores. Every morning the girls' schools go for their constitutional walks; there seem no end of these schools – the place has a garrison of girls, and the same thing is noticeable in their ranks. Too young to have developed actual loveliness, some in each band distinctly promise future success. After long residence the people become accustomed to good looks, and do not see anything especial around them, but on going away for a few days soon miss these pleasant faces.

In reconstructing Brighton station, one thing was omitted – a balcony from which to view the arrival and departure of the trains in summer and autumn. The scene is as lively and interesting as the stage when a good play is proceeding. So many happy expectant faces, often very beautiful; such a mingling of colours, and succession of different figures; now a brunette, now golden hair: it is a stage, only it is real. The bustle, which is not the careworn anxious haste of business; the rushing to and fro; the greetings of friends; the smiles; the shifting of the groups, some coming, and some going – plump and rosy, – it is really charming. One has a fancy dog, another a bright-bound novel; very many have cavaliers; and look at the piles of luggage! What dresses, what changes and elegance concealed therein! conjurors' trunks out of which wonders will spring. Can anything look jollier than a cab overgrown with luggage, like huge barnacles, just starting away with its freight? One can imagine such a fund of enjoyment on its way in that cab. This happy throng seems to express something that delights the heart. I often used to walk up to the station just to see it, and left feeling better.

10 The Breeze on Beachy Head

The waves coming round the promontory before the west wind still give the idea of a flowing stream, as they did in Homer's days. Here beneath the cliff, standing where beach and sand meet, it is still; the wind passes six hundred feet overhead. But yonder, every larger wave rolling before the breeze breaks over the rocks; a white line of spray rushes along them, gleaming in the sunshine; for a moment the dark rock-wall disappears, till the spray sinks.

The sea seems higher than the spot where I stand, its surface on a higher level – raised like a green mound – as if it could burst in and occupy the space up to the foot of the cliff in a moment. It will not do so, I know; but there is an infinite possibility about the sea; it may do what it is not recorded to have done. It is not to be ordered, it may overleap the bounds human observation has fixed for it. It has a potency unfathomable. There is still something in it not quite grasped and understood – something still to be discovered – a mystery.

So the white spray rushes along the low broken wall of rocks, the sun gleams on the flying fragments of the wave, again it sinks, and the rhythmic motion holds the mind, as an invisible force holds back the tide. A faith of expectancy, a sense that something may drift up from the unknown, a large belief in the unseen resources of the endless space out yonder, soothes the mind with dreamy hope.

The little rules and little experiences, all the petty ways of narrow life, are shut off behind by the ponderous and impassable cliff; as if we had dwelt in the dim light of a cave, but coming out at last to look at the sun, a great stone had fallen and closed the entrance, so that there was no return to the shadow. The impassable precipice shuts off our former selves of yesterday, forcing us to look out over the sea only, or up to the deeper heaven.

These breadths draw out the soul; we feel that we have wider thoughts than we knew; the soul has been living, as it were, in a nutshell, all unaware of its own power, and now suddenly finds freedom in the sun and the sky. Straight, as if sawn down from turf to beach, the cliff shuts off the human world, for the sea knows no time and no era; you cannot tell what century it is from the face of the sea. A Roman trireme suddenly rounding the white edge-line of chalk, borne on wind and oar from the Isle of Wight towards the grey castle at Pevensey (already old in olden days), would not seem strange. What wonder could surprise us coming from the wonderful sea?

The little rills winding through the sand have made an islet of a detached rock by the beach; limpets cover it, adhering like rivet-heads. In the stillness here, under the roof of the wind so high above, the sound of the sand draining itself is audible. From the cliff blocks of chalk have fallen, leaving hollows as when a knot drops from a beam. They lie crushed together at the base, and on the point of this jagged ridge a wheatear perches.

There are ledges three hundred feet above, and from these now and then a jackdaw glides out and returns again to his place, where, when still and with folded wings, he is but a speck of black. A spire of chalk still higher stands out from the wall, but the rains have got behind it and will cut the crevice deeper and deeper into its foundation. Water, too, has carried the soil from under the turf at the summit over the verge, forming brown streaks.

Upon the beach lies a piece of timber, part of a wreck; the wood is torn and the fibres rent where it was battered against the dull edge of the rocks. The heat of the sun burns, thrown back by the dazzling chalk; the river of ocean flows ceaselessly, casting the spray over the stones; the unchanged sky is blue.

Let us go back and mount the steps at the Gap, and rest on the sward there. I feel that I want the presence of grass. The sky is a softer blue, and the sun genial now the eye and the mind alike are relieved – the one of the strain of too great solitude (not the solitude of the woods), the other of too brilliant and hard a contrast of colours. Touch but the grass, and the harmony returns; it is repose after exaltation.

A vessel comes round the promontory; it is not a trireme of old Rome, nor the 'fair and stately galley' Count Arnaldus hailed with its seamen singing the mystery of the sea. It is but a brig in ballast, high out of the water, black of hull and dingy of sail: still, it is a ship, and there is always an interest about a ship. She is so near, running along but just outside the reef, that the deck is visible. Up rises her stern as the billows come fast and roll under; then her bow lifts, and immediately she rolls, and, loosely swaying with the sea, drives along.

The slope of the billow now behind her is white with the bubbles of her passage, rising, too, from her rudder. Steering athwart with a widening angle from the land, she is laid to clear the distant point of Dungeness. Next, a steamer glides forth, unseen till she passed the cliff; and thus each vessel that comes from the westward has the charm of the unexpected. Eastward there is many a sail working slowly into the wind, and as they approach talking in the language of flags with the watch on the summit of the Head.

Once now and then the great *Orient* pauses on her outward route to Australia, slowing her engines: the immense length of her hull contains every adjunct of modern life; science, skill, and civilization are there. She starts, and is lost sight of round the cliff, gone straight away for the very ends of the world. The incident is forgotten, when one morning, as you turn over the newspaper, there is the *Orient* announced to start again. It is like a tale of enchantment; it seems but yesterday that the Head hid her from view; you have scarcely moved, attending to the daily routine of life, and scarce recognize that time has passed at all. In so few hours has the earth been encompassed.

The seagulls as they settle on the surface ride high out of the water, like the mediaeval caravals, with their sterns almost as tall as the masts. Their unconcerned flight, with crooked wings unbent, as if it were no matter to them whether they flew or floated, in its peculiar jerking motion somewhat reminds one of the lapwing – the heron has it, too, a little – as if aquatic or water-side birds had a common and distinct action of the wing.

Sometimes a porpoise comes along, but just beyond the reef; looking down on him from the verge of the cliff, his course can be watched. His dark body, wet and oily, appears on the surface for two seconds; and then, throwing up his tail like the fluke of an anchor, down he goes. Now look forward, along the waves, some fifty yards or so, and he will come up, the sunshine gleaming on the water as it runs off his back, to again dive, and reappear after a similar interval. Even when the eye can no longer distinguish the form, the spot where he rises is visible, from the slight change in the surface.

The hill receding in hollows leaves a narrow plain between the foot of the sward and the cliff; it is ploughed, and the teams come to the footpath which follows the edge; and thus those who plough the sea and those who plough the land look upon each other. The one sees the vessel change her tack, the other notes the plough turning at the end of the furrow. Bramble bushes project over the dangerous wall of chalk, and grasses fill up the interstices, a hedge suspended in air; but be careful not to reach too far for the blackberries.

The green sea is on the one hand, the yellow stubble on the other. The porpoise dives along beneath, the sheep graze above. Green seaweed lines the reef over which the white spray flies, blue lucerne dots the field. The pebbles of the beach seen from the height mingle in a faint blue tint, as if the distance ground them into coloured sand. Leaving the footpath now, and crossing the stubble to 'France', as the wide open hollow in the down is called by the shepherds, it is no easy matter in dry summer weather to climb the steep turf to the furze line above.

Dry grass is as slippery as if it were hair, and the sheep have fed it too close for a grip of the hand. Under the furze (still far from the summit) they have worn a path – a narrow ledge, cut by their cloven feet – through the sward. It is time to rest; and already, looking back, the sea has extended to an indefinite horizon. This climb of a few hundred feet opens a view of so many miles more. But the ships lose their individuality and human character; they are so far, so very far, away, they do not take hold of the sympathies; they seem like sketches – cunningly executed, but only sketches – on the immense canvas of the ocean. There is something unreal about them.

On a calm day, when the surface is smooth as if the brimming ocean had been straked – the rod passed across the top of the measure, thrusting off the irregularities of wave; when the distant green from long simmering under the sun becomes pale; when the sky, without cloud, but with some slight haze in it, likewise loses its hue, and the two so commingle in the pallor of heat that they cannot be separated – then the still ships appear suspended in space. They are as much held from above as upborne from beneath.

They are motionless, midway in space – whether it

is sea or air is not to be known. They neither float nor fly, they are suspended. There is no force in the flat sail, the mast is lifeless, the hull without impetus. For hours they linger, changeless as the constellations, still, silent, motionless, phantom vessels on a voïd sea.

Another climb up from the sheep path, and it is not far then to the terrible edge of that tremendous cliff which rises straighter than a ship's side out of the sea, six hundred feet above the detached rock below, where the limpets cling like rivet-heads, and the sand rills run around it. But it is not possible to look down to it – the glance of necessity falls outwards, as a raindrop from the eaves is deflected by the wind, because it *is* the edge where the mould crumbles; the rootlets of the grass are exposed; the chalk is about to break away in flakes.

You cannot lean over as over a parapet, lest such a flake should detach itself – lest a mere trifle should begin to fall, awakening a dread and dormant inclination to slide and finally plunge like it. Stand back; the sea there goes out and out, to the left and to the right, and how far is it to the blue overhead? The eye must stay here a long period, and drink in these distances, before it can adjust the measure, and know exactly what it sees.

The vastness conceals itself, giving us no landmark or milestone. The fleck of cloud yonder, does it part it in two, or is it but a third of the way? The world is an immense cauldron, the ocean fills it, and we are merely on the rim – this narrow land is but a ribbon to the limitlessness yonder. The wind rushes out upon it with wild joy; springing from the edge of the earth, it leaps out over the ocean. Let us go back a few steps and recline on the warm, dry turf.

It is pleasant to look back upon the green slope and the hollows and narrow ridges, with sheep and stubble and some low hedges, and oxen, and that old, old sloth – the plough – creeping in his path. The sun is bright on the stubble and the corners of furze; there are bees humming yonder, no doubt, and flowers, and hares crouching – the dew dried from around them long since, and waiting for it to fall again; partridges, too, corn-ricks, and the roof of a farmhouse by them. Lit with sunlight are the fields, warm autumn garnering all that is dear to the heart of man, blue heaven above – how sweet the wind comes from these! – the sweeter for the knowledge of the profound abyss behind.

Here, reclining on the grass – the verge of the cliff rising a little, shuts out the actual sea – the glance goes forth into the hollow unsupported. It is sweeter towards the corn-ricks, and yet the mind will not be satisfied, but ever turns to the unknown. The edge and the abyss recall us; the boundless plain, for it appears solid as the waves are levelled by distance, demands the gaze. But with use it becomes easier, and the eye labours less. There is a promontory standing out from the main wall, whence you can see the side of the cliff, getting a flank view, as from a tower.

The jackdaws occasionally floating out from the ledge are as mere specks from above, as they were from below. The reef running out from the beach, though now covered by the tide, is visible as you look down on it through the water; the seaweed, which lay matted and half dry on the rocks, is now under the wave. Boats have come round, and are beached; how helplessly little they seem beneath the cliff by the sea!

On returning homewards towards Eastbourne stay awhile by the tumulus on the slope. There are others hidden among the furze; butterflies flutter over them, and the bees hum round by day; by night the night-hawk passes, coming up from the fields and even skirting the sheds and houses below. The rains beat on them, and the storm drives the dead leaves over their low green domes; the waves boom on the shore far down.

How many times has the morning star shone yonder in the East? All the mystery of the sun and of the stars centres around these lowly mounds.

But the glory of these glorious Downs is the breeze. The air in the valleys immediately beneath them is pure and pleasant; but the least climb, even a hundred feet, puts you on a plane with the atmosphere itself, uninterrupted by so much as the tree-tops. It is air without admixture. If it comes from the south, the waves refine it; if inland, the wheat and flowers and grass distil it. The great headland and the whole rib of the promontory is wind-swept and washed with air; the billows of the atmosphere roll over it.

The sun searches out every crevice amongst the grass, nor is there the smallest fragment of surface which is not sweetened by air and light. Underneath, the chalk itself is pure, and the turf thus washed by wind and rain, sun-dried and dew-scented, is a couch prepared with thyme to rest on. Discover some excuse to be up there always, to search for stray mushrooms – they will be stray, for the crop is gathered extremely early in the morning – or to make a list of flowers and grasses; to do anything, and, if not, go always without any pretext. Lands of gold have been found, and lands of spices and precious merchandise; but this is the land of health.

There is the sea below to bathe in, the air of the sky up hither to breathe, the sun to infuse the invisible magnetism of his beams. These are the three potent medicines of nature, and they are medicines that by degrees strengthen not only the body but the unquiet mind. It is not necessary to always look out over the sea. By strolling along the slopes of the ridge a little way inland there is another scene where hills roll on after hills till the last and largest hides those that succeed behind it.

Vast cloud-shadows darken one, and lift their veil from another; like the sea, their tint varies with the hue of the sky over them. Deep narrow valleys – lanes in the hills – draw the footsteps downwards into their solitude, but there is always the delicious air, turn whither you will, and there is always the grass, the touch of which refreshes. Though not in sight, it is pleasant to know that the sea is close at hand, and that you have only to mount to the ridge to view it. At sunset the curves of the shore westward are filled with a luminous mist.

Or if it should be calm, and you should like to look at the massive headland from the level of the sea, row out a mile from the beach. Eastwards a bank of red vapour shuts in the sea, the wavelets – no larger than those raised by the oar – on that side are purple as if wine had been spilt upon them, but westwards the ripples shimmer with palest gold.

The sun sinks behind the summit of the Downs, and slender streaks of purple are drawn along above them. A shadow comes forth from the cliff; a duskiness dwells on the water; something tempts the eye upwards, and near the zenith there is a star.

11 The Pigeons at the British Museum

The front of the British Museum stands in the sunlight clearly marked against the firm blue of the northern sky. The blue appears as if solid above the angle of the stonework, for while looking towards it – towards the north – the rays do not come through the azure, which is therefore colour without life. It seems nearer than the southern sky, it descends and forms a close background to the building; as you approach you seem to come nearer to the blue surface rising at its rear. The dark edges of sloping stone are distinct and separate, but not sharp; the hue of the stone is toned by time and weather, and is so indefinite as to have lost its hardness. Those small rounded bodies upon the cornice are pigeons resting in the sun, so motionless and neutral-tinted that they might be mistaken for some portion of the carving. A double gilt ring, a circle in a circle, at the feet of an allegorical figure gleams brightly against the dark surface. The sky already seems farther away seen between the boles of stone, perpetual shade dwells in their depth, but two or three of the pigeons fluttering down are searching for food on the sunlit gravel at the bottom of the steps. To them the building is merely a rock, pierced with convenient caverns; they use its exterior for their purpose, but penetrate no farther. With air and light, the sunlit gravel, the green lawn between it and the outer railings – with these they are concerned, and with these only. The heavy roll of the traffic in Oxford Street, audible here, is nothing to them; the struggle for money does not touch them, they let it go by. Nor the many minds searching and re-searching in the great Library, this mental toil is no more to them than the lading of the waggons in the street. Neither the tangible product nor the intellectual attainment is of any value – only the air and light. There are idols in the galleries within upon whose sculptured features the hot Eastern sun shone thousands of years since. They were made by human effort, however mistaken, and they were the outcome of human thought and handiwork. The doves fluttered about the temples in those days, full only of the air and light. They fluttered about the better temples of Greece and round the porticos where philosophy was born. Still only the light, the sunlight, the air of heaven. We labour on and think, and carve our idols and the pen never ceases from its labour; but the lapse of the centuries has left us in the same place. The doves who have not laboured nor travailed in thought possess the sunlight. Is not theirs the preferable portion?

The shade deepens as I turn from the portico to the hall and vast domed house of books. The half-hearted light under the dome is stagnant and dead. For it is the nature of light to beat and throb; it has a pulse and undulation like the swing of the sea. Under the trees in the woodlands it vibrates and lives; on the hills there is a resonance of light. It beats against every leaf, and, thrown back, beats again; it is agitated with the motion of the grass blades; you can feel it ceaselessly streaming on your face. It is renewed and fresh every moment, and never twice do you see the same ray. Stayed and checked by the dome and book-built walls, the beams lose their elasticity, and the ripple ceases in the motionless pool. The eyes, responding, forget to turn quickly, and only partially see. Deeper thought and inspiration quit the heart, for they can only exist where the light vibrates and communicates its tone to the soul. If any imagine they shall find thought in many books, certainly they will be disappointed. Thought dwells by the stream and sea, by the hill and in the woodland, in the sunlight and free wind, where the wild dove haunts. Walls and roof shut it off as they shut off the undulation of light. The very lightning cannot penetrate here. A murkiness marks the coming of the cloud, and the dome becomes vague, but the fierce flash is shorn to a pale reflection, and the thunder is no more than the rolling of a heavier truck loaded with tomes. But in closing out the sky, with it is cut off all that the sky can tell you with its light, or in its passion of storm.

Sitting at these long desks and trying to read, I soon find that I have made a mistake; it is not here I shall find that which I seek. Yet the magic of books draws me here time after time, to be as often disappointed. Something in a book tempts the mind as pictures tempt the eye; the eye grows weary of pictures, but looks again. The mind wearies of books, yet cannot forget that once when they were first opened in youth they gave it hope of knowledge. Those first books exhausted, there is nothing left but words and covers. It seems as if all the books in the world – really books – can be bought for £10. Man's whole thought is purchaseable at that small price, for the value of a watch, of a good dog. For the rest it is repetition and paraphrase. The grains of wheat were threshed out and garnered two thousand years since. Except the receipts of chemists, except specifications for the steam-engine, or the electric motor, there is nothing in these millions of books that was not known at the commencement of our era. Not a thought has been added. Continual threshing has widened out the heap of straw and spread it abroad, but it is empty. Nothing will ever be found in it. Those original grains of true thought were found beside the stream, the sea, in the sunlight, at the shady verge of woods. Let us leave this beating and turning over of empty straw; let us return to the stream and the hills; let us ponder by night in view of the stars.

It is pleasant to go out again into the portico under the great columns. On the threshold I feel nearer knowledge than when within. The sun shines, and southwards above the houses there is a statue crowning the summit of some building. The figure is in the midst of the light: it stands out clear and white as if in Italy. The southern blue is luminous – the beams of light flow through it – the air is full of the undulation and life of light. There is rest in gazing at the sky: a sense that wisdom does exist and may be found, a hope returns that was taken away among the books. The green lawn is pleasant to look at, though it is mown so ruthlessly. If they would only let the grass spring up, there would be a thought somewhere entangled in the long blades as a dewdrop sparkles in their depths. Seats should be placed here, under the great columns or by the grass, so that one might enjoy the sunshine after books and watch the pigeons. They have no fear of the people, they come to my feet, but the noise of a door heavily swinging-to in the great building alarms them; they rise and float around, and return again. The sunlight casts a shadow of the pigeon's head and neck upon his shoulder; he turns his head, and the shadow of his beak falls on his breast. Iridescent gleams of bronze and green and blue play about his neck; blue predominates. His pink feet step so near, the red round his eye is visible. As he rises vertically, forcing his way in a straight line upwards, his wings almost meet above his back and again beneath the body; they are put forth to his full stroke. When his flight inclines and becomes gradually horizontal, the effort is less and the wing tips do not approach so closely.

They have not laboured in mental searching as we have; they have not wasted their time looking among empty straw for the grain that is not there. They have been in the sunlight. Since the days of ancient Greece the doves have remained in the sunshine; we who have laboured have found nothing. In the sunshine, by the shady verge of woods, by the sweet waters where the wild dove sips, there alone will thought be found.

12 One of the New Voters

I

If any one were to get up about half-past five on an August morning and look out of an eastern window in the country, he would see the distant trees almost hidden by a white mist. The tops of the larger groups of elms would appear above it, and by these the line of the hedgerows could be traced. Tier after tier they stretch along, rising by degrees on a gentle slope, the space between filled with haze. Whether there were corn-fields or meadows under this white cloud he could not tell – a cloud that might have come down from the sky, leaving it a clear azure. This morning haze means intense heat in the day. It is hot already, very hot, for the sun is shining with all his strength, and if you wish the house to be cool it is time to set the sunblinds.

Roger, the reaper, had slept all night in the cow-house, lying on the raised platform of narrow planks put up for cleanliness when the cattle were there. He had set the wooden window wide open and left the door ajar when he came stumbling in overnight, long after the late swallows had settled in their nests on the beams, and the bats had wearied of moth catching. One of the swallows twittered a little, as much as to say to his mate, 'My love, it is only a reaper, we need not be afraid,' and all was silence and darkness. Roger did not so much as take off his boots but flung himself on the boards crash, curled himself up hedgehog fashion with some old sacks, and immediately began to breathe heavily. He had no difficulty in sleeping, first because his muscles had been tired to the utmost, and next because his skin was full to the brim, not of jolly 'good ale and old', but of the very smallest and poorest of wish-washy beer. In his own words, it 'blowed him up till he very nigh bust'. Now the great authorities on dyspepsia, so eagerly studied by the wealthy folk whose stomachs are deranged, tell us that a very little flatulence will make the heart beat irregularly and cause the most distressing symptoms.

Roger had swallowed at least a gallon of a liquid chemically designed, one might say, on purpose to utterly upset the internal economy. Harvest beer is probably the vilest drink in the world. The men say it is made by pouring muddy water into empty casks returned sour from use, and then brushing them round and round inside with a besom. This liquid leaves a stickiness on the tongue and a harsh feeling at the back of the mouth which soon turns to thirst, so that having once drunk a pint the drinker must go on drinking. The peculiar dryness caused by this beer is not like any other throat drought – worse than dust, or heat, or thirst from work; there is no satisfying it. With it there go down the germs of fermentation, a sour, yeasty, and, as it were, secondary fermentation; not that kind which is necessary to make beer, but the kind that unmakes and spoils beer. It is beer rotting and decomposing in the stomach. Violent diarrhoea often follows, and then the exhaustion thus caused induces the men to drink more in order to regain the strength necessary to do their work. The great heat of the sun and the heat of hard labour, the strain and perspiration, of course try the body and weaken the digestion. To distend the stomach with half a gallon of this liquor, expressly compounded to ferment, is about the most murderous thing a man could do – murderous because it exposes him to the risk of sunstroke. So vile a drink there is not elsewhere in the world; arrack, and potato-spirit, and all the other killing extracts of the distiller are not equal to it. Upon this abominable mess the golden harvest of English fields is gathered in.

Some people have in consequence endeavoured to induce the harvesters to accept a money payment in place of beer, and to a certain extent successfully. Even then, however, they must drink something. Many manage on weak tea after a fashion, but not so well as the abstainers would have us think. Others have brewed for their men a miserable stuff in buckets, an infusion of oatmeal, and got a few to drink it; but English labourers will never drink oatmeal-water unless they are paid to do it. If they are paid extra beer-money and oatmeal-water is made for them gratis, some will, of course, imbibe it, especially if they see that thereby they may obtain little favours from their employer by yielding to his fad. By drinking the crotchet perhaps they may get a present now and then – food for themselves, cast-off clothes for their families, and so on. For it is a remarkable feature of human natural history, the desire to proselytize. The spectacle of John Bull – jovial John Bull – offering his men a bucket of oatmeal liquor is not a pleasant one. Such a John Bull ought to be ashamed of himself.

The truth is the English farmer's man was and is, and will be, a drinker of beer. Neither tea, nor oatmeal, nor vinegar and water (coolly recommended by indoor folk) will do for him. His natural constitution rebels against such 'peevish' drink. In winter he wants beer against the cold and the frosty rime and the heavy raw mist that hangs about the hollows; in spring and autumn against the rain, and in summer to support him under the pressure of additional work and prolonged hours. Those who really wish well to the labourer cannot do better than see that he really has beer to drink – real beer, genuine brew of malt and hops, a moderate quantity of which will supply force to his thews and sinews, and will not intoxicate or injure. If by giving him a small money payment in lieu of such large quantities you can induce him to be content with a little, so much the better. If an employer followed that plan, and at the same time once or twice a day sent out a moderate supply of genuine beer as a gift to his men, he would do them all the good in the world, and at the same time obtain for himself their goodwill and hearty assistance, that hearty work which is worth so much.

Roger breathed heavily in his sleep in the cowhouse, because the vile stuff he had taken puffed him up and obstructed nature. The tongue in his open mouth became parched and cracked, swollen and dry; he slept indeed, but he did not rest; he groaned heavily at times and rolled aside. Once he awoke choking – he could not swallow, his tongue was so dry and large; he sat up, swore, and again lay down. The rats in the sties had already discovered that a man slept in the cowhouse, a place they rarely visited, as there was nothing there to eat; how they found it out no one knows. They are clever creatures, the despised rats. They came across in the night and looked under his bed, supposing that he might have eaten his bread-and-cheese for supper there, and that fragments might have dropped between the boards. There were none. They mounted the boards and sniffed round him; they would have stolen the food from his very pocket if it had been there. Nor could they find a bundle in a handkerchief, which they would have gnawn through speedily. Not a scrap of food was there to be smelt at, so they left him. Roger had indeed gone supperless, as usual; his supper he had swilled and not eaten. His own fault; he should have exercised self-control. Well, I don't know; let us consider further before we judge.

In houses the difficulty often is to get the servants up in the morning; one cannot wake, and the rest sleep too sound – much the same thing; yet they have clocks and alarums. The reapers are never behind. Roger got off his planks, shook himself, went outside the shed, and tightened his shoelaces in the bright light. His rough hair he just pushed back from his forehead, and that was his toilet. His dry throat sent him to the pump, but he did not swallow much of the water – he washed his mouth out, and that was enough; and so without breakfast he went to his work. Looking down from the stile on the high ground there seemed to be a white cloud resting on the valley, through which the tops of the high trees penetrated; the hedgerows beneath were concealed, and their course could only be traced by the upper branches of the elms. Under this cloud the wheat-fields were blotted out; there seemed neither corn nor grass, work for man nor food for animal; there could be nothing doing there surely. In the stillness of the August morning, without song of bird, the sun, shining brilliantly high above the mist, seemed to be the only living thing, to possess the whole and reign above absolute peace. It is a curious sight to see the early harvest morn – all hushed under the burning sun, a morn that you know is full of life and meaning, yet quiet as if man's foot had never trodden the land. Only the sun is there, rolling on his endless way.

Roger's head was bound with brass, but had it not been he would not have observed anything in the aspect of the earth. Had a brazen band been drawn firmly round his forehead it could not have felt more stupefied. His eyes blinked in the sunlight; every now and then he stopped to save himself from staggering; he was not in a condition to think. It would have mattered not at all if his head had been clear; earth, sky, and sun were nothing to him; he knew the footpath, and saw that the day would be fine and hot, and that was sufficient for him, because his eyes had never been opened.

The reaper had risen early to his labour, but the birds had preceded him hours. Before the sun was up the swallows had left their beams in the cow-shed and twittered out into the air. The rooks and wood-pigeons and doves had gone to the corn, the blackbird to the stream, the finch to the hedgerow, the bees to the heath on the hills, the humble-bees to the clover in the plain. Butterflies rose from the flowers by the footpath, and fluttered before him to and fro and round and back again to the place whence they had been driven. Goldfinches tasting the first thistledown rose from the corner where the thistles grew thickly. A hundred sparrows came rushing up into the hedge, suddenly filling the boughs with brown fruit; they chirped and quarrelled in their talk, and rushed away again back to the corn as he stepped nearer. The boughs were stripped of their winged brown berries as quickly as they had grown. Starlings ran before the cows feeding in the aftermath, so close to their mouths as to seem in danger of being licked up by their broad tongues. All creatures, from the tiniest insect upward, were in reality busy under that curtain of white-heat haze. It looked so still, so quiet, from afar; entering it and passing among the fields, all that lived was found busy at its long day's work. Roger did not interest himself in these things, in the wasps that left the gate as he approached – they were making *papier-maché* from the wood of the top bar, – in the bright poppies brushing against his drab unpolished boots, in the hue of the wheat or the white convolvulus; they were nothing to him.

Why should they be? His life was work without skill or thought, the work of the horse, of the crane that lifts stones and timber. His food was rough, his drink rougher, his lodging dry planks. His books were – none; his picture-gallery a coloured print at the alehouse – a dog, dead, by a barrel, 'Trust is dead; Bad Pay killed him'. Of thought he thought nothing; of hope his idea was a shilling a week more wages; of any future for himself of comfort such as even a good cottage can give – of any future whatever – he had no more conception than the horse in the shafts of the waggon. A human animal simply in all this, yet if you reckoned upon him as simply an animal – as has been done these centuries – you would now be mistaken. But why should he note the colour of the butterfly, the bright light of the sun, the hue of the wheat? This loveliness gave him no cheese for breakfast; of beauty in itself, for itself, he had no idea. How should he ? To many of us the harvest – the summer – is a time of joy in light and colour; to him it was a time for adding yet another crust of hardness to the thick skin of his hands.

Though the haze looked like a mist it was perfectly dry; the wheat was as dry as noon; not a speck of dew, and the pimpernels wide open for a burning day. The reaping-machine began to rattle as he came up, and work was ready for him. At breakfast-time his fellows lent him a quarter of a loaf, some young onions, and a drink from their tea. He ate little, and the tea slipped from his hot tongue like water from the bars of a grate; his tongue was like the heated iron the housemaid tries before using it on the linen. As the reaping-machine went about the gradually decreasing square of corn, narrowing it by a broad band each time, the wheat fell flat on the short stubble. Roger stooped, and, gathering sufficient together, took a few straws, knotted them to another handful as you might tie two pieces of string, and twisted the band round the sheaf. He worked stooping to gather the wheat, bending to tie it in sheaves; stooping, bending – stooping, bending, – and so across the field. Upon his head and back the fiery sun poured down the ceaseless and increasing heat of the August day. His face grew red, his neck black; the drought of the dry ground rose up and entered his mouth and nostrils, a warm air seemed to rise from the earth and fill his chest. His body ached from the ferment of the vile beer, his back ached with stooping, his forehead was bound tight with a brazen band. They brought some beer at last; it was like the spring in the desert to him. The vicious liquor – 'a hair of the dog that bit him' – sank down his throat, grateful and refreshing to his disordered palate as if he had drunk the very shadow of green boughs. Good ale would have seemed nauseous to him at that moment, his taste and stomach destroyed by so many gallons of this. He was 'pulled together', and worked easier; the slow hours went on, and it was luncheon. He could have borrowed more food, but he was content instead with a screw of tobacco for his pipe and his allowance of beer.

They sat in the corner of the field. There were no trees for shade; they had been cut down as injurious to corn, but there were a few maple bushes and thin ash sprays, which seemed better than the open. The bushes cast no shade at all, the sun being so nearly overhead, but they formed a kind of enclosure, an open-air home, for men seldom sit down if they can help it on the bare and level plain; they go to the bushes, to the corner, or even to some hollow. It is not really any advantage; it is habit; or shall we not rather say that it is nature? Brought back as it were in the open field to the primitive conditions of life, they resumed the same instincts that controlled man in the ages past. Ancient man sought the shelter of trees and banks, of caves and hollows, and so the labourers under somewhat the same conditions came to the corner where the bushes grew. There they left their coats and slung up their luncheon-bundles to the branches; there the children played and took charge of the infants; there the women had their hearth and hung their kettle over a fire of sticks.

II

In August the unclouded sun, when there is no wind, shines as fervently in the harvest-field as in Spain. It is doubtful if the Spanish people feel the heat so much as our reapers; they have their siesta; their habits have become attuned to the sun, and it is no special strain upon them. In India our troops are carefully looked after in the hot weather, and everything made as easy for them as possible; without care and special clothing and coverings for the head they could not long endure. The English simoon of heat drops suddenly on the heads of the harvesters and finds them entirely unprepared; they have not so much as a cooling drink ready; they face it, as it were, unarmed. The sun spares not; it is fire from morn till night. Afar in the town the sunblinds are up, there is a tent on the lawn in the shade, people drink claret-cup and use ice; ice has never been seen in the harvest-field. Indoors they say they are melting lying on a sofa in a darkened room, made dusky to keep out the heat. The fire falls straight from the sky on the heads of the harvesters – men, women, and children – and the white-hot light beats up again from the dry straw and the hard ground.

The tender flowers endure; the wide petal of the poppy, which withers between the fingers, lies afloat on the air as the lilies on water, afloat and open to the weight of the heat. The red pimpernel looks straight up at the sky from the early morning till its hour of closing in the afternoon. Pale blue speedwell does not fade; the pale blue stands the warmth equally with the scarlet. Far in the thick wheat the streaked convolvulus winds up the stalks, and is not smothered for want of air though wrapped and circled with corn. Beautiful though they are, they are bloodless, not sensitive; we have given to them our feelings, they do not share our pain or pleasure. Heat has gone into the hollow stalks of the wheat and down the yellow tubes to the roots, drying them in the earth. Heat has dried the leaves upon the hedge, and they touch rough – dusty rough, as books touch that have been lying unused; the plants on the bank are drying up and turning white. Heat has gone down into the cracks of the ground; the bar of the stile is so dry and powdery in the crevices that if a reaper chanced to drop a match on it there would seem risk of fire. The still atmosphere is laden with heat, and does not move in the corner of the field between the bushes.

Roger the reaper smoked out his tobacco; the children played round and watched for scraps of food; the women complained of the heat; the men said nothing. It is seldom that a labourer grumbles much at the weather, except as interfering with his work. Let the heat increase, so it would only keep fine. The fire in the sky meant money. Work went on again; Roger had now to go to another field to pitch – that is, help to load the waggon; as a young man, that was one of the jobs allotted to him. This was the reverse. Instead of stooping he had now to strain himself upright and lift sheaves over his head. His stomach empty of everything but small ale did not like this any more than his back had liked the other; but those who work for bare food must not question their employment. Heavily the day drove on; there was more beer, and again more beer, because it was desired to clear some fields that evening. Monotonously pitching the sheaves, Roger laboured by the waggon till the last had been loaded – till the moon was shining. His brazen forehead was unbound now; in spite of the beer the work and the perspiration had driven off the aching. He was weary but well. Nor had he been dull during the day; he had talked and joked – cumbrously in labourers' fashion – with his fellows. His aches, his empty stomach, his labour, and the heat had not overcome the vitality of his spirits. There was life enough left for a little rough play as the group gathered together and passed out through the gateway. Life enough left in him to go with the rest to the alehouse; and what else, oh moralist, would you have done in his place? This, remember, is not a fancy sketch of rural poetry; this is the reaper's real existence.

He had been in the harvest-field fourteen hours, exposed to the intense heat, not even shielded by a pith helmet; he had worked the day through with thew and sinew; he had had for food a little dry bread and a few onions, for drink a little weak tea and a great deal of small beer. The moon was now shining in the sky, still bright with sunset colours. Fourteen hours of sun and labour and hard fare! Now tell him what to do. To go straight to his plank-bed in the cowhouse; to eat a little more dry bread, borrow some cheese or greasy bacon, munch it alone, and sit musing till sleep came – he who had nothing to muse about. I think it would need a very clever man indeed to invent something for him to do, some way for him to spend his evening. Read! To recommend a man to read after fourteen hours' burning sun is indeed a mockery; darn his stockings would be better. There really is nothing whatsoever that the cleverest and most benevolent person could suggest. Before any benevolent or well-meaning suggestions could be effective the preceding circumstances must be changed – the hours and conditions of labour, everything; and can that be done? The world has been working these thousands of years, and still it is the same; with our engines, our electric light, our printing press, still the coarse labour of the mine, the quarry, the field has to be carried out by human hands. While that is so, it is useless to recommend the weary reaper to read. For a man is not a horse: the horse's day's work is over; taken to his stable he is content, his mind goes no deeper than the bottom of his manger, and so long as his nose does not feel the wood, so long as it is met by corn and hay, he will endure happily. But Roger the reaper is not a horse.

Just as his body needed food and drink, so did his mind require recreation, and that chiefly consists of conversation. The drinking and the smoking are in truth but the attributes of the labourer's public-house evening. It is conversation that draws him thither, just as it draws men with money in their pockets to the club and the houses of their friends. Any one can drink or smoke alone; it needs several for conversation, for company. You pass a public-house – the reaper's house – in the summer evening. You see a number of men grouped about trestle-tables out of doors, and others sitting at the open window; there is an odour of tobacco, a chink of glasses and mugs. You can smell the tobacco and see the ale; you cannot see the indefinite power which holds men there – the magnetism of company and conversation. *Their* conversation, not *your* conversation; not the last book, the last play; not saloon conversation; but theirs – talk in which neither you nor any one of your condition could really join. To us there would seem nothing at all in that conversation, vapid and subjectless; to them it means much. We have not been through the same circumstances: our day has been differently spent, and the same words have therefore a varying value. Certain it is, that it is conversation that takes men to the public-house. Had Roger been a horse he would have hastened to borrow some food, and having eaten that, would have cast himself at once upon his rude bed. Not being an animal, though his life and work were animal, he went with his friends to talk. Let none unjustly condemn him as a blackguard for that – no, not even though they had seen him at ten o'clock unsteadily walking to his shed, and guiding himself occasionally with his hands to save himself from stumbling. He blundered against the door, and the noise set the swallows on the beams twittering. He reached his bedstead, and sat down and tried to unlace his boots, but could not. He threw himself upon the sacks and fell asleep. Such was one twenty-four hours of harvest-time.

The next and the next, for weeks, were almost exactly similar; now a little less beer, now a little more; now tying up, now pitching, now cutting a small field or corner with a fagging-hook. Once now and then there was a great supper at the farm. Once he fell out with another fellow, and they had a fight; Roger, however, had had so much ale, and his opponent so much whisky, that their blows were soft and helpless. They both fell – that is, they stumbled – they were picked up, there was some more beer, and it was settled. One afternoon Roger became suddenly giddy, and was so ill that he did no more work that day, and very little on the following. It was something like a sunstroke, but fortunately a slight attack; on the third day he resumed his place. Continued labour in the sun, little food and much drink, stomach derangement, in short, accounted for his illness. Though he resumed his place and worked on, he was not so well afterwards; the work was more of an effort to him, and his face lost its fulness, and became drawn and pointed. Still he laboured, and would not miss an hour, for harvest was coming to an end, and the extra wages would soon cease. For the first week or so of haymaking or reaping the men usually get drunk, delighted with the prospect before them, then they settle down fairly well. Towards the end they struggle hard to recover lost time and the money spent in ale.

As the last week approached, Roger went up into the village and ordered the shoemaker to make him a good pair of boots. He paid partly for them then, and the rest next pay-day. This was a tremendous effort. The labourer usually pays a shilling at a time, but Roger mistrusted himself. Harvest was practically over, and after all the labour and the long hours, the exposure to the sun and the rude lodging, he found he should scarcely have thirty shillings. With the utmost ordinary care he could have saved a good lump of money. He was a single man, and his actual keep cost but little. Many married labourers, who had been forced by hard necessity to economy, contrived to put by enough to buy clothes for their families. The single man, with every advantage, hardly had thirty shillings, and even then it showed extraordinary prudence on his part to go and purchase a pair of boots for the winter. Very few in his place would have been as thoughtful as that; they would have got boots somehow in the end, but not beforehand. This life of animal labour does not grow the spirit of economy. Not only in farming, but in navvy work, in the rougher work of factories and mines, the same fact is evident. The man who labours with thew and sinew at horse labour – crane labour – not for himself, but for others, is not the man who saves. If he worked for his own hand possibly he might, no matter how rough his labour and fare; not while working for another. Roger reached his distant home among the meadows at last, with one golden half-sovereign in his pocket. That and his new pair of boots, not yet finished, represented the golden harvest to him. He lodged with his parents when at home; he was so far fortunate that he had a bed to go to; therefore in the estimation of his class he was not badly off. But if we consider his position as regards his own life we must recognize that he was very badly off indeed, so much precious time and the strength of his youth having been wasted.

Often it is stated that the harvest wages recoup the labourer for the low weekly receipts of the year, and if the money be put down in figures with pen and ink it is so. But in actual fact the pen-and-ink figures do not represent the true case; these extra figures have been paid for, and gold may be bought too dear. Roger had paid heavily for his half-sovereign and his boots; his pinched face did not look as if he had benefited greatly. His cautious old father, rendered frugal by forty years of labour, had done fairly well; the young man not at all. The old man, having a cottage, in a measure worked for his own hand. The young man, with none but himself to think of, scattered his money to the winds. Is money earned with such expenditure of force worth the having? Look at the arm of a woman labouring in the harvest-field – thin, muscular, sinewy, black almost, it tells of continual strain. After much of this she becomes pulled out of shape, the neck loses its roundness and shows the sinews, the chest flattens. In time the women find the strain of it tells severely. I am not trying to make out a case of special hardship, being aware that both men, women, and children work as hard and perhaps suffer more in cities; I am simply describing the realities of rural life behind the scenes. The golden harvest is the first scene; the golden wheat, glorious under the summer sun. Bright poppies flower in its depths, and convolvulus climbs the stalks. Butterflies float slowly over the yellow surface as they might over a lake of colour. To linger by it, to visit it day by day, at even to watch the sunset by it, and see it pale under the changing light, is a delight to the thoughtful mind. There is so much in the wheat, there are books of meditation in it, it is dear to the heart. Behind these beautiful aspects comes the reality of human labour – hours upon hours of heat and strain; there comes the reality of a rude life, and in the end little enough of gain. The wheat is beautiful, but human life is labour.

13 *From* Amaryllis at the Fair

I

Amaryllis found the first daffodil flowering by the damask rose, and immediately ran to call her father to come and see it.

There are no damask roses now, like there used to be in summer at Coombe Oaks. I have never seen one since I last gathered one from that very bush. There are many grand roses, but no fragrance – the fragrance is gone out of life. Instinctively as I pass gardens in summer I look under the shade of the trees for the old roses, but they are not to be found. The dreary nurseries of evergreens and laurels – cemeteries they should be called, cemeteries in appearance and cemeteries of taste – are innocent of such roses. They show you an acre of what they call roses growing out of dirty straw, spindly things with a knob on the top, which even dew can hardly sweeten. 'No call for damask roses – wouldn't pay to grow they. Single they was, I thinks. No good. These be cut every morning and fetched by the flower-girls for gents' button-holes and ladies' jackets. You won't get no damask roses; they be died out.'

I think in despite of the nurseryman, or cemetery-keeper, that with patience I could get a damask rose even now by inquiring about from farmhouse to farmhouse. In time some old farmer, with a good old taste for old roses and pinks, would send me one; I have half a mind to try. But, alas! it is no use, I have nowhere to put it; I rent a house which is built in first-rate modern style, though small, of course, and there is a 'garden' to it, but no place to put a damask rose. No place, because it is not 'home', and I cannot plant except round 'home'. The plot or 'patch' the landlord calls 'the garden' – it is about as wide as the border round a patch, old style – is quite vacant, bare, and contains nothing but mould. It is nothing to me, and I cannot plant it.

Not only are there no damask roses, but there is no place for them now-a-days, no 'home', only villas and rented houses. Anything rented in a town can never be 'home'.

Farms that were practically taken on a hundred and twenty, or fifty, or perhaps two hundred years' leases were 'homes'. Consequently they had damask roses, bees, and birds about them.

There had been daffodils in that spot at least a century, opening every March to the dry winds that shrivel up the brown dead leaves of winter, and carry them out from the bushes under the trees, sending them across the meadow – fleeing like a routed army before the bayonets of the East. Every spring for a century at least the daffodils had bloomed there.

Amaryllis did not stay to think of the century, but ran round the corner of the house, and came face to face with the east wind, which took her with such force as to momentarily stay her progress. Her skirts were blown out horizontally, her ankles were exposed, and the front line of her shape (beginning to bud like spring) was sketched against the red brick wall. She laughed, but the strong gale filled her throat as if a hand had been thrust down it; the wind got its edge like a knife under her eyelids, between them and the eyeballs, and seemed as if it would scoop them out; her eyes were wet with involuntary tears; her lips dried up and parched in a moment. The wind went through her thick stockings as if the wool was nothing. She lifted her hand to defend her eyes, and the skin of her arm became 'goosey' directly. Had she worn hat or bonnet it would have flown. Stooping forwards, she pushed step by step, and gradually reached the shelter of the high garden wall; there she could stand upright and breathe again.

Her lips, which had been whitened by the keen blast, as if a storm of ice particles had been driven against them, now resumed their scarlet, but her ears were full of dust and reddened, and her curly dark hair was dry and rough and without gloss. Each separate hair separated itself from the next, and would not lie smooth – the natural unctuous essence which usually caused them to adhere was dried up.

The wind had blown thus round that corner every March for a century, and in no degree abated its bitter force because a beautiful human child, full of the happiness of a flower, came carelessly into its power. Nothing ever shows the least consideration for human creatures.

The moss on the ridge of the wall under which she stood to breathe looked shrivelled and thin, the green tint dried out of it. A sparrow with a straw tried hard to reach the eaves of the house to put it in his nest, but the depending straw was caught by the breeze as a sail, and carried him past.

Under the wall was a large patch recently dug, beside the patch a grass path, and on the path a wheelbarrow. A man was busy putting in potatoes; he wore the raggedest coat ever seen on a respectable back. As the wind lifted the tails it was apparent that the lining was loose and only hung by threads, the cuffs were worn through, there was a hole beneath each arm, and on each shoulder the nap of the cloth was gone; the colour, which had once been grey, was now a mixture of several soils and numerous kinds of grit.

The hat he had on was no better; it might have been made of some hard pasteboard, it was so bare. Every now and then the wind brought a few handfuls of dust over the wall from the road, and dropped it on his stooping back.

The way in which he was planting potatoes was wonderful, every potato was placed at exactly the right distance apart, and a hole made for it in the general trench; before it was set it was looked at and turned over, and the thumb rubbed against it to be sure that it was sound, and when finally put in, a little mould was delicately adjusted round to keep it in its right position till the whole row was buried. He carried the potatoes in his coat pocket – those, that is, for the row – and took them out one by one; had he been planting his own children he could not have been more careful. The science, the skill, and the experience brought to this potato-planting you would hardly credit; for all this care was founded upon observation, and arose from very large abilities on the part of the planter, though directed to so humble a purpose at that moment.

So soon as Amaryllis had recovered breath, she ran down the grass path and stood by the wheelbarrow, but although her shadow fell across the potato row, he would not see her.

'Pa,' she said, not very loud. 'Pa,' growing bolder. 'Do come – there's a daffodil out, the very, very first.'

'Oh,' a sound like a growl – 'oh,' from the depth of a vast chest heaving out a doubtful note.

'It is such a beautiful colour!'

'Where is your mother?' looking at her askance and still stooping.

'Indoors – at least – I think – no – '

'Haven't you got no sewing? Can't you help her? What good be you on?'

'But this is such a lovely daffodil, and the very first – now do come!'

'Flowers bean't no use on; such trumpery as that;

what do'ee want a-messing about arter thaay? You'll never be no good on; you ain't never got a apron on.'

'But – just a minute now.'

'Go on in, and be some use on.'

Amaryllis' lip fell; she turned and walked slowly away along the path, her head drooping forward.

Did ever anyone have a beautiful idea or feeling without being repulsed?

She had not reached the end of the path, however, when the father began to change his attitude; he stood up, dropped his 'dibbler', scraped his foot on his spade, and, grumbling to himself, went after her. She did not see or hear him till he overtook her.

'Please, I'll go and do the sewing,' she said.

'Where be this yer flower?' gruffly.

'I'll show you,' taking his ragged arm, and brightening up immediately. 'Only think, to open in all this wind, and so cold – isn't it beautiful? It's much more beautiful than the flowers that come in the summer.'

'Trumpery rubbish – mean to dig'em all up – would if I had time,' muttered the father. 'Have 'em carted out and drowed away – do for ashes to drow on the fields. Never no good on to nobody, thaay thengs. You can't eat'em, can you, like you can potatoes?'

'But it's lovely. Here it is,' and Amaryllis stepped on the patch tenderly, and lifted up the drooping face of the flower.

'Ah, yes,' said Iden, putting his left hand to his chin, a habit of his when thinking, and suddenly quite altering his pronunciation from that of the country folk and labourers amongst whom he dwelt to the correct accent of education. 'Ah, yes; the daffodil was your great-uncle's favourite flower.'

'Richard?' asked Amaryllis.

'Richard,' repeated Iden. And Amaryllis, noting how handsome her father's intellectual face looked, wandered in her mind from the flower as he talked, and marvelled how he could be so rough sometimes, and why he talked like the labourers, and wore a ragged coat – he who was so full of wisdom in his other moods, and spoke, and thought, and indeed acted as a perfect gentleman.

'Richard's favourite flower,' he went on. 'He brought the daffodils down from Luckett's; every one in the garden came from there. He was always reading poetry, and writing, and sketching, and yet he was such a capital man of business; no one could understand that. He built the mill, and saved heaps of money; he bought back the old place at Luckett's, which belonged to us before Queen Elizabeth's days; indeed, he very nearly made up the fortunes Nicholas and the rest of them got rid of. He was, indeed, a man. And now it is all going again – faster than he made it. He used to take you on his knee and say you would walk well, because you had a good ankle.'

Amaryllis blushed and smoothed her dress with her hands, as if that would lengthen the skirt and hide the ankles which Richard, the great-uncle, had admired when she was a child, being a man, but which her feminine acquaintances told her were heavy.

'Here, put on your hat and scarf; how foolish of you to go out in this wind without them!' said Mrs Iden, coming out. She thrust them into Amaryllis' unwilling hands, and retired indoors again immediately.

'He was the only one of all the family,' continued her father, 'who could make money; all the rest could do nothing but spend it. For ten generations he was the only money-maker and saver, and yet he was as free and liberal as possible. Very curious, wasn't it? – only one in ten generations – difficult to understand why none of the others – why –' He paused, thinking.

Amaryllis, too, was silent, thinking – thinking how easily her papa could make money, great heaps of money. She was sure he could if he tried, instead of planting potatoes.

'If only another Richard would rise up like him!' said Iden.

This was a very unreasonable wish, for, having had one genius in the family, and that, too, in the memory of man, they could not expect another. Even vast empires rarely produce more than one great man in all the course of their history. There was but one Caesar in the thousand years of Rome; Greece never had one as a nation, unless we except Themistocles, or unless we accept Alexander, who was a Macedonian; Persia had a Cyrus; there was a Tamerlane somewhere, but few people know anything of the empire he overshadows with his name; France has had two mighty warriors, Charlemagne and Napoleon – unfortunate France! As for ourselves, fortunate islanders! we have never had a great man so immensely great as to overtop the whole, like Charlemagne in his day. Fortunate for us, indeed, that it has been so. But the best example to the point is the case of the immense empire of Russia, which has had one Peter the Great, and one only. Great-uncle Richard was the Peter the Great of his family, whose work had been slowly undone by his successors.

'I wonder whether any of us will ever turn out like Richard,' continued Iden. 'No one could deny him long; he had a way of persuading and convincing people, and always got his own will in the end. Wonderful man!' he pondered, returning towards his work.

Suddenly the side door opened, and Mrs Iden just peered out, and cried, 'Put your hat and scarf on directly.'

Amaryllis put the hat on, and wound the scarf very loosely about her neck. She accompanied her father to the potato patch, hoping that he would go on talking, but he was quickly absorbed in the potatoes. She watched him stooping till his back was an arch; in fact, he had stooped so much that now he could not stand upright, though still in the prime of life; if he stood up and stretched himself, still his back was bowed at the shoulders. He worked so hard – ever since she could remember she had seen him working like this; he was up in the morning while it was yet dark tending the cattle; sometimes he was up all night with them, wind or weather made no difference. Other people stopped indoors if it rained much, but it made no difference to her father, nor did the deep snow or the sharp frosts. Always at work, and he could talk so cleverly, too, and knew everything, and yet they were so short of money. How could this be?

What a fallacy it is that hard work is the making of money; I could show you plenty of men who have worked the whole of their lives as hard as ever could possibly be, and who are still as far off independence as when they began. In fact, that is the rule; the winning of independence is rarely the result of work, else nine out of ten would be well-to-do.

II

Presently Amaryllis wandered indoors, and was met in the hall by her mother.

'What has he been talking to you about?' she said, angrily. 'Don't listen to him. He will never do any good. Just look at his coat; it's a disgrace, a positive disgrace. Telling you about the old people? What's the use of talking of people who have been dead all this time? Why doesn't he do something himself? Don't listen to his rubbish – wasting his time there with potatoes, it is enough to make one wild! Why doesn't he go in to market and buy and sell cattle, and turn over money in that way? Not he! he'd rather muddle with a few paltry potatoes, as if it mattered an atom how they were stuck in the ground.'

Not liking to hear her father abused, Amaryllis went upstairs, and when she was alone lifted her skirt and looked at the ankles which great-uncle Richard had admired. Other girls had told her they were thick, and she was ashamed of them.

Instead of the slender things which seem as if a sudden strain would snap them, and are nothing but mere bone, she had a pair of well-shaped ankles, justly proportioned to what would soon be a fine form; strong, but neither thick, nor coarse, nor heavy, ankles that would carry her many a mile without weariness, that ended good legs with plenty of flesh on them. The stupidity of calling such coarse or heavy! They were really ideal ankles, such as a sculptor would carve. Yet these ill-instructed girls called them coarse! It was not their fault, it was the lack of instruction; as they did not know what was physically perfect, of course they could not recognize it.

Let every girl who has such ankles be proud of them, for they will prove a blessing to her for the whole of her life.

Amaryllis could not get her hair smooth, though she brushed it for some time; it would not lie close, so much had the east wind dried it. She opened a drawer, and took out a little bottle of macassar, and held it in her hand, balancing probabilities. Would her father see it if she used it, or might he, perhaps, fail to notice? She dared not leave the bottle on the dressing-table, for if he had chanced to pass through the room he would certainly have thrown it out of window, so bitter was his antagonism to all oils and perfumes, scents, pomades, and other resources of the hairdresser, which he held defiled the hair and ruined it, to the deception of woman and the disgust of man. Not one drop of scent did Amaryllis dare to sprinkle on her handkerchief, not one drop of oil did she dare put on her beautiful hair unless surreptitiously, and then she could not go near him, for he was certain to detect it and scorch her with withering satire.

Yet, however satirized, feminine faith in perfumes and oils and so forth is like a perennial spring, and never fails.

Such splendid hair as Amaryllis possessed needed no dressing – nothing could possibly improve it, and the chances therefore were that whatever she used would injure – yet in her heart she yearned to rub it with oil.

But the more she considered the more probable it seemed that her father would detect her; she had better wait till he went out for the afternoon somewhere, an event that seldom occurred, for Iden was one of those who preferred working at home to rambling abroad. He was, indeed, too attached to his home work. So she returned the bottle to the drawer, and hid it under some stockings.

Immediately afterwards it was dinner-time. At all meals the rule was that there must be no talking, but at dinner the law was so strict that even to ask for anything, as a piece of bread, or to say so much as 'Give me the salt, please,' was a deadly sin. There must be absolute silence while the master ate. The least infringement was visited with a severe glance from his keen and brilliant blue eyes – there are no eyes so stern as blue eyes when angry – or else he uttered a deep sigh like a grunt, and sat rigidly upright for a moment. For he usually stooped, and to sit upright showed annoyance. No laws of the Medes and Persians were ever obeyed as was this law of silence in that house.

Anything that disturbed the absolute calm of the dinner hour was worse than sacrilege; anything that threatened to disturb it was watched intently by that repressive eye. No one must come in or go out of the room; if anyone knocked at the door (there are no bells in old country houses) there was a frown immediately, it necessitated someone answering it, and then Mrs Iden or Amaryllis had to leave the table, to go out and open and shut the sitting-room door as they went, and again as they returned. Amaryllis dreaded a knock at the door, it was so awful to have to stir once they had sat down to dinner, and the servant was certain not to know what reply to give. Sometimes it happened – and this was very terrible – that the master himself had to go, someone wanted him about some hay or a horse and cart, and no one could tell what to do but the master. A dinner broken up in this way was a very serious matter indeed.

That day they had a leg of mutton – a special occasion – a joint to be looked on reverently. Mr Iden had walked into the town to choose it himself some days previously, and brought it home on foot in a flag basket. The butcher would have sent it, and if not, there were men on the farm who could have fetched it, but it was much too important to be left to a second person. No one could do it right but Mr Iden himself. There was a good deal of reason in this personal care of the meat, for it is a certain fact that unless you do look after such things yourself, and that persistently, too, you never get it first-rate. For this cause people in grand villas scarcely ever have anything worth eating on their tables. Their household expenses reach thousands yearly, and yet they rarely have anything eatable, and their dinner-tables can never show meat, vegetables, or fruit equal to Mr Iden's. The meat was dark brown, as mutton should be, for if it is the least bit white it is sure to be poor; the grain was short, and ate like bread and butter, firm, and yet almost crumbling to the touch; it was full of juicy red gravy, and cut pleasantly, the knife went through it nicely; you can tell good meat directly you touch it with the knife. It was cooked to a turn, and had been done at a wood fire on a hearth; no oven taste, no taint of coal gas or carbon; the pure flame of wood had browned it. Such emanations as there may be from burning logs are odorous of the woodland, of the sunshine, of the fields and fresh air; the wood simply gives out as it burns the sweetness it has imbibed through its leaves from the atmosphere which floats above grass and flowers. Essences of this order, if they do penetrate the fibres of the meat, add to its flavour a delicate aroma. Grass-fed meat, cooked at a wood fire, for me.

Wonderful it is that wealthy people can endure to have their meat cooked over coal or in a shut-up iron box, where it kills itself with its own steam, which ought to escape. But then wealthy villa people do do odd things. *Les Misérables* who have to write like myself must put up with anything and be thankful for permission to exist; but people with mighty incomes from tea, or crockeryware, or mud, or bricks and mortar – why on earth these happy and favoured mortals do not live like the gods passes understanding.

Parisian people use charcoal: perhaps Paris will convert some of you who will not listen to a farmer.

Mr Iden had himself grown the potatoes that were placed before him. They were white, floury, without a drop of water in the whole dish of them. They were equal to the finest bread – far, far superior to the bread with which the immense city of London permits itself to be poisoned. (It is not much better, for it destroys the digestion.) This, too, with wheat at thirty shillings the quarter, a price which is in itself one of the most wonderful things of the age. The finest bread ought to be cheap.

'They be forty-folds,' said Mr Iden, helping himself to half a dozen. 'Look at the gravy go up into um like tea up a knob of sugar.'

The gravy was drawn up among the dry, floury particles of the potatoes as if they had formed capillary tubes.

'Forty-folds,' he repeated; 'they comes forty to one. It be an amazing theng how thengs do that; forty grows for one. Thaay be an old-fashioned potato; you won't find many of thaay, not true forty-folds. Mine comes true, 'cause I saves um every year a' purpose. Better take more than that (to Amaryllis) – you haven't got but two' (to Mrs Iden).

What he ate other people at his table must eat, and the largest quantity possible. No one else must speak, hardly to say 'Yes' or 'No', but the master could talk, talk, talk without end. The only talking that might be done by others was in praise of the edibles on the table by Iden so carefully provided. You might admire the potatoes or the mutton, but you must not talk on any other subject. Nor was it safe even to do that, because if you said, 'What capital potatoes!' you were immediately helped to another plateful, and had to finish them, want them or not. If you praised the mutton several thick slices were placed on your plate, and woe to you if you left a particle. It was no use to try and cover over what you could not manage with knife and fork; it was sure to be seen. 'What bean't you going to yet (eat) up that there juicy bit, you?'

Amaryllis and Mrs Iden, warned by previous experience, discreetly refrained from admiring either mutton or potatoes.

III

'Forty-folds,' went on the master, 'be the best keeping potatoes. Thur be so many new sorts now, but they bean't no good; they be very good for gentlefolk as doan't know no better, and poor folk as can't help theirselves. They won't grow everywhere neither; there bean't but one patch in our garden as ull grow 'um well. It's that's big middle patch. Summat different in the soil thur. There's a lot, bless you! to be learned before you can grow a potato, for all it looks such a simple thing. Farty-folds – '

'Farty-folds!' said Mrs Iden, imitating his provincial pronunciation with extreme disgust in her tone.

'Aw, yes, too,' said Iden. 'Varty-volds be ould potatoes, and thur bean't none as can beat um.'

The more she showed her irritation at his speech or ways, the more he accentuated both language and manner.

'Talking with your mouth full,' said Mrs Iden. It was true, Iden did talk with his mouth full, very full indeed, for he fed heartily. The remark annoyed him; he grunted and spluttered and choked a little – floury things are choky. He got it down by taking a long draught at his quart of strong ale. Splendid ale it was, too, the stuff to induce you to make faces at Goliath. He soon began to talk again.

'Th' ould shepherd fetched me these swede greens; I axed un three days ago; I know'd we was going to have this yer mutton. You got to settle these yer things aforehand.'

'Axed,' muttered Mrs Iden.

'Th' pigeons have been at um, they be 'mazing

fond of um, so be the larks. These be the best as thur was. They be the best things in the world for the blood. Swede greens be the top of all physic. If you can get fresh swede tops you don't want a doctor within twenty miles. There's nothing in all the chemists' shops in England equal to swede greens' – helping himself to a large quantity of salt.

'What a lot of salt you *do* eat!' muttered Mrs Iden.

'Only you must have the real swedes – not thuck stuff they sells in towns; greens they was once p'rhaps, but they be tough as leather, and haven't got a drop of sap in um. Swedes is only to be got about March.'

'Pooh! you can get them at Christmas in London,' said Mrs Iden.

'Aw, can 'ee? Call they swede tops? They bean't no good; you might as well eat dried leaves. I tell you these are the young fresh green shoots of spring' – suddenly changing his pronunciation as he became interested in his subject and forgot the shafts of irritation shot at him by his wife. 'They are full of sap – fresh sap – the juice which the plant extracts from the earth as the active power of the sun's rays increases. It is this sap which is so good for the blood. Without it the vegetable is no more than a woody fibre. Why the sap should be so powerful I cannot tell you; no one knows, any more than they know *how* the plant prepares it. This is one of those things which defy analysis – the laboratory is at fault, and can do nothing with it.' ('More salt!' muttered Mrs Iden. 'How can you eat such a quantity of salt?') 'There is something beyond what the laboratory can lay hands on; something that cannot be weighed, or seen, or estimated, neither by quantity, quality, or by any means. They analyse champagne, for instance; they find so many parts water, so much sugar, so much this, and so much that; but out of the hundred parts there remain ten – I think it is ten – at all events so many parts still to be accounted for. They escape, they are set down as volatile – the laboratory has not even a distinct name for this component; the laboratory knows nothing at all about it, cannot even name it. But this unknown constituent is the real champagne. So it is with the sap. In spring the sap possesses a certain virtue; at other times of the year the leaf is still green, but useless to us.'

'I shall have some vinegar,' said Mrs Iden, defiantly, stretching out her hand to the cruet.

Mr Iden made a wry face, as if the mere mention of vinegar had set his teeth on edge. He looked the other way and ate as fast as he could, to close his eyes to the spectacle of any one spoiling the sappy swede greens with nauseous vinegar. To his system of edible philosophy vinegar was utterly antagonistic – destructive of the sap-principle, altogether wrong, and, in fact, wicked, as destroying good and precious food.

Amaryllis would not have dared to have taken the vinegar herself, but as her mother passed the cruet to her, she, too, fell away, and mixed vinegar with the green vegetables. All women like vinegar.

When the bottle was restored to the cruet-stand Mr Iden deigned to look round again at the table.

'Ha! you'll cut your thumb!' he shouted to Amaryllis, who was cutting a piece of bread. She put the loaf down with a consciousness of guilt. 'Haven't I told you how to cut bread twenty times? Cutting towards your thumb like that! Hold your left hand lower down, so that if the knife slips it will go over. Here, like this. Give it to me.'

He cut a slice to show her, and then tossed the slice across the table so accurately that it fell exactly into its proper place by her plate. He had a habit of tossing things in that way.

'Why ever couldn't you pass it on the tray?' said Mrs Iden. 'Flinging in that manner! I hate to see it.'

Amaryllis, as in duty bound, in appearance took the lesson in bread-cutting to heart, as she had done twenty times before. But she knew she should still cut a loaf in the same dangerous style when out of his sight. She could not do it in the safe way – it was so much easier in the other; and if she did cut her hand she did not greatly care.

‘Now perhaps you’ll remember,’ said the master, getting up with his plate in his hand.

‘Whatever *are* you going to do now?’ asked Mrs Iden, who knew perfectly well.

‘Going to warm the plate.’ He went out into the kitchen, sat down by the fire, and carefully warmed his plate for a second helping.

‘I should think you couldn’t want any more,’ said Mrs Iden when he came back. ‘You had enough the first time for three.’

But Iden, who had the appetite of a giant, and had never ruined his digestion with vinegar or sauces, piled another series of thick slices on his plate, now hot to liquefy the gravy, and added to the meat a just proportion of vegetables. In proportion and a just mixture the secret of eating successfully consisted, according to him.

First he ate a piece of the dark brown mutton, this was immediately followed by a portion of floury potato, next by a portion of swede tops, and then, lest a too savoury taste should remain in the mouth, he took a fragment of bread, as it were to sweeten and cleanse his teeth. Finally came a draught of strong ale, and after a brief moment the same ingredients were mixed in the same order as before. His dinner was thus eaten in a certain order, and with a kind of rhythm, duly exciting each particular flavour like a rhyme in its proper position, and duly putting it out with its correct successor. Always the savour of meat and gravy and vegetables had to be toned down by the ultimate bread, a vast piece of which he kept beside him. He was a great bread eater – it was always bread after everything, and if there were two courses then bread between to prepare the palate, and to prevent the sweets from quarrelling with the acids. Organization was the chief characteristic of his mind – his very dinner was organized and well planned, and any break or disturbance was not so much an annoyance in itself as destructive of a clever design, like a stick thrust through the web of a geometrical spider.

This order of mouthfuls had been explained over and over again to the family, and if they felt that he was in a more than usually terrible mood, and if they felt his gaze upon them, the family to some extent submitted. Neither Mrs Iden nor Amaryllis, however, could ever educate their palates into this fixed sequence of feeding; and, if Iden was not in a very awful and Jovelike mood, they wandered about irregularly in their eating. When the dinner was over (and, indeed, before it began) they had a way of visiting the larder, and 'picking' little fragments of pies, or cold fowl, even a cold potato, the smallest mug – a quarter of a pint of the Goliath ale between them, or, if it was to be had, a sip of port wine. These women were very irrational in their feeding; they actually put vinegar on cold cabbage; they gloated over a fragment of pickled salmon about eleven o'clock in the morning. They had a herring sometimes for tea – the smell of it cooking sent the master into fits of indignation, he abominated it so, but they were so hardened and lost to righteousness they always repeated the offence next time the itinerant fish-dealer called. You could not drum them into good solid, straightforward eating.

They generally had a smuggled bit of pastry to eat in the kitchen after dinner, for Mr Iden considered that no one could need a second course after first-rate mutton and forty-folds. A morsel of cheese if you liked – nothing more. In summer the great garden abounded with fruit; he would have nothing but rhubarb, rhubarb, rhubarb, day after day, or else black-currant pudding. He held that black currants were the most wholesome fruit that grew; if he fancied his hands were not quite clean he would rub them with black-currant leaves to give them a pleasant aromatic odour (as ladies use scented soap). He rubbed them with walnut-leaves for the same purpose.

Of salad in its season he was a great eater, cucumber especially and lettuce and celery; but a mixed salad (oil and a flash, as it were, of Worcester sauce) was a horror to him. A principle ran through all his eating – an idea, a plan and design.

I assure you it is a very important matter this eating, a man's fortune depends on his dinner. I should have been as rich as Croesus if I could only have eaten what I liked all my time; I am sure I should, now I come to look back.

The soundest and most wholesome food in the world was set on Mr Iden's table; you may differ from his system, but you would have enjoyed the dark brown mutton, the floury potatoes, the fresh vegetables and fruit and salad, and the Goliath ale.

When he had at last finished his meal he took his knife and carefully scraped his crumbs together, drawing the edge along the cloth, first one way then the other, till he had a little heap; for, eating so much bread, he made many crumbs. Having got them together, he proceeded to shovel them into his mouth with the end of his knife, so that not one was wasted. Sometimes he sprinkled a little moist sugar over them with his finger and thumb. He then cut himself a slice of bread and cheese, and sat down with it in his armchair by the fire, spreading his large red-and-yellow silk handkerchief on his knee to catch the fragments in lieu of a plate.

'Why can't you eat your cheese at the table, like other people?' said Mrs Iden, shuffling her feet with contemptuous annoyance. A deep grunt in the throat was the answer she received; at the same time he turned his armchair more towards the fire, as much as to say, 'Other people are nothing to me.'

IV

This armchair, of old-fashioned make, had lost an arm – the screw remained sticking up, but the woodwork on that side was gone. It had been accidentally broken some ten years since; yet, although he used the chair every day, the arm had never been mended. Awkward as it was, he let it alone.

'Hum! where's *The Standard,* then?' he said presently, as he nibbled his cheese and sipped the ale which he had placed on the hob.

'Here it is, Pa,' said Amaryllis, hastening with the paper.

'Thought you despised the papers?' said Mrs Iden. 'Thought there was nothing but lies and rubbish in them, according to you?'

'No more thur bean't.'

'You always take good care to read them, though.'

'Hum!' Another deep grunt, and another slight turn of the chair. He could not answer this charge of inconsistency, for it was a fact that he affected to despise the newspaper and yet read it with avidity, and would almost as soon have missed his ale as his news.

However, to settle with his conscience, he had a manner of holding the paper half aslant a good way from him, and every now and then as he read uttered a dissentient or disgusted grunt.

The master's taking up his paper was a signal for all other persons to leave the room, and not to return till he had finished his news and his nap.

Mrs Iden and Amaryllis, as they went out, each took as many of the dishes as they could carry, for it was uncertain when they could come in again to clear the table. The cloth must not be moved, the door opened, or the slightest sound heard till the siesta was over.

'Can't clear the dinner things till four o'clock,' said Mrs Iden as she went, 'and then you want your tea – senseless!' Amaryllis shut the door, and the master was left to himself.

By-and-by, his cheese being finished, he dropped his newspaper, and arranged himself for slumber. His left elbow he carefully fitted to the remnant of the broken woodwork of the chair. The silk handkerchief, red and yellow, he gathered into a loose pad in his left hand for his cheek and temple to rest on. His face was thus supported by his hand and arm, while the side of his head touched and rested against the wainscot of the wall.

Just where his head touched it the wainscot had been worn away by the daily pressure, leaving a round spot. The wood was there exposed – a round spot, an inch or two in diameter, being completely bare of varnish. So many nods – the attrition of thirty years and more of nodding – had gradually ground away the coat with which the painter had originally covered the wood. It even looked a little hollow – a little depressed – as if his head had scooped out a shallow crater; but this was probably an illusion, the eye being deceived by the difference in colour between the wood and the varnish around it.

This human mark reminded one of the grooves worn by the knees of generations of worshippers in the sacred steps of the temple which they ascended on all-fours. It was, indeed, a mark of devotion, as Mrs Iden and others, not very keen observers, would have said, to the god of Sleep; in truth, it was a singular instance of continued devotion at the throne of the god of Thought.

It was to think that Mr Iden in the commencement assumed this posture of slumber, and commanded silence. But thought which has been cultivated for a third of a century is apt to tone down to something very near somnolence.

That panel of wainscot was, in fact, as worthy of preservation as those on which the early artists delineated the Madonna and Infant, and for which high prices are now paid. It was intensely – superlatively – human. Worn in slow time by a human head within which a great mind was working under the most unhappy conditions, it had the deep value attaching to inanimate things which have witnessed intolerable suffering.

I am not a Roman Catholic, but I must confess that if I could be assured any particular piece of wood had really formed a part of the Cross I should think it the most valuable thing in the world, to which Koh-i-noors would be mud.

I am a pagan, and think the heart and soul above crowns.

That panel was in effect a cross on which a heart had been tortured for a third of a century, that is, for the space of time allotted to a generation.

That mark upon the panel had still a further meaning, it represented the unhappiness, the misfortunes, the Nemesis of two hundred years. This family of Idens had endured already two hundred years of unhappiness and discordance for no original fault of theirs, simply because they had once been fortunate of old time, and therefore they had to work out that hour of sunshine to the utmost depths of shadow.

The panel of the wainscot upon which that mark had been worn was in effect a cross upon which a human heart had been tortured – and thought can, indeed, torture – for a third of a century. For Iden had learned to know himself, and despaired.

Not long after he had settled himself and closed his eyes the handle of the door was very softly turned, and Amaryllis stole in for her book, which she had forgotten. She succeeded in getting it on tiptoe without a sound, but in shutting the door the lock clicked, and she heard him kick the fender angrily with his iron-shod heel.

After that there was utter silence, except the ticking of the American clock – a loud and distinct tick in the still (and in that sense vacant) room.

Presently a shadow somewhat darkened the window, a noiseless shadow; Mrs Iden had come quietly round the house, and stood in the March wind, watching the sleeping man. She had a shawl about her shoulders – she put out her clenched hand from under its folds, and shook her fist at him, muttering to herself, 'Never *do* anything; nothing but sleep, sleep, sleep: talk, talk, talk; never *do* anything. That's what I hate.'

The noiseless shadow disappeared; the common American clock continued its loud tick, tick.

Slight sounds, faint rustlings, began to be audible among the cinders in the fender. The dry cinders were pushed about by something passing between them. After a while a brown mouse peered out at the end of the fender under Iden's chair, looked round a moment, and went back to the grate. In a minute he came again, and ventured somewhat farther across the width of the white hearthstone to the verge of the carpet. This advance was made step by step, but on reaching the carpet the mouse rushed home to cover in one run – like children at 'touch wood', going out from a place of safety very cautiously, returning swiftly. The next time another mouse followed, and a third appeared at the other end of the fender. By degrees they got under the table, and helped themselves to the crumbs; one mounted a chair and reached the cloth, but soon descended, afraid to stay there. Five or six mice were now busy at their dinner.

The sleeping man was as still and quiet as if carved.

A mouse came to the foot, clad in a great rusty-hued iron-shod boot – the foot that rested on the fender, for he had crossed his knees. His ragged and dingy trouser, full of March dust, and earthstained by labour, was drawn up somewhat higher than the boot. It took the mouse several trials to reach the trouser, but he succeeded, and audaciously mounted to Iden's knee. Another quickly followed, and there the pair of them feasted on the crumbs of bread and cheese caught in the folds of his trousers.

One great brown hand was in his pocket, close to them – a mighty hand, beside which they were pigmies indeed in the land of the giants. What would have been the value of their lives between a finger and thumb that could crack a ripe and strong-shelled walnut?

The size – the mass – the weight of his hand alone was as a hill overshadowing them; his broad frame like the Alps; his head high above as a vast rock that overhung the valley.

His thumb-nail – widened by labour with spade and

axe – his thumb-nail would have covered either of the tiny creatures as his shield covered Ajax.

Yet the little things fed in perfect confidence. He was so still, so *very* still – quiescent – they feared him no more than they did the wall; they could not hear his breathing.

Had they been gifted with human intelligence that very fact would have excited their suspicions. Why so very, *very* still? Strong men, wearied by work, do not sleep quietly; they breathe heavily. Even in firm sleep we move a little now and then, a limb trembles, a muscle quivers, or stretches itself.

But Iden was so still it was evident he was really wide awake and restraining his breath, and exercising conscious command over his muscles, that this scene might proceed undisturbed.

Now the strangeness of the thing was in this way: Iden set traps for mice in the cellar and the larder, and slew them there without mercy. He picked up the trap, swung it round, opening the door at the same instant, and the wretched captive was dashed to death upon the stone flags of the floor. So he hated them and persecuted them in one place, and fed them in another.

A long psychological discussion might be held on this apparent inconsistency, but I shall leave analysis to those who like it, and go on recording facts. I will only make one remark. That nothing is consistent that is human. If it was not inconsistent it would have no association with a living person.

From the merest thin slit, as it were, between his eyelids, Iden watched the mice feed and run about his knees till, having eaten every crumb, they descended his leg to the floor.

V

He was not asleep – he was thinking. Sometimes, of course, it happened that slumber was induced by the position in which he placed himself; slumber, however, was not his intent. He liked to rest after his midday meal and think. There was no real loss of time in it – he had been at work since half past five.

His especial and striking characteristic was a very large, high and noble forehead – the forehead attributed to Shakespeare and seen in his busts. Shakespeare's intellect is beyond inquiry, yet he was not altogether a man of action. He was, indeed, an actor upon the stage; once he stole the red deer (delightful to think of that!), but he did not sail to the then new discovered lands of America, nor did he fight the Spaniards. So much intellect is, perhaps, antagonistic to action, or rather it is averse to those arts by which a soldier climbs to the position of commander. If Shakespeare by the chance of birth, or other accident, had had the order of England's forces, we should have seen generalship such as the world had not known since Caesar.

His intellect was too big to climb backstairs till opportunity came. We have great thoughts instead of battles.

Iden's forehead might have been sculptured for Shakespeare's. There was too much thought in it for the circumstances of his life. It is possible to think till you cannot act.

After the mice descended Iden did sleep for a few minutes. When he awoke he looked at the clock in a guilty way, and then opening the oven of the grate, took out a baked apple. He had one there ready for him almost always – always, that is, when they were not ripe on the trees.

A baked apple, he said, was the most wholesome thing in the world; it corrected the stomach, prevented acidity, improved digestion, and gave tone to all the food that had been eaten previously. If people would only eat baked apples they would not need to be for ever going to the chemists' shops for drugs and salines to put them right. The women were always at the chemists' shops – you could never pass the chemists' shops in the town without seeing two or three women buying something.

The apple was the apple of fruit, the natural medicine of man – and the best flavoured. It was compounded of the sweetest extracts and essences of air and light, put together of sunshine and wind and shower in such a way that no laboratory could imitate: and so on in a strain and with a simplicity of language that reminded you of Bacon and his philosophy of the Elizabethan age.

Iden in a way certainly had a tinge of the Baconian culture, naturally, and not from any study of that author, whose books he had never seen. The great Bacon was, in fact, a man of orchard and garden, and gathered his ideas from the fields.

Just look at an apple on the tree, said Iden. Look at a Blenheim orange, the inimitable mixture of colour, the gold and bronze, and ruddy tints, not bright colours – undertones of bright colours – smoothed together and polished, and made the more delightful by occasional roughness in the rind. Or look at the brilliant King Pippin. Now he was getting older he found, however, that the finest of them all was the russet. For eating, at its proper season, it was good, but for cooking it was simply the Imperial Caesar and Sultan of apples; whether for baking, or pies, or sauce, there was none to equal it. Apple-sauce made of the real true russet was a sauce for Jove's own table. It was necessary that it should be the real russet. Indeed in apple trees you had to be as careful of breeding and pedigree as the owners of racing stables were about their horses.

Ripe apples could not be got all the year round in any variety; besides which, in winter and cold weather the crudity of the stomach needed to be assisted with a little warmth; therefore bake them.

People did not eat nearly enough fruit now-a-days; they had too much butcher's meat, and not enough fruit – that is, home-grown fruit, straight from orchard or garden, not the half-sour stuff sold in the shops, picked before it was ready.

The Americans were much wiser (he knew a good deal about America – he had been there in his early days, before thought superseded action) – the Americans had kept up many of the fine old English customs of two or three hundred years since, and among these was the eating of fruit. They were accused of being so modern, so very, very modern, but, in fact, the country Americans, with whom he had lived (and who had taught him how to chop) maintained much of the genuine antique life of old England.

They had first-rate apples, yet it was curious that the same trees produced an apple having a slightly different flavour to what it had in this country. You could always distinguish an American apple by its peculiar piquancy – a sub-acid piquancy, a wild strawberry piquancy, a sort of woodland, forest, backwoods delicacy of its own. And so on, and so on – 'talk, talk, talk', as Mrs Iden said.

After his baked apple he took another guilty look at the clock, it was close on four, and went into the passage to get his hat. In farmhouses these places are called passages; in the smallest of villas, wretched little villas not fit to be called houses, they are always 'halls'.

In the passage Mrs Iden was waiting for him, and began to thump his broad though bowed back with all her might.

'Sleep, sleep, sleep!' she cried, giving him a thump at each word. 'You've slept two hours. (Thump.) You sleep till you stupefy yourself (thump), and then you go and dig. What's the use of digging? (Thump.) Why don't you make some money? (Thump.) Talk and sleep! (Thump.) I hate it. (Thump.) You've rubbed the paint off the wainscot with your sleep, sleep, sleep (thump) – there's one of your hairs sticking to the paint where your head goes. (Thump.) Anything more hateful – sleep (thump), talk (thump), sleep (thump). Go on!'

She had thumped him down the passage, and across the covered-in court to the door opening on the garden. There he paused to put on his hat – an aged, battered hat – some sort of nondescript bowler, broken, grey, weather-stained, very battered and very aged – a pitiful hat to put above that broad, Shakespearian forehead. While he fitted it on he was thumped severely: when he opened the door he paused, and involuntarily looked up at the sky to see about the weather – a habit all country people have – and so got more thumping, ending as he started out with a tremendous push. He did not seem to resent the knocks, nor did the push accelerate his pace; he took it very much as he took the March wind.

Mrs Iden slammed the door, and went in to clear the dinner things, and make ready for tea. Amaryllis helped her.

'He'll want his tea in half an hour,' said Mrs Iden. 'What's the use of his going out to work for half an hour?'

Amaryllis was silent. She was very fond of her father; he never did anything wrong in her eyes, and she could have pointed out that when he sat down to dinner at one he had already worked as many hours as Mrs Iden's model City gentleman in a whole day. His dinner at one was, in effect, equivalent to their dinner at seven or eight, over which they frequently lingered an hour or two. He would still go on labouring, almost another half day. But she held her peace, for, on the other hand, she could not contradict and argue with her mother, whom she knew had had a wearisome life and perpetual disappointments.

Mrs Iden grumbled on to herself, working herself into a more fiery passion, till at last she put down the tea-pot, and rushed into the garden. There as she came round the first thing she saw was the daffodil, the beautiful daffodil Amaryllis had discovered. Beside herself with indignation – what was the use of flowers or potatoes? – Mrs Iden stepped on the border and trampled the flower underfoot till it was shapeless.

After this she rushed indoors again and upstairs to her bedroom, where she locked herself in, and fumbled about in the old black oak chest of drawers till she found a faded lavender glove.

That glove had been worn at the old 'Ship' at Brighton years and years ago on the honeymoon trip: in those days bridal parties went down by coach. Faded with years, it had also faded from the tears that had fallen upon it. She turned it over in her hands, and her tears spotted it once more.

Amaryllis went on with the tea-making; for her mother to rush away in that manner was nothing new. She toasted her father a piece of toast – he affected to despise toast, but he always ate it if it was there, and looked about for it if it was not, though he never said anything. The clock struck five, and out she went to tell him tea was ready. Coming round the house she found her daffodil crushed to pieces.

'Oh!' The blood rushed to her forehead; then her beautiful lips pouted and quivered; tears filled her eyes, and her breast panted. She knew immediately who had done it; she ran to her bedroom to cry and to hide her grief and indignation.

14 Hours of Spring

It is sweet on awaking in the early morn to listen to the small bird singing on the tree. No sound of voice or flute is like to the bird's song; there is something in it distinct and separate from all other notes. The throat of woman gives forth a more perfect music, and the organ is the glory of man's soul. The bird upon the tree utters the meaning of the wind – a voice of the grass and wild flower, words of the green leaf; they speak through that slender tone. Sweetness of dew and rifts of sunshine, the dark hawthorn touched with breadths of open bud, the odour of the air, the colour of the daffodil – all that is delicious and beloved of spring-time are expressed in his song. Genius is nature, and his lay, like the sap of the bough from which he sings, rises without thought. Nor is it necessary that it should be a song; a few short notes in the sharp spring morning are sufficient to stir the heart. But yesterday the least of them all came to a bough by my window, and in his call I heard the sweet-briar wind rushing over the young grass. Refulgent fall the golden rays of the sun; a minute only, the clouds cover him and the hedge is dark. The bloom of the gorse is shut like a book; but it is there – a few hours of warmth and the covers will fall open. The meadow is bare, but in a little while the heart-shaped celandine leaves will come in their accustomed place. On the pollard willows the long wands are yellow-ruddy in the passing gleam of sunshine, the first colour of spring appears in their bark. The delicious wind rushes among them and they bow and rise; it touches the top of the dark pine that looks in the sun the same now as in summer; it lifts and swings the arching trail of bramble; it dries and crumbles the earth in its fingers; the hedge-sparrow's feathers are fluttered as he sings on the bush.

I wonder to myself how they can all get on without me – how they manage, bird and flower, without me to keep the calendar for them. For I noted it so carefully and lovingly, day by day, the seed-leaves on the mounds in the sheltered places that come so early, the pushing up of the young grass, the succulent dandelion, the coltsfoot on the heavy, thick clods, the trodden chickweed despised at the foot of the gate-post, so common and small, and yet so dear to me. Every blade of grass was mine, as though I had planted it separately. They were all my pets, as the roses the lover of his garden tends so faithfully. All the grasses of the meadow were my pets, I loved them all; and perhaps that was why I never had a 'pet', never cultivated a flower, never kept a caged bird, or any creature. Why keep pets when every wild free hawk that passed overhead in the air was mine? I joyed in his swift, careless flight, in the throw of his pinions, in his rush over the elms and miles of woodland; it was happiness to see his unchecked life. What more beautiful than the sweep and curve of his going through the azure sky? These were my pets, and all the grass. Under the wind it seemed to dry and become grey, and the starlings running to and fro on the surface that did not sink now stood high above it and were larger. The dust that drifted along blessed it and it grew. Day by day a change; always a note to make. The moss drying on the tree trunks, dog's-mercury stirring under the ash-poles, bird's-claw buds of beech lengthening; books upon books to be filled with these things. I cannot think how they manage without me.

To-day through the window-pane I see a lark high up against the grey cloud, and hear his song. I cannot walk about and arrange with the buds and gorse-bloom; how does he know it is the time for him to sing? Without my book and pencil and observing eye, how does he understand that the hour has come? To sing high in the air, to chase his mate over the low stone wall of the ploughed field, to battle with his high-crested rival, to balance himself on his trembling wings outspread a few yards above the earth, and utter the sweet little loving kiss, as it were, of song – oh, happy, happy days! So beautiful to watch as if he were my own, and I felt it all! It is years since I went out amongst them in the old fields, and saw them in the green corn; they must be dead, dear little things, by now. Without me to tell him, how does this lark to-day that I hear through the window know it is his hour?

The green hawthorn buds prophesy on the hedge; the reed pushes up in the moist earth like a spear thrust through a shield; the eggs of the starling are laid in the knot-hole of the pollard elm – common eggs, but within each a speck that is not to be found in the cut diamond of two hundred carats – the dot of proto-plasm, the atom of life. There was one row of pollards where they always began laying first. With a big stick in his beak the rook is blown aside like a loose feather in the wind; he knows his building-time from the fathers of his house – hereditary knowledge handed down in settled course: but the stray things of the hedge, how do they know? The great blackbird has planted his nest by the ash-stole, open to every one's view, without a bough to conceal it and not a leaf on the ash – nothing but the moss on the lower end of the branches. He does not seek cunningly for conceal-ment. I think of the drift of time, and I see the apple bloom coming and the blue veronica in the grass. A thousand thousand buds and leaves and flowers and blades of grass, things to note day by day, increasing so rapidly that no pencil can put them down and no book hold them, not even to number them – and how to write the thoughts they give? All these without me – how can they manage without me?

For they were so much to me, I had come to feel that I was as much in return to them. The old, old error: I love the earth, therefore the earth loves me – I am her child – I am Man, the favoured of all creatures. I am the centre, and all for me was made.

In time past, strong of foot, I walked gaily up the noble hill that leads to Beachy Head from Eastbourne, joying greatly in the sun and the wind. Every step crumbled up numbers of minute grey shells, empty and dry, that crunched under foot like hoar-frost or fragile beads. They were very pretty; it was a shame to crush them – such vases as no king's pottery could make. They lay by millions in the depths of the sward, and I thought as I broke them unwillingly that each of these had once been a house of life. A living creature dwelt in each and felt the joy of existence, and was to itself all in all – as if the great sun over the hill shone for it, and the width of the earth under was for it, and the grass and plants put on purpose for it. They were dead, the whole race of them, and these their skeletons were as dust under my feet. Nature sets no value upon life neither of minute hill-snail nor of human being.

I thought myself so much to the earliest leaf and the first meadow orchis – so important that I should note the first zee-zee of the titlark – that I should pronounce it summer, because now the oaks were green; I must not miss a day nor an hour in the fields lest something should escape me. How beautiful the droop of the great brome-grass by the wood! But to-day I have to listen to the lark's song – not out of doors with him, but through the window-pane, and the bullfinch carries the rootlet fibre to his nest without me. They manage without me very well; they know their times and seasons – not only the civilized rooks, with their libraries of knowledge in their old nests of reference, but the stray things of the hedge and the chiffchaff from over sea in the ash wood. They go on without me. Orchis flower and cowslip – I cannot number them all – I hear, as it were, the patter of their feet – flower and bud and the beautiful clouds that go over, with the sweet rush of rain and burst of sun glory among the leafy trees. They go on, and I am no more than the least of the empty shells that strewed the sward of the hill. Nature sets no value upon life, neither of mine nor of the larks that sang years ago. The earth is all in all to me, but I am nothing to the earth: it is bitter to know this before you are dead. These delicious violets are sweet for themselves; they were not shaped and coloured and gifted with that exquisite proportion and adjustment of odour and hue for me. High up against the grey cloud I hear the lark through the window singing, and each note falls into my heart like a knife.

Now this to me speaks as the roll of thunder that cannot be denied – you must hear it; and how can you shut your ears to what this lark sings, this violet tells, this little grey shell writes in the curl of its spire? The bitter truth that human life is no more to the universe than that of the unnoticed hill-snail in the grass should make us think more and more highly of ourselves as human – as men – living things that think. We must look to ourselves to help ourselves. We must think ourselves into an earthly immortality. By day and by night, by years and by centuries, still striving, studying, searching to find that which shall enable us to live a fuller life upon the earth – to have a wider grasp upon its violets and loveliness, a deeper draught of the sweet-briar wind. Because my heart beats feebly today, my trickling pulse scarcely notating the passing of the time, so much the more do I hope that those to come in future years may see wider and enjoy fuller than I have done; and so much the more gladly would I do all that I could to enlarge the life that shall be then. There is no hope on the old lines – they are dead, like the empty shells; from the sweet delicious violets think out fresh petals of thought and colours, as it were, of soul.

Never was such a worshipper of earth. The commonest pebble, dusty and marked with the stain of the ground, seems to me so wonderful; my mind works round it till it becomes the sun and centre of a system of thought and feeling. Sometimes moving aside the tufts of grass with careless fingers while resting on the sward, I found these little pebble-stones loose in the crumbly earth among the rootlets. Then, brought out from the shadow, the sunlight shone and glistened on the particles of sand that adhered to it. Particles adhered to my skin – thousands of years between finger and thumb, these atoms of quartz, and sunlight shining all that time, and flowers blooming and life glowing in all, myriads of living things, from the cold still limpet on the rock to the burning, throbbing heart of man. Sometimes I found them among the sand of the heath, the sea of golden brown surging up yellow billows six feet high about me, where the dry lizard hid, or basked, of kin, too, to old time. Or the rush of the sea wave brought them to me, wet and gleaming, up from the depths of what unknown Past? where they nestled in the root crevices of trees forgotten before Egypt. The living mind opposite the dead pebble – did you ever consider the strange and wonderful problem there? Only the thickness of the skin of the hand between them. The chief use of matter is to demonstrate to us the existence of the soul. The pebble-stone tells me I am a soul because I am not that that touches the nerves of my hand. We are distinctly two, utterly separate, and shall never come together. The little pebble and the great sun overhead – millions of miles away: yet is the great sun no more distinct and apart than this which I can touch. Dull-surfaced matter, like a polished mirror, reflects back thoughts to thought's self within.

I listened to the sweet-briar wind this morning; but for weeks and weeks the stark black oaks stood straight out of the snow as masts of ships with furled sails frozen and ice-bound in the haven of the deep valley. Each was visible to the foot, set in the white slope, made individual in the wood by the brilliance of the background. Never was such a long winter. For fully two months they stood in the snow in black armour of iron bark unshaken, the front rank of the forest army that would not yield to the northern invader. Snow in broad flakes, snow in semi-flakes, snow raining down in frozen specks, whirling and twisting in fury, ice raining in small shot of frost, howling, sleeting, groaning; the ground like iron, the sky black and faintly yellow – brutal colours of despotism – heaven striking with clenched fist. When at last the general surface cleared, still there remained the trenches and traverses of the enemy, his ramparts drifted high, and his roads marked with snow. The black firs on the ridge stood out against the frozen clouds, still and hard; the slopes of leafless larches seemed withered and brown; the distant plain far down gloomy with the same dull yellowish blackness. At a height of seven hundred feet the air was sharp as a scythe – a rude barbarian giant wind knocking at the walls of the house with a vast club, so that we crept sideways even to the windows to look out upon the world. There was everything to repel – the cold, the frost, the hardness, the snow, dark sky and ground, leaflessness; the very furze chilled and all benumbed. Yet the forest was still beautiful. There was no day that we did not, all of us, glance out at it and admire it, and say something about it. Harder and harder grew the frost, yet still the forest-clad hills possessed a something that drew the mind open to their largeness and grandeur. Earth is always beautiful – always. Without colour, or leaf, or sunshine, or song of bird and flutter of butterfly's wing; without anything sensuous, without advantage or gilding of summer – the power is ever there. Or shall we not say that the desire of the mind is ever there, and *will* satisfy itself, in a measure at least, even with the barren wild? The heart from the moment of its first beat instinctively longs for the beautiful; the means we possess to gratify it are limited – we are always trying to find the statue in the rude block. Out of the vast block of earth the mind endeavours to carve itself loveliness, nobility, and grandeur. We strive for the right and the true: it is circumstance that thrusts wrong upon us.

One morning a labouring man came to the door with a spade, and asked if he could dig the garden, or try to, at the risk of breaking the tool in the ground. He was starving; he had had no work for two months; it was just six months, he said, since the first frost started the winter. Nature and the earth and the gods did not trouble about *him,* you see; he might grub the rock-frost ground with his hands if he chose – the yellowish black sky did not care. Nothing for man! The only good he found was in his fellow-men; they fed him after a fashion – still they fed him. There was no good in anything else. Another aged man came once a week regularly; white as the snow through which he walked. In summer he worked; since the winter began he had had no employment, but supported himself by going round to the farms in rotation. They all gave him a trifle – bread and cheese, a penny, a slice of meat – something; and so he lived, and slept the whole of that time in outhouses wherever he could. He had no home of any kind. Why did he not go into the work-house? 'I be afeared if I goes in there they'll put me with the rough uns, and very likely I should get some of my clothes stole.' Rather than go into the work-house he would totter round in the face of the blasts that might cover his weak old limbs with drift. There was a sense of dignity and manhood left still; his clothes were worn, but clean and decent; he was no companion of rogues; the snow and frost, the straw of the outhouses, was better than that. He was struggling against age, against nature, against circumstance; the entire weight of society, law, and order pressed upon him to force him to lose his self-respect and liberty. He would rather risk his life in the snowdrift. Nature, earth, and the gods did not help him; sun and stars, where were they? He knocked at the doors of the farms and found good in man only – not in Law or Order, but in individual man alone.

The bitter north wind drives even the wild fieldfare to the berries in the garden hedge; so it drives stray human creatures to the door. A third came – an old gipsy woman – still stout and hearty, with green fresh brooms to sell. We bought some brooms – one of them was left on the kitchen floor, and the tame rabbit nibbled it; it proved to be heather. The true broom is as green and succulent in appearance in January as June. She would see the 'missis'. 'Bless you, my good lady, it be weather, bean't it? I hopes you'll never know what it be to want, my good lady. Ah, well, you looks good-tempered if you don't want to buy nothing. Do you see if you can't find me an old body, now, for my girl – now do'ee try; she's confined in a tent on the common – nothing but one of our tents, my good lady – that's true – and she's doing jest about well' (with briskness and an air of triumph), 'that she is! She's got twins. you see, my lady, but she's all right, and as well as can be. She wants to get up; and she says to me, "Mother, do'ee try and get me a body; 'tis hard to lie here abed and be well enough to get up, and be obliged to stay here because I've got nothing but a bedgown." For you see, my good lady, we managed pretty well with the first baby; but the second bothered us, and we cut up all the bits of things we could find, and there she ain't got nothing to put on. Do'ee see if 'ee can't find her an old body.' The common is an open piece of furze and heath at the verge of the forest; and here, in a tent just large enough to creep in, the gipsy woman had borne twins in the midst of the snow and frost. They could not make a fire of the heath and gorse even if they cut it, the snow and whirling winds would not permit. The old gipsy said if they had little food they could not do without fire, and they were compelled to get coke and coal somehow – apologizing for such a luxury. There was no whining – not a bit of it, they were evidently quite contented and happy, and the old woman proud of her daughter's hardihood. By-and-by the husband came round with straw beehives to sell, and cane to mend chairs – a strong, respectable-looking man. Of all the north wind drove to the door, the outcasts were the best off – much better off than the cottager who was willing to break his spade to earn a shilling; much better off than the white-haired labourer, whose strength was spent, and who had not even a friend to watch with him in the dark hours of the winter evening – not even a fire to rest by. The gipsy nearest to the earth was the best off in every way; yet not even for primitive man and woman did the winds cease. Broad flakes of snow drifted up against the low tent, beneath which the babes were nestling to the breast. Not even for the babes did the snow cease or the keen wind rest; the very fire could scarcely struggle against it. Snow-rain and ice-rain; frost-formed snow-granules, driven along like shot, stinging and rattling against the tent-cloth, hissing in the fire; roar and groan of the great wind among the oaks of the forest. No kindness to man, from birth-hour to ending; neither earth, sky, nor gods care for him, innocent at the mother's breast. Nothing good to man but man. Let man, then, leave his gods and lift up his ideal beyond them.

Something grey and spotted and puffy, not unlike a toad, moved about under the gorse of the garden hedge one morning, half hidden by the stalks of old grasses. By-and-by it hopped out – the last thrush, so distended with puffed feathers against the frost as to be almost shapeless. He searched about hopelessly round the stones and in the nooks, all hard and frostbound; there was the shell of a snail, dry and whitened and empty, as was apparent enough even at a distance. His keen eye must have told him that it was empty; yet such was his hunger and despair that he took it and dashed it to pieces against a stone. Like a human being, his imagination was stronger than his experience; he tried to persuade himself that there might be something there; hoping against hope. Mind, you see, working in the bird's brain, and overlooking facts. A mere mechanism would have left the empty and useless shell untouched – would have accepted facts at once, however bitter, just as the balance of the heaviest side declines immediately, obeying the fact of an extra grain of weight. The bird's brain was not mechanical, and therefore he was not wholly mastered by experience. It was a purely human action – just what we do ourselves. Next he came across to the door to see if a stray berry still remained on a creeper. He saw me at the window, and he came to the window – right to it – and stopped and looked full at me some minutes, within touch almost, saying as plainly as could be said, 'I am starving – help me.' I never before knew a thrush make so unmistakable an appeal for assistance, or deliberately approach so near (unless previously encouraged). We tried to feed him, but we fear little of the food reached him. The wonder of the incident was that a thrush should still be left – there had not been one in the garden for two months. Berries all gone, ground hard and foodless, streams frozen, snow lying for weeks, frost stealing away the vital heat – ingenuity could not devise a more terrible scene of torture to the birds. Neither for the thrushes nor for the new-born infants in the tent did the onslaught of the winter slacken. No pity in earth or heaven. This one thrush did, indeed, by some exceptional fortune, survive; but where were the family of thrushes that had sung so sweetly in the rainy autumn? Where were the blackbirds?

Looking down from the stilts of seven hundred feet into the deep coombe of black oaks standing in the white snow, day by day, built round about with the rugged mound of the hills, doubly locked with the key of frost – it seemed to me to take on itself the actuality of the ancient faith of the Magi. How the seeds of all living things – the germs – of bird and animal, man and insect, tree and herb, of the whole earth – were gathered together into a four-square rampart, and there laid to sleep in safety, shielded by a spell-bound fortification against the coming flood, not of water, but of frost and snow! With snow and frost and winter the earth was overcome, and the world perished, stricken dumb and dead, swept clean and utterly destroyed – a winter of the gods, the silence of snow and universal death. All that had been passed away, and the earth was depopulated. Death triumphed. But under the snow, behind the charmed rampart, slept the living germs. Down in the deep coombe, where the dark oaks stood out individually in the whiteness of the snow, fortified round about with immovable hills, there was the actual presentment of Zoroaster's sacred story. Locked in sleep lay bud and germ – the butterflies of next summer were there somewhere, under the snow. The earth was swept of its inhabitants, but the seeds of life were not dead. Near by were the tents of the gipsies – an Eastern race, whose forefathers perhaps had seen that very Magian worship of the Light; and in those tents birth had already taken place. Under the Night of winter – under the power of dark Ahriman, the evil spirit of Destruction – lay bud and germ in bondage, waiting for the coming of Ormuzd, the Sun of Light and Summer. Beneath the snow, and in the frozen crevices of the trees, in the chinks of the earth, sealed up by the signet of frost, were the seeds of the life that would replenish the air in time to come. The buzzing crowds of summer were still under the snow.

This forest land is marked by the myriads of insects that roam about it in the days of sunshine. Of all the million million heathbells – multiply them again by a million million more – that purple the acres of rolling hills, mile upon mile, there is not one that is not daily visited by these flying creatures. Countless and incalculable hosts of the yellow-barred hover-flies come to them; the heath and common, the moor and forest, the hedgerow and copse, are full of insects. They rise under foot, they rise from the spray brushed by your arm as you pass, they settle down in front of you – a rain of insects, a coloured shower. Legion is a little word for the butterflies; the dry pastures among the woods are brown with meadow-brown; blues and coppers float in endless succession; all the nations of Xerxes' army were but a handful to these. In their millions they have perished; but somewhere, coiled up, as it were, and sealed under the snow, there must have been the mothers and germs of the equally vast crowds that will fill the atmosphere this year. The great humble-bee that shall be mother of hundreds, the yellow wasp that shall be mother of thousands, were hidden there somewhere. The food of the migrant birds that are coming from over sea was there dormant under the snow. Many nations have a tradition of a former world destroyed by a deluge of water, from the East to the West, from Greece to Mexico, where the tail of a comet was said to have caused the flood; but in the strange characters of the Zend is the legend of an ark (as it were) prepared against the snow. It may be that it is the dim memory of a glacial epoch. In this deep coombe, amid the dark oaks and snow, was the fable of Zoroaster. For the coming of Ormuzd, the Light and Life Bringer, the leaf slept folded, the butterfly was hidden, the germ concealed, while the sun swept upwards towards Aries.

There is nothing so wearying as a long frost – the endless monotony, which makes one think that the very fault we usually find with our climate – its changeableness – is in reality its best quality. Rain, mist, gales – anything; give us anything but weary, weary frost. But having once fixed its mind, the weather will not listen to the usual signs of alteration.

The larks sang at last high up against the grey cloud over the frost-bound earth. They could not wait longer; love was strong in their little hearts – stronger than the winter. After a while the hedge-sparrows, too, began to sing on the top of the gorse-hedge about the garden. By-and-by a chaffinch boldly raised his voice, ending with the old story, 'Sweet, will you, will you kiss – me – dear?' Then there came a hoar-frost, and the earth which had been black, became white, as its evaporated vapours began to gather and drops of rain to fall. Even then the obstinate weather refused to quite yield, wrapping its cloak, as it were, around it in bitter enmity. But in a day or two white clouds lit up with sunshine appeared drifting over from the southward, and that was the end. The old pensioner came to the door for his bread and cheese: 'The wind's in the south,' he said, 'and I hopes she'll stay there.' Five dull yellow spots on the hedge – gorse bloom – that had remained unchanged for so many weeks, took a fresh colour and became golden. By the constant passing of the waggons and carts along the road that had been so silent it was evident that the busy time of spring was here. There would be rough weather, doubtless, now and again, but it would not again be winter.

Dark patches of cloud – spots of ink on the sky, the 'messengers' – go drifting by; and after them will follow the water-carriers, harnessed to the south and west winds, drilling the long rows of rain like seed into the earth. After a time there will be a rainbow. Through the bars of my prison I can see the catkins thick and sallow-grey on the willows across the field, visible even at that distance; so great the change in a few days, the hand of spring grows firm and takes a strong grasp of the hedges. My prison bars are but a sixteenth of an inch thick; I could snap them with a fillip – only the windowpane, to me as impenetrable as the twenty-foot wall of the Tower of London. A cart has just gone past bearing a strange load among the carts of spring; they are talking of poling the hops. In it there sat an old man, with the fixed stare, the animal-like eye, of extreme age; he is over ninety. About him there were some few chairs and articles of furniture, and he was propped against a bed. He was being moved – literally carted – to another house, not home, and he said he could not go without his bed; he had slept on it for seventy-three years. Last Sunday his son – himself old – was carted to the churchyard, as is the country custom, in an open van; to-day the father, still living, goes to what will be to him a strange land. His home is broken up – he will potter no more with maize for the chicken; the gorse hedges will become solid walls of golden bloom, but there will never again be a spring for him. It is very hard, is it not, at ninety? It is not the tyranny of any one that has done it; it is the tyranny of circumstance, the lot of man. The song of the Greeks is full of sorrow; man was to them the creature of grief, yet theirs was the land of violets and pellucid air. This has been a land of frost and snow, and here too, it is the same. A stranger, I see, is already digging the old man's garden.

How happy the trees must be to hear the song of birds again in their branches! After the silence and the leaflessness, to have the birds back once more and to feel them busy at the nest-building; how glad to give them the moss and fibres and the crutch of the boughs to build in! Pleasant it is now to watch the sunlit clouds sailing onwards; it is like sitting by the sea. There is voyaging to and fro of birds; the strong wood-pigeon goes over – a long course in the air, from hill to distant copse; a blackbird starts from an ash, and, now inclining this way and now that, traverses the meadows to the thick corner hedge; finches go by, and the air is full of larks that sing without ceasing. The touch of the wind, the moisture of the dew, the sun-stained raindrop, have in them the magic force of life – a marvellous something that was not there before. Under it the narrow blade of grass comes up freshly green between the old white fibres the rook pulled; the sycamore bud swells and opens, and takes the eye instantly in the still dark wood; the starlings go to the hollow pollards; the lambs leap in the mead. You never know what a day may bring forth – what new thing will come next. Yesterday I saw the ploughman and his team, and the earth gleam smoothed behind the share; to-day a butterfly has gone past; the farm-folk are bringing home the fagots from the hedgerows; to-morrow there will be a merry, merry note in the ash copse, the chiffchaffs' ringing call to arms, to arms, ye leaves! By-and-by a bennet, a bloom of the grass; in time to come the furrow, as it were, shall open, and the great buttercup of the waters will show a broad palm of gold. You never know what will come to the net of the eye next – a bud, a flower, a nest, a curled fern, or whether it will be in the woodland or by the meadow path, at the water's side or on the dead dry heap of fagots. There is no settled succession, no fixed and formal order – always the unexpected; and you cannot say, 'I will go and find this or that.' The sowing of life in the spring time is not in the set straight line of the drill, nor shall you find wild flowers by a foot measure. There are great woods without a lily of the valley; the nightingale does not sing everywhere. Nature has no arrangement, no plan, nothing judicious even; the walnut trees bring forth their tender buds, and the frost burns them – they have no mosaic of time to fit in, like a Roman tessellated pavement; nature is like a child, who will sing and shout though you may be never so deeply pondering in the study, and does not wait for the hour that suits your mind. You do not know what you may find each day; perhaps you may only pick up a fallen feather, but it is beautiful, every filament. Always beautiful! everything beautiful! And are these things new – the ploughman and his team, the lark's song, the green leaf? Can they be new? Surely they have been of old time! They are, indeed, new – the only things that are so; the rest is old and grey, and a weariness.

15 My Old Village

'John Brown is dead,' said an aged friend and visitor in answer to my inquiry for the strong labourer.

'Is he really dead?' I asked, for it seemed impossible.

'He is. He came home from his work in the evening as usual, and seemed to catch his foot in the threshold and fell forward on the floor. When they picked him up he was dead.'

I remember the doorway; a raised piece of wood ran across it, as is commonly the case in country cottages, such as one might easily catch one's foot against if one did not notice it; but he knew that bit of wood well. The floor was of brick, hard to fall on and die. He must have come down over the crown of the hill, with his long slouching stride, as if his legs had been half pulled away from his body by his heavy boots in the furrows when a ploughboy. He must have turned up the steps in the bank to his cottage, and so, touching the threshold, ended. He is gone through the great doorway, and one pencil-mark is rubbed out. There used to be a large hearth in that room, a larger room than in most cottages; and when the fire was lit and the light shone on the yellowish red brick beneath and the large rafters overhead, it was homely and pleasant. In

the only hospital worthy of the name. People have a chance to get well in such places; they have very great difficulty in the huge buildings that are put up expressly for them. I have a Convalescent Home in my mind at the moment, a vast building. In these great blocks what they call ventilation is a steady draught, and there is no 'home' about it. It is all walls and regulations and draughts, and altogether miserable. I would infinitely rather see any friend of mine in John Brown's cottage. That terrible disease, however, seemed to quite spoil the violet bank opposite, and I never picked one there afterwards. There is something in disease so destructive, as it were, to flowers.

The hundreds of times I saw the tall chimney of that cottage rise out of the hill-side as I came home at all hours of the day and night! the first chimney after a long journey, always comfortable to see, especially so in earlier days, when we had a kind of halting belief in John Brown's ghosts, several of which were dotted along that road according to him. The ghosts die as we grow older, they die and their places are taken by real ghosts. I wish I had sent John Brown a pound or two when I was in good health; but one is selfish then, and puts off things till it is too late – a lame excuse verily. I can scarcely believe now that he is really dead, gone as you might casually pluck a hawthorn leaf from the hedge.

The next cottage was a very marked one, for houses grow to their owners. The low thatched roof had rounded itself and stooped down to fit itself to Job's shoulders; the walls had got short and thick to suit him, and they had a yellowish colour, like his complexion, as if chewing tobacco had stained his cheeks right through. Tobacco juice had likewise penetrated and tinted the wall. It was cut off as it seemed by a party-wall into one room, instead of which there were more rooms beyond which no one would have suspected. Job had a way of shaking hands with you with his right hand, while his left hand was casually doing something else in a detached sort of way. 'Yes, sir,' and

'No, sir,' and nodding to everything you said all so complaisant, but at the end of the bargain you generally found yourself a few shillings in some roundabout manner on the wrong side. Job had a lot of shut-up rooms in his house and in his character, which never seemed to be opened to daylight. The eaves hung over and beetled like his brows, and he had a forelock, a regular antique forelock, which he used to touch with the greatest humility. There was a long bough of an elm hanging over one gable just like the forelock. His face was a blank, like the broad end wall of the cottage, which had no window – at least you might think so until you looked up and discovered one little arrow slit, one narrow pane, and woke with a start to the idea that Job was always up there watching and listening. That was how he looked out of his one eye so intensely cunning, the other being a wall eye – that is, the world supposed so, as he kept it half shut, always between the lights; but whether it was really blind or not I cannot say. Job caught rats and rabbits and moles, and bought fagots or potatoes, or fruit or rabbit-skins, or rusty iron: wonderful how he seemed to have command of money. It was done probably by buying and selling almost simultaneously, so that the cash passed really from one customer to another, and was never his at all. Also he worked as a labourer, chiefly piecework; also Mrs Job had a shop window about two feet square: snuff and tobacco, bread and cheese, immense big round jumbles and sugar, kept on the floor above, and reached down by hand, when wanted, through the opening for the ladder stairs. The front door – Job's right hand – was always open in summer, and the flagstones of the floor chalked round their edges; a clean table, clean chairs, decent crockery, an old clock about an hour slow, a large hearth with a minute fire to boil the kettle without heating the room. Tea was usually at half past three, and it is a fact that many well-to-do persons, as they came along the road hot and dusty, used to drop in and rest and take a cup – very little milk and much gossip. Two paths met just there, and people used to step in out of a storm of rain, a sort of thatched house club. Job was somehow on fair terms with nearly everybody, and that is a wonderful thing in a village, where everybody knows everybody's business, and petty interests continually cross. The strangest fellow and the strangest way of life, and yet I do not believe a black mark was ever put against him; the shiftiness was all for nothing. It arose, no doubt, out of the constant and eager straining to gain a little advantage and make an extra penny. Had Job been a Jew he would have been rich. He was the exact counterpart of the London Jew dealer, set down in the midst of the country. Job should have been rich. Such immense dark brown jumbles, such cheek-distenders – never any French sweetmeats or chocolate or bonbons to equal these. I really think I could eat one now. The pennies and fourpenny bits – there were fourpenny bits in those days – that went behind that two-foot window, goodness! there was no end. Job used to chink them in a pint pot sometimes before the company, to give them an idea of his great hoards. He always tried to impress people with his wealth, and would talk of a fifty-pound contract as if it was nothing to him. Jumbles are eternal, if nothing else is. I thought then there was not such another shop as Job's in the universe. I have found since that there is a Job shop in every village, and in every street in every town – that is to say, a window for jumbles and rubbish; and if you don't know it, you may be quite sure your children do, and spend many a sly penny there. Be as rich as you may, and give them gilded sweetmeats at home, still they will slip round to the Job shop.

It was a pretty cottage, well backed with trees and bushes, with a south-east mixture of sunlight and shade, and little touches that cannot be suggested by writing. Job had not got the Semitic instinct of keeping. The art of acquisition he possessed to some extent, that was his right hand; but somehow the half-crowns slipped away through his unstable left hand, and fortune was a greasy pole to him. His left hand was too cunning for him, it wanted to manage things too cleverly. If it had only had the Semitic grip, digging the nails into the flesh to hold tight each separate coin, he would have been village rich. The great secret is the keeping. Finding is by no means keeping. Job did not flourish in his old days; the people changed round about. Job is gone, and I think every one of that cottage is either dead or moved. Empty.

The next cottage was the water-bailiff's, who looked after the great pond or 'broad'. There were one or two old boats, and he used to leave the oars leaning against a wall at the side of the house. These oars looked like fragments of a wreck, broken and irregular. The right-hand scull was heavy, as if made of ironwood, the blade broad and spoon-shaped, so as to have a most powerful grip of the water. The left-hand scull was light and slender, with a narrow blade like a marrow scoop; so when you had the punt, you had to pull very hard with your left hand and gently with the right to get the forces equal. The punt had a list of its own, and no matter how you rowed, it would still make leeway. Those who did not know its character were perpetually trying to get this crooked wake straight, and consequently went round and round exactly like the whirligig beetle. Those who knew used to let the leeway proceed a good way and then alter it, so as to act in the other direction like an elongated zigzag. These sculls the old fellow would bring you as if they were great treasures, and watch you off in the punt as if he was parting with his dearest. At that date it was no little matter to coax him round to unchain his vessel. You had to take an interest in the garden, in the baits, and the weather, and be very humble; then perhaps he would tell you he did not want it for the trimmers, or the withy, or the flags, and you might have it for an hour as far as he could see; 'did not think my lord's steward would come over that morning; of course, if he did you must come in', and so on; and if the stars were propitious, by-and-by the punt was got afloat. These sculls were tilted up against the wall, and as you innocently went to take one, Wauw! – a dirty little ill-tempered mongrel poodle rolled himself like a ball to your heels and snapped his teeth – Wauw! At the bark, out rushed the old lady, his housekeeper, shouting in the shrillest key to the dog to lie still, and to you that the bailiff would be there in a minute. At the sound of her shrewish 'yang-yang' down came the old man from the bank, and so one dog fetched out the lot. The three were exactly alike somehow. Beside these diamond sculls he had a big gun, with which he used to shoot the kingfishers that came for the little fish; the number he slaughtered was very great; he persecuted them as Domitian did the flies: he declared that a kingfisher would carry off a fish heavier than itself. Also he shot rooks, once now and then strange wild fowl with this monstrous iron pipe, and something happened with this gun one evening which was witnessed, and after that the old fellow was very benevolent, and the punt was free to one or two who knew all about it. There is an old story about the stick that would not beat the dog, and the dog would not bite the pig, and so on; and so I am quite sure that ill-natured cur could never have lived with that 'yang-yang' shrew, nor could any one else but he have turned the gear of the hatch, nor have endured the dog and the woman, and the constant miasma from the stagnant waters. No one else could have shot anything with that cumbrous weapon, and no one else could row that punt straight. He used to row it quite straight, to the amazement of a wondering world, and somehow supplied the motive force – the stick – which kept all these things going. He is gone, and, I think, the housekeeper too, and the house has had several occupants since, who have stamped down the old ghosts and thrust them out of doors.

After this the cottages and houses came in little groups, some up crooked lanes, hidden away by elms as if out of sight in a cupboard, and some dotted along the brooks, scattered so that, unless you had connected them all with a very long rope, no stranger could have told which belonged to the village and which did not. They drifted into various tithings, and yet it was all the same place. They were all thatched. It was a thatched village. This is strictly accurate and strictly inaccurate, for I think there were one or two tiled and one 'slated', and perhaps a modern one slated. Nothing is ever quite rigid or complete that is of man; all rules have a chip in them. The way they builded the older thatched farm-houses was to put up a very high wall in front and a very low one behind, and then the roof in a general way sloped down from the high wall to the low wall, an acre broad of thatch. These old thatched houses seemed to be very healthy so long as the old folk lived in them in the old-fashioned way. Thatch is believed to give an equable temperature. The air blew all round them, and it might be said all through them; for the front door was always open three parts of the year, and at the back the dairies were in a continual blow. Upstairs the houses were only one room thick, so that each wall was an outside wall, or rather it was a wall one side and thatched the other, so that the wind went through if a window was open. Modern houses are often built two rooms thick, so that the air does not circulate from one side to the other. No one seemed to be ill, unless he brought it home with him from some place where he had been visiting. The diseases they used to have were long-lived, such as rheumatism, which may keep a man comfortably in aches and pains forty years. My dear old friend, however, taking them one by one, went through the lot and told me of the ghosts. The forefathers I knew are all gone – the stout man, the lame man, the paralysed man, the gruff old stick: not one left. There is not one left of the old farmers, not a single one. The fathers, too, of our own generation have been dropping away. The strong young man who used to fill us with such astonishment at the feats he would achieve without a thought, no gymnastic training, to whom a sack of wheat was a toy. The strong young man went one day into the harvest-field, as he had done so many times before.

Suddenly he felt a little dizzy. By-and-by he went home and became very ill with sunstroke; he recovered, but he was never strong again; he gradually declined for twelve months, and next harvest-time he was under the daisies. Just one little touch of the sun, and the strength of man faded as a leaf. The hardy dark young man, built of iron, broad, thick, and short, who looked as if frost, snow, and heat were all the same to him, had something go wrong in his lung: one twelvemonth, and there was an end. This was a very unhappy affair. The pickaxe and the spade have made almost a full round to every door; I do not want to think any more about this. Family changes and the pressure of these hard times have driven out most of the rest; some seem to have quite gone out of sight; some have crossed the sea; some have abandoned the land as a livelihood. Of the few, the very few that still remain, still fewer abide in their original homes. Time has shuffled them about from house to house like a pack of cards. Of them all, I verily believe there is but one soul living in the same old house. If the French had landed in the mediaeval way to harry with fire and sword, they could not have swept the place more clean.

Almost the first thing I did with pen and ink as a boy was to draw a map of the hamlet with the roads and lanes and paths, and I think some of the ponds, and with each of the houses marked and the occupier's name. Of course it was very roughly done, and not to any scale, yet it was perfectly accurate and full of detail. I wish I could find it, but the confusion of time has scattered and mixed these early papers. A map by Ptolemy would bear as much resemblance to the same country in a modern atlas as mine to the present state of that locality. It is all gone – rubbed out. The names against the whole of those houses have been altered, one only excepted, and changes have taken place there. Nothing remains. This is not in a century, half a century, or even in a quarter of a century, but in a few ticks of the clock.

I think I have heard that the oaks are down. They may be standing or down, it matters nothing to me; the leaves I last saw upon them are gone for evermore, nor shall I ever see them come there again ruddy in spring. I would not see them again even if I could; they could never look again as they used to do. There are too many memories there. The happiest days become the saddest afterwards; let us never go back, lest we too die. There are no such oaks anywhere else, none so tall and straight, and with such massive heads, on which the sun used to shine as if on the globe of the earth, one side in shadow, the other in bright light. How often I have looked at oaks since, and yet have never been able to get the same effect from them! Like an old author printed in another type, the words are the same, but the sentiment is different. The brooks have ceased to run. There is no music now at the old hatch where we used to sit in danger of our lives, happy as kings, on the narrow bar over the deep water. The barred pike that used to come up in such numbers are no more among the flags. The perch used to drift down the stream, and then bring up again. The sun shone there for a very long time, and the water rippled and sang, and it always seemed to me that I could feel the rippling and the singing and the sparkling back through the centuries. The brook is dead, for when man goes nature ends. I dare say there is water there still, but it is not the brook; the brook is gone like John Brown's soul. There used to be clouds over the fields, white clouds in blue summer skies. I have lived a good deal on clouds; they have been meat to me often; they bring something to the spirit which even the trees do not. I see clouds now sometimes when the iron grip of hell permits for a minute or two; they are very different clouds, and speak differently. I long for some of the old clouds that had no memories. There were nights in those times over those fields, not darkness, but Night, full of glowing suns and glowing richness of life that sprang up to meet them. The nights are there still; they are everywhere, nothing local in the night; but it is not the Night to me seen through the window.

There used to be footpaths. Following one of them, the first field always had a good crop of grass; over the next stile there was a great oak standing alone in the centre of the field, generally a great cart-horse under it, and a few rushes scattered about the furrows; the fourth was always full of the finest clover; in the fifth you could scent the beans on the hill, and there was a hedge like a wood, and a nest of the long-tailed tit; the sixth had a runnel and blue forget-me-nots; the seventh had a brooklet and scattered trees along it; from the eighth you looked back on the slope and saw the thatched houses you had left behind under passing shadows, and rounded white clouds going straight for the distant hills, each cloud visibly bulging and bowed down like a bag. I cannot think how the distant thatched houses came to stand out with such clear definition and etched outline and bluish shadows; and beyond these was the uncertain vale that had no individuality, but the trees put their arms together and became one. All these were meadows, every step was among grass, beautiful grass, and the cuckoos sang as if they had found paradise. A hundred years ago a little old man with silver buckles on his shoes used to walk along this footpath once a week in summer, taking his children over to drink milk at the farm; but though he set them every time to note the number of fields, so busy were they with the nests and the flowers, they could never be sure at the end of the journey whether there were eight or nine. To make quite sure at last, he took with them a pocket full of apples, one of which was eaten in each field, and so they came to know for certain that the number of meadows was either eight or nine, I forget which; and so you see this great experiment did not fix the faith of mankind. Like other great truths, it has grown dim, but it seems strange to think how this little incident could have been borne in mind for a century. There was another footpath that led through the peewit field, where the green plovers for evermore circle round in spring; then past the nightingale field, by the largest maple trees that grew in that country; this too was all grass. Another led along the water to bluebell land; another into the coombs of the hills; all meadows, which was the beauty of it; for though you could find wheat in plenty if you liked, you always walked in grass. All round the compass you could still step on sward. This is rare. Of one other path I have a faded memory, like a silk marker in an old book; in truth, I don't want to remember it except the end of it where it came down to the railway. So full was the mind of romance in those days, that I used to get there specially in time to see the express go up, the magnificent engine of the broad gauge that swept along with such ease and power to London. I wish I could feel like that now. The feeling is not quite gone even now, and I have often since seen these great broad-gauge creatures moving alive to and fro like Ezekiel's wheel dream beside the platforms of Babylon with much of the same old delight. Still I never went back with them to the faded footpath. They are all faded now, these footpaths.

The walnut trees are dead at home. They gave such a thick shade when the fruit was juicy ripe, and the hoods cracked as they fell; they peeled as easy as taking off a glove; the sweetest and nuttiest of fruit. It was delicious to sit there with a great volume of Sir Walter Scott, half in sunshine, half in shade, dreaming of *Kenilworth* and Wayland Smith's cave; only the difficulty was to balance the luxuries, when to peel the walnuts and when to read the book, and how to adjust oneself to perfection so as to get the exact amount of sunshine and shadow. Too much luxury. There was a story, too, told by one Abu-Kaka ibn Ja'is, of the caravan that set forth in 1483 to cross the desert, and being overwhelmed by a sandstorm, lost their way. They wandered for some time till hunger and thirst began to consume them, and then suddenly lit on an oasis unknown to the oldest merchant of Bagdad.

There they found refreshing waters and palms and a caravanserai; and, what was most pleasant, the people at the bazaar and the prince hastened to fill them with hospitality; sheep were killed, and kids were roasted, and all was joy. They were not permitted to depart till they had feasted, when they set out again on their journey, and each at leaving was presented with strings of pearls and bags of rubies, so that at last they came home with all the magnificence of kings. They found, however, that instead of having been absent only a month or two they had been gone twenty years, so swiftly had time sped. As they grew old, and their beards grey, and their frames withered, and the pearls were gone, and the rubies spent, they said, 'We will go back to the city of the oasis.' They set out, each on his camel, one lame, the other paralytic, and the third blind, but still the way was plain, for had they not trodden it before? and they had with them the astrolabe of the astronomer that fixes the track by the stars. Time wore on, and presently the camels' feet brought them nearer and nearer the wished-for spot. One saw the water, and another the palms, but when they came near, it was the mirage, and deep sand covered the place. Then they separated, and each hastened home; but the blind had no leader, and the lame fell from his camel, and the paralytic had no more dates, and their whited bones have disappeared.* Many another tale, too, I read under the trees that are gone like human beings. Sometimes I went forth to the nooks in the deep meadows by the hazel mounds,

* The Arabian commentator thinks this story a myth: the oasis in the desert is the time of youth, which passes so quickly, and is not recognized till it is gone; the pearls and rubies, the joys of love, which make the fortunate lover as a king. In old age every man is afflicted with disease or infirmity, every one is paralytic, lame, or blind. They set out to find a second youth – the dream of immortality – with the astrolabe, which is the creed or Koran all take as their guide. And death separated the company. This is only his pragmatic way; the circumstance is doubtless historic.

and sometimes I parted the ash-tree wands. In my waistcoat pocket I had a little red book, made square; I never read it out of doors, but I always carried it in my pocket till it was frayed and the binding broken; the smallest of red books, but very much therein – the poems and sonnets of Mr William Shakespeare. Some books are alive. The book I have still, it cannot die; the ash copses are cut, and the hazel mounds destroyed.

Was every one, then, so pleasant to me in those days? were the people all so beneficent and kindly that I must needs look back; all welcoming with open hand and open door? No, the reverse; there was not a single one friendly to me. Still that has nothing to do with it; I never thought about them, and I am quite certain they never thought about me. They are all gone, and there is an end. Incompatibility would describe our connection best. Nothing to do with them at all; it was me. I planted myself everywhere – in all the fields and under all the trees. The curious part of it is that though they are all dead, and 'worms have eaten them, but not for love', we continually meet them in other shapes. We say, 'Holloa, here is old So-and-so coming; that is exactly his jaw, that's his Flemish face'; or, 'By Jove, yonder is So-and-so; that's his very walk': one almost expects them to speak as one meets them in the street. There seem to be certain set types which continually crop up again whithersoever you go, and even certain tricks of speech and curves of the head – a set of family portraits walking about the world. It was not the people, neither for good, for evil, nor indifference.

I planted myself everywhere under the trees in the fields and footpaths, by day and by night, and that is why I have never put myself into the charge of the many wheeled creatures that move on the rails and gone back thither, lest I might find the trees look small, and the elms mere switches, and the fields shrunken, and the brooks dry, and no voice anywhere. Nothing but my own ghost to meet me by every hedge. I fear lest I should find myself more dead than all the rest. And verily I wish, could it be without injury to others, that the sand of the desert would rise and roll over and obliterate the place for ever and ever.

I need not wish, for I have been conversing again with learned folk about this place, and they begin to draw my view to certain considerations. These very learned men point out to me a number of objections, for the question they sceptically put is this: are you quite certain that such a village ever existed? In the first place, they say, you have only got one other witness beside yourself, and she is aged, and has defective sight; and really we don't know what to say to accepting such evidence unsupported. Secondly, John Brown cannot be found to bear testimony. Thirdly, there are no ghosts there; that can be demonstrated. It renders a case unsubstantial to introduce these flimsy spirits. Fourthly, the map is lost, and it might be asked was there ever such a map? Fifthly, the people are all gone. Sixthly, no one ever saw any particular sparkle on the brook there, and the clouds appear to be of the same commonplace order that go about everywhere. Seventhly, no one can find these footpaths, which probably led nowhere; and as for the little old man with silver buckles on his shoes, it is a story only fit for some one in his dotage. You can't expect grave and considerate men to take your story as it stands; they must consult the Ordnance Survey and Domesday Book; and the fact is, you have not got the shadow of a foundation on which to carry your case into court. I may resent this, but I cannot deny that the argument is very black against me, and I begin to think that my senses have deceived me. It is as they say. No one else seems to have seen the sparkle on the brook, or heard the music at the hatch, or to have felt back through the centuries; and when I try to describe these things to them they look at me with stolid incredulity. No one seems to understand how I got food from the clouds, nor what there was in the night, nor why it is not so good to look at it out of window. They turn their faces away from me, so that perhaps after all I was mistaken, and there never was any such place or any such meadows, and I was never there. And perhaps in course of time I shall find out also, when I pass away physically, that as a matter of fact there never was any earth.

16 Nature and Eternity

The goldfinches sing so sweetly hidden in the topmost boughs of the apple trees that heart of man cannot withstand them. These four walls, though never so well decorated with pictures, this flat white ceiling, feels all too small, and dull and tame. Down with books and pen, and let us away with the goldfinches, the princes of the birds. For thirty of their generations they have sung and courted and built their nests in those apple trees, almost under the very windows – a time in their chronology equal to a thousand years. For they are so very busy, from earliest morn till night – a long summer's day is like a year. Now flirting with a gaily-decked and coy lady-love, chasing her from tree to tree; now splashing at the edge of a shallow stream till the golden feathers glisten and the red top-knot shines. Then searching in and out the hedgerow for favourite seeds, and singing, singing all the while, verily a 'song without an end'. The wings never still, the bill never idle, the throat never silent, and the tiny heart within the proud breast beating so rapidly that, reckoning time by change and variety, an hour must be a day. A life all joy and freedom, without thought, and full of love. What a great god the sun must be to the finches from whose wings his beams are reflected in glittering gold! The abstract idea of a deity apart, as they feel their life-blood stirring, their eyelids opening, with the rising sun; as they fly to satisfy their hunger with those little fruits they use; as they revel in the warm sunshine, and utter soft notes of love to their beautiful mates, they cannot but feel a sense, unnamed, indefinite, of joyous gratitude towards that great orb which is very nearly akin to the sensual worship of ancient days. Darkness and cold are Typhon and Ahriman, light and warmth, Osiris and Ormuzd, indeed to them; with song they welcome the spring and celebrate the awakening of Adonis. Lovely little idolaters, my heart goes with them. Deep down in the mysteries of organic life there are causes for the marvellously extended grasp which the worship of light once held upon the world, hardly yet guessed at, and which even now play a part unsuspected in the motives of men. Even yet, despite our artificial life, despite railroads, telegraphs, printing-press, in the face of firm monotheistic convictions, once a year the old, old influence breaks forth, driving thousands and thousands from cities and houses out into field and forest, to the seashore and mountain-top, to gather fresh health and strength from the Sun, from the Air-Jove and old Ocean. So the goldfinches rejoice in the sunshine, and who can sit indoors when they sing?

Foolish fashion has banished the orchard from the mansion – the orchard which Homer tells us kings once valued as part of their demesne – and has substituted curious evergreens to which the birds do not take readily. But this orchard is almost under the windows, and in summer the finches wake the sleeper with their song, and in autumn the eye looks down upon the yellow and rosy fruit. Up the scaling bark of the trunks the brown tree-climbers run, peering into every cranny, and few are the insects which escape those keen eyes. Sitting on a bench under a pear tree, I saw a spider drop from a leaf fully nine feet above the ground, and disappear in the grass, leaving a slender rope of web, attached at the upper end to a leaf, and at the lower to a fallen pear. In a few minutes a small white caterpillar, barely an inch long, began to climb this rope. It grasped the thread in the mouth and drew up its body about a sixteenth of an inch at a time, then held tight with the two fore-feet, and, lifting its head, seized the rope a sixteenth higher; repeating this operation incessantly, the rest of the body swinging in the air. Never pausing, without haste and without rest, this creature patiently worked its way upwards, as a man might up a rope. Let anyone seize a beam overhead and attempt to lift the chest up to a level with it, the expenditure of strength is very great; even with long practice, to 'swarm' up a pole or rope to any distance is the hardest labour the human muscles are capable of. This despised 'creeping' thing, without the slightest apparent effort, without once pausing to take breath, reached the leaf overhead in rather under half an hour, having climbed a rope fully 108 times its own length. To equal this a man must climb 648 feet, or more than half as high again as St Paul's. The insect on reaching the top at once began feeding, and easily bit through the hard pear-leaf: how delicately then it must have grasped the slender spider's web, which a touch would destroy! The thoughts which this feat call forth do not end here, for there was no necessity to go up the thread; the insect could to all appearance have travelled up the trunk of the tree with ease, and it is not to be supposed that its mouth and feet were specially adapted to climb a web, a thing which I have never seen done since, and which was to all appearance merely the result of the *accident* of the insect coming along just after the spider had left the thread. Another few minutes, and the first puff of wind would have carried the thread away – as a puff actually did soon afterwards. I claim a wonderful amount of *original* intelligence – as opposed to the ill-used term, instinct – of patience and perseverance for this creature. It is so easy to imagine that because man is big, brain power cannot exist in tiny organizations; but even in man the seat of thought is so minute that it escapes discovery, and his very life may be said to lie in the point of contact of two bones of the neck. Put the mind of man within the body of a caterpillar – what more could it have done? Accustomed to bite and eat its way through hard leaves, why did not the insect snip off and destroy its rope? These are matters to think over dreamily while the finches sing overhead in the apple tree.

They are not the only regular inhabitants, still less the only visitors. As there are wide plains even in thickly populated England where man has built no populous city, so in birdlife there are fields and weeds almost deserted by the songsters, who at the same time congregate thickly in a few favourite resorts, where experience gathered in slow time has shown them they need fear nothing from human beings. Such a place, such a city of the birds and beasts, is this old orchard. The bold and handsome bullfinch builds in the low hawthorn hedge which bounds it upon one side. In the walls of the arbour formed of thick ivy and flowering creepers, the robin and thrush hide their nests. On the topmost branches of the tall pear trees the swallows rest and twitter. The noble blackbird, with full black eye, pecks at the decaying apples upon the sward, and takes no heed of a footstep. Sometimes the loving pair of squirrels who dwell in the fir-copse at the end of the meadow find their way down the hedges – staying at each tree as an inn by the road – into the orchard, and play their fantastic tricks upon the apple-boughs. The flycatchers perch on a branch clear from the tree, and dart at the passing flies. Merriest of all, the tomtits chatter and scold, hanging under the twigs, head downwards, and then away to their nest in the crumbling stone wall which encloses one side of the orchard. They have worked their way by a cranny deep into the thick wall. On the other side runs the king's highway, and ever and anon the teams go by, making music with their bells. One day a whole nation of martins savagely attacked this wall. Pressure of population probably had compelled them to emigrate from the sand quarry, and the chinks in the wall pleased their eyes. Five-and-thirty brown little birds went to work like miners at twelve or fourteen holes, tapping at the mortar with their bills, scratching out small fragments of stone, twittering and talking all the time, and there undoubtedly they would have founded a colony had not the jingling teams and now and then a barking dog disturbed them. Resting on the bench and leaning back against an apple tree, it is easy to watch the eager starlings on the chimney-top, and see them tear out the straw of the thatch to form their holes. They are all orators born. They live in a democracy, and fluency of speech leads the populace. Perched on the top of the chimney, his bronze-tinted wings flapping against his side to give greater emphasis – as a preacher moves his hands – the starling pours forth a flood of eloquence, now rising to screaming-pitch, now modulating his tones to soft persuasion, now descending to deep, low, complaining, regretful sounds – a speech without words – addressed to a dozen birds gravely listening on the ash tree yonder. He is begging them to come with him to a meadow where food is abundant. In the ivy close under the window there, within reach of the hand, a water-wagtail built its nest. To this nest one lovely afternoon came a great bird like a hawk, to the fearful alarm and intense excitement of all the bird population. It was a cuckoo, and after three or four visits, despite a curious eye at the window, there was a strange egg in that nest. Inside that window, huddled fearfully in the darkest corner of the room, there was once a tiny heap of blue and yellow feathers. A tomtit straying through the casement had been chased by the cat until it dropped exhausted, and the cat was fortunately frightened by a footstep. The bird was all but dead – the feathers awry and ruffled, the eyelids closed, the body limp and helpless – only a faint fluttering of the tiny heart. When placed tenderly on the ledge of the casement, where the warm sunshine fell and the breeze came softly, it dropped listlessly on one side. But in a little while the life-giving rays quickened the blood, the eyelids opened, and presently it could stand perched upon the finger. Then, lest with returning consciousness fear should again arise, the clinging claws were transferred from the finger to a twig of wall-pear. A few minutes more, and with a chirp the bird was gone into the flood of sunlight. What intense joy there must have been in that little creature's heart as it drank the sweet air and felt the loving warmth of its great god Ra, the Sun!

Throwing open the little wicket-gate, by a step the greensward of the meadow is reached. Though the grass has been mown and the ground is dry, it is better to carry a thick rug, and cast it down in the shadow under the tall chestnut tree. It is only while in a dreamy, slumbrous, half-mesmerized state that nature's ancient papyrus roll can be read – only when the mind is at rest, separated from care and labour; when the body is at ease, luxuriating in warmth and delicious languor; when the soul is in accord and sympathy with the sunlight, with the leaf, with the slender blades of grass, and can feel with the tiniest insect which climbs up them as up a mighty tree. As the genius of the great musicians, without an articulated word or printed letter, can carry with it all the emotions, so now, lying prone upon the earth in the shadow, with quiescent will, listening, thoughts and feelings rise respondent to the sunbeams, to the leaf, the very blade of grass. Resting the head upon the hand, gazing down upon the ground, the strange and marvellous inner sight of the mind penetrates the solid earth, grasps in part the mystery of its vast extension upon either side, bearing its majestic mountains, its deep forests, its grand oceans, and almost feels the life which in ten thousand thousand forms revels upon its surface. Returning upon itself, the mind joys in the knowledge that it too is a part of this wonder – akin to the ten thousand thousand creatures, akin to the very earth itself. How grand and holy is this life! how sacred the temple which contains it!

Out from the hedge, not five yards distant, pours a rush of deep luscious notes, succeeded by the sweetest trills heard by man. It is the nightingale, which tradition assigns to the night only, but which in fact sings as loudly, and to my ear more joyously, in the full sunlight, especially in the morning, and always close to the nest. The sun has moved onward upon his journey, and this spot is no longer completely shaded, but the foliage of a great oak breaks the force of his rays, and the eye can even bear to gaze at his disc for a few moments. Living for this brief hour at least in unalloyed sympathy with nature, apart from all disturbing influences, the sight of that splendid disc carries the soul with it till it feels as eternal as the sun. Let the memory call up a picture of the desert sands of Egypt – upon the kings with the double crown, upon Rameses, upon Sesostris, upon Assurbanipal the burning beams of this very sun descended, filling their veins with tumultuous life, three thousand years ago. Lifted up in absorbing thought, the mind feels that these three thousand years are in truth no longer past than the last beat of the pulse. It throbbed – the throb is gone; their pulse throbbed, and it seems but a moment since, for to thought, as to the sun, there is no time. This little petty life of seventy years, with its little petty aims and hopes, its despicable fears and contemptible sorrows, is no more the life with which the mind is occupied. This golden disc has risen and set, as the graven marks of man alone record, full eight thousand years. The hieroglyphs of the rocks speak of a fiery sun shining inconceivable ages before that. Yet even this almost immortal sun had a beginning – perhaps emerging as a ball of incandescent gas from chaos: how long ago was that? And onwards, still onwards goes the disc, doubtless for ages and ages to come. It is time that our measures should be extended; these paltry divisions of hours and days and years – aye, of centuries – should be superseded by terms conveying some faint idea at least of the vastness of space. For in truth, when thinking thus, there is no *time* at all. The mind loses the sense of time and reposes in eternity. This hour, this instant, is eternity; it extends backwards, it extends forwards, and we are in it. It is a grand and an ennobling feeling to know that at this moment illimitable time extends on either hand. No conception formed in the brain has ever or will ever surpass the mystery of this endless existence as exemplified – as made manifest by the physical sun – a visible sign of immortality. This – this hour is part of the immortal life. Reclining upon this rug under the chestnut tree, while the grateful shadows dance, a passing bee hums and the nightingale sings, while the oak foliage sprinkles the sunshine over us, we are really and in truth in the midst of eternity. Only by walking hand in hand with nature, only by a reverent and loving study of the mysteries for ever around us, is it possible to disabuse the mind of the narrow view, the contracted belief that time is now and eternity to-morrow. Eternity is to-day. The goldfinches and the tiny caterpillars, the brilliant sun, if looked at lovingly and thoughtfully, will lift the soul out of the smaller life of human care that is of selfish aims, bounded by seventy years, into the greater, the limitless life which has been going on over universal space from endless ages past, which is going on now, and which will for ever and for ever, in one form or another, continue to proceed.

Dreamily listening to the nightingale's song, let us look down upon the earth as the sun looks down upon it. In this meadow how many millions of blades of grass are there, each performing wonderful operations which the cleverest chemist can but poorly indicate, taking up from the earth its sap, from the air its gases, in a word living, living as much as ourselves, though in a lower form? On the oak tree yonder, how many leaves are doing the same? Just now we felt the vastness of the earth – its extended majesty, bearing mountain, forest and sea. Not a blade of grass but has its insect, not a leaf; the very air as it softly woos the cheek bears with it living germs, and upon all these mountains, within those forests, and in every drop of those oceans, life in some shape moves and stirs. Nay, the very solid earth itself, the very chalk and clay and stone and rock has been built up by once living organisms. But at this instant, looking down upon the earth as the sun does, how can words depict the glowing wonder, the marvellous beauty of all the plant, the insect, the animal life, which presses upon the mental eye? It is impossible. But with these that are more immediately around us – with the goldfinch, the caterpillar, the nightingale, the blades of grass, the leaves – with these we may feel, into their life we may in part enter, and find our own existence thereby enlarged. Would that it were possible for the heart and mind to enter into *all* the life that glows and teems upon the earth – to feel with it, hope with it – and thereby to become a grander, nobler being. Such a being, with such a sympathy and larger existence, must hold in scorn the feeble, cowardly, selfish desire for an immortality of pleasure only, whose one great hope is to escape pain. No. Let me joy with all living creatures; let me suffer with them all – the reward of feeling a deeper, grander life would be amply sufficient.

What wonderful patience the creatures called 'lower' exhibit! Watch this small red ant travelling among the grass-blades. To it they are as high as the oak trees to us, and they are entangled and matted together as a forest overthrown by a tornado. The insect overcomes all the difficulties of its route – now climbing over the creeping roots of the buttercups, now struggling under a fallen leaf, now getting up a bennet, up and down, making one inch forward for three vertically, but never pausing, always onwards at racing speed. A shadow sweeps rapidly over the grass – it is that of a rook which has flown between us and the sun. Looking upwards into the deep azure of the sky, intently gazing into space and forgetting for a while the life around and beneath, there comes into the mind an intense desire to rise, to penetrate the height, to become part and parcel of that wondrous infinity which extends overhead as it extends along the surface. The soul full of thought grows concentrated in itself, marvels only at its own destiny, labours to behold the secret of its own existence, and, above all, utters without articulate words a prayer forced from it by the bright sun, by the blue sky, by bird and plant: Let me have wider feelings, more extended sympathies, let me feel with all living things, rejoice and praise with them. Let me have deeper knowledge, a nearer insight, a more reverent conception. Let me see the mystery of life – the secret of the sap as it rises in the tree – the secret of the blood as it courses through the vein. Reveal the broad earth and the ends of it – make the majestic ocean open to the eye down to its utmost recesses. Expand the mind till it grasps the idea of the unseen forces which hold the globe suspended and draw the vast suns and stars through space. Let it see the life, the organisms which dwell in those great worlds, and feel with them their hopes and joys and sorrows. Ever upwards, onwards, wider, deeper, broader, till capable of all – all. Never did vivid imagination stretch out the powers of deity with such a fulness, with such intellectual grasp, vigour, omniscience as the human mind could reach to, if only its organs, its means, were equal to its thought. Give us, then, greater strength of body, greater length of days; give us more vital energy, let our limbs be mighty as those of the giants of old. Supplement such organs with nobler mechanical engines – with extended means of locomotion; add novel and more minute methods of analysis and discovery. Whoso gave the gift of the mind gave also an infinite space, an infinite matter for it to work upon, an infinite time in which to work. Let no one presume to define the boundaries of that divine gift – that mind – for all the experience of eight thousand years proves beyond a question that the limits of its powers will never be reached, though the human race dwell upon the globe for eternity. Up, then, and labour: and let that labour be sound and holy. Not for immediate and petty reward, not that the appetite or the vanity may be gratified, but that the sum of human perfection may be advanced; labouring as consecrated priests, for true science is religion. All is possible. A grand future awaits the world. When man has only partially worked out his own conception – when only a portion of what the mind foresees and plans is realized – then already earth will be as a paradise.

Full of love and sympathy for this feeble ant climbing over grass and leaf, for yonder nightingale pouring forth its song, feeling a community with the finches, with bird, with plant, with animal, and reverently studying all these and more – how is it possible for the heart while thus wrapped up to conceive the desire of crime? For ever anxious and labouring for perfection, shall the soul, convinced of the divinity of its work, halt and turn aside to fall into imperfection? Lying thus upon the rug under the shadow of the oak and horse-chestnut tree, full of the joy of life – full of the joy which all organisms feel in living alone – lifting the eye far, far above the sphere even of the sun, shall we ever conceive the idea of murder, of violence, of aught that degrades ourselves? It is impossible while in this frame. So thus reclining, and thus occupied, we require no judge, no prison, no law, no punishment – and, further, no army, no monarch. At this moment, did neither of these institutions exist our conduct would be the same. Our whole existence at this moment is permeated with a reverent love, an aspiration – a desire of a more perfect life. It is but a simple transition to conclude that with more extended knowledge, with wider sympathies, with greater powers – powers more equal to the vague longings of their minds, the human race would be as we are at this moment in the shadow of the chestnut tree. No need of priest and lawyer; no need for armies or kings. It is probable that with the progress of knowledge it will be possible to satisfy the necessary wants of existence much more easily than now, and thus to remove one great cause of discord. And all these thoughts because the passing shadow of a rook caused the eye to gaze upwards into the deep azure of the sky. There is no limit, no number to the thoughts which the study of nature may call forth, any more than there is a limit to the number of the rays of the sun.

This blade of grass grows as high as it can, the nightingale there sings as sweetly as it can, the goldfinches feed to their full desire and lay down no arbitrary rules of life; the great sun above pours out its heat and light in a flood unrestrained. What is the meaning of this hieroglyph, which is repeated in a thousand thousand other ways and shapes, which meets us at every turn? It is evident that all living creatures, from the zoophyte upwards, plant, reptile, bird, animal, and in his natural state – in his physical frame – man also, strive with all their powers to obtain as perfect an existence as possible. It is the one great law of their being, followed from birth to death. All the efforts of the plant are put forth to obtain more light, more air, more moisture – in a word, more food – upon which to grow, expand, and become more beautiful and perfect. The aim may be unconscious, but the result is evident. It is equally so with the animal; its lowest appetites subserve the one grand object of its advance. Whether it be eating, drinking, sleeping, procreating, all tends to one end, a fuller development of the individual, a higher condition of the species; still further, to the production of new races capable of additional progress. Part and parcel as we are of the great community of living beings, indissolubly connected with them from the lowest to the highest by a thousand ties, it is impossible for us to escape from the operation of this law; or if, by the exertion of the will, and the resources of the intellect, it is partially suspended, then the individual may perhaps pass away unharmed, but the race must suffer. It is, rather, the province of that inestimable gift, the mind, to aid nature, to smooth away the difficulties, to assist both the mental and the physical man to increase his powers and widen his influence. Such efforts have been made from time to time, but unfortunately upon purely empirical principles, by arbitrary interference, without a long previous study of the delicate organization it was proposed to amend. If there is one thing our latter-day students have demonstrated beyond all reach of cavil, it is that both the physical and the mental man are, as it were, a mass of inherited structures – are built up of partially absorbed rudimentary organs and primitive conceptions, much as the trunks of certain trees are formed by the absorption of the leaves. He is made up of the Past. This is a happy and inspiriting discovery, insomuch as it holds out a resplendent promise that there may yet come a man of the future made out of our present which will then be the past. It is a discovery which calls upon us for new and larger moral and physical exertion, which throws upon us wider and nobler duties, for upon us depends the future. At one blow this new light casts aside those melancholy convictions which, judging from the evil blood which seemed to stain each new generation alike, had elevated into a faith the depressing idea that man could not advance. It explains the causes of that stain, the reason of those imperfections, not necessary parts of the ideal man, but inherited from a lower order of life, and to be gradually expunged.

But this marvellous mystery of inheritance has brought with it a series of mental instincts, so to say; a whole circle of ideas of moral conceptions, in a sense belonging to the Past – ideas which were high and noble in the rudimentary being, which were beyond the capacity of the pure animal, but which are now in great part, merely obstructions to advancement. Let these perish. We must seek for enlightenment and for progress, not in the dim failing traditions of a period but just removed from the time of the rudimentary or primeval man – we must no longer allow the hoary age of such traditions to blind the eye and cause the knee to bend – we must no longer stultify the mind by compelling it to receive as infallible what in the very nature of things must have been fallible to the highest degree. The very plants are wiser far. They seek the light of to-day, the heat of the sun which shines at this hour; they make no attempt to guide their life by the feeble reflection of rays which were extinguished ages ago. This slender blade of grass, beside the edge of our rug under the chestnut tree, shoots upwards in the fresh air of to-day; its roots draw nourishment from the moisture of the dew which heaven deposited this morning. If it does make use of the past – of the soil, the earth that has accumulated in centuries – it is to advance its present growth. Root out at once and for ever these primeval, narrow, and contracted ideas; fix the mind upon the sun of the present, and prepare for the sun that must rise to-morrow. It is our duty to develop both mind and body and soul to the utmost: as it is the duty of this blade of grass and this oak tree to grow and expand as far as their powers will admit. But the blade of grass and the oak have this great disadvantage to work against – they can only labour in the lines laid down for them, and unconsciously; while man can think, foresee, and plan. The greatest obstacle to progress is the lack now beginning to be felt all over the world, but more especially in the countries most highly civilized, of a true ideal to work up to. It is necessary that some far-seeing master-mind, some giant intellect, should arise, and sketch out in bold, unmistakable outlines the grand and noble future which the human race should labour for. There have been weak attempts – there are contemptible makeshifts now on their trial, especially in the new world – but the whole of these, without exception, are simply diluted reproductions of systems long since worn out. These can only last a little while; if anything, they are worse than the prejudices and traditions which form the body of wider-spread creeds. The world cries out for an intellect which shall draw its inspiration from the unvarying and infallible laws regulating the universe; which shall found its faith upon the teaching of grass, of leaf, of bird, of beast, of hoary rock, great ocean, star and sun; which shall afford full room for the development of muscle, sense, and above all of the wondrous brain; and which without fettering the individual shall secure the ultimate apotheosis of the race. No such system can spring at once, complete, perfect in detail, from any one mind. But assuredly, when once a firm basis has been laid down, when an outline has been drawn, the converging efforts of a thousand thousand thinkers will be brought to bear upon it, and it will be elaborated into something approaching a reliable guide. The faiths of the past, of the ancient world, now extinct or feebly lingering on, were each inspired by one mind only. The faith of the future, in strong contrast, will spring from the researches of a thousand thousand thinkers, whose minds, once brought into a focus, will speedily burn up all that is useless and worn out with a fierce heat, and evoke a new and brilliant light. This converging thought is one of the greatest blessings of our day made possible by the vastly extended means of communication, and almost seems specially destined for this very purpose. Thought increases with the ages. At this moment there are probably as many busy brains studying, reflecting, collecting scattered truths, as there were thinkers – effectual thinkers – in all the recorded eighty centuries gone by. Daily and hourly the noble army swells its numbers, and the sound of its mighty march grows louder; the inscribed roll of its victories fills the heart with exultation.

There is a slight rustle among the bushes and the fern upon the mound. It is a rabbit who has peeped forth into the sunshine. His eye opens wide with wonder at the sight of us; his nostrils work nervously as he watches us narrowly. But in a little while the silence and stillness reassure him; he nibbles in a desultory way at the stray grasses on the mound, and finally ventures out into the meadow almost within reach of the hand. It is so easy to make the acquaintance – to make friends with the children of Nature. From the tiniest insect upwards they are ready to dwell in sympathy with us – only be tender, quiet, considerate, in a word, *gentlemanly*, towards them and they will freely wander around. And they have all such marvellous tales to tell – intricate problems to solve for us. This common wild rabbit has an ancestry of almost unsearchable antiquity. Within that little body there are organs and structures which, rightly studied, will throw a light upon the mysteries hidden in our own frames. It is a peculiarity of this search that nothing is despicable; nothing can be passed over – not so much as a fallen leaf, or a grain of sand. Literally everything bears stamped upon it characters in the hieratic, the sacred hand-writing, not one word of which shall fall to the ground.

Sitting indoors, with every modern luxury around, rich carpets, artistic furniture, pictures, statuary, food and drink brought from the uttermost ends of the earth, with the telegraph, the printing-press, the railway at immediate command, it is easy to say, 'What have I to do with all this? I am neither an animal nor a plant, and the sun is nothing to me. This is *my* life which I have created: I am apart from the other inhabitants of the earth.' But go to the window. See – there is but a thin, transparent sheet of brittle glass between the artificial man and the air, the light, the trees, and grass. So between him and the other innumerable organisms which live and breathe there is but a thin feeble crust of prejudice and social custom. Between him and those irresistible laws which keep the sun upon its course there is absolutely no bar whatever. Without air he cannot live. Nature cannot be escaped. Then face the facts, and having done so, there will speedily arise a calm pleasure beckoning onwards.

The shadows of the oak and chestnut tree no longer shelter our rug; the beams of the noon-day sun fall vertically on us; we will leave the spot for a while. The nightingale and the goldfinches, the thrushes and blackbirds, are silent for a time in the sultry heat. But they only wait for evening to burst forth in one exquisite chorus, praising this wondrous life and the beauties of the earth.

Bibliography

Chief Works of Richard Jefferies:

The Scarlet Shawl, A Novel, 1874
Restless Human Hearts, A Novel, 1875
World's End: A Story in Three Books, 1877
The Gamekeeper at Home: Or, Sketches of Natural History and Rural Life, 1878. Illustrated Edition by Charles Whymper, 1880
Wild Life in a Southern County, 1879
The Amateur Poacher, 1879
Greene Ferne Farm, 1880
Hodge and His Masters, 1880
Round About a Great Estate, 1880
Wood Magic, A Fable, 1881
Bevis: the Story of a Boy, 1882
Nature near London, 1883
The Story of My Heart: My Autobiography, 1883
Red Deer, 1884
The Life of the Fields, 1884
The Dewy Morn, A Novel, 1884
After London: Or, Wild England, 1885
The Open Air, 1885
Amaryllis at the Fair, A Novel, 1887

Published posthumously:

Field and Hedgerow: being the Last Essays of Richard Jefferies, collected by his widow, 1889

The Toilers of the Field, 1892

The Hills and the Vale, with an introduction by Edward Thomas, 1909

The Nature Diaries and Note-Books of Richard Jefferies, edited with an introduction and notes by Samuel J. Looker, 1948

Chief books and articles relating to Richard Jefferies:

The Eulogy of Richard Jefferies, Sir Walter Besant, Chatto and Windus, 1888

Nature in Books: Some Studies in Biography, P. Anderson Graham, Methuen and Co., 1891

Richard Jefferies: a Study, H. S. Salt, Swan Sonnenschein and Co., 1894

Richard Jefferies: his Life and Work, Edward Thomas, Hutchinson and Co., 1909; Aldine Library Edition, J. M. Dent and Sons Ltd., 1938; Faber and Faber, 1978

Richard Jefferies, T. Reginald Arkell, Rich and Cowan, 1933

Richard Jefferies, Selections of his work, with details of his life and circumstance, his death and immortality, Henry Williamson, Faber and Faber, 1937

Lives and Works of Richard Jefferies, by Q. D. Leavis, Scrutiny, March 1938

Richard Jefferies: A Critical Study, W. J. Keith, Oxford University Press/University of Toronto Press, 1965

References also in:

Nature in Downland, W. H. Hudson, J. M. Dent and Sons Ltd., 1900

Portrait of Wiltshire, Pamela Street, Robert Hale, 1971

Thomas Hardy and Rural England, Merryn Williams, Macmillan, 1972

The Oldest Road, An Exploration of the Ridgeway, text by J. R. L. Anderson, photography by Fay Godwin, Wildwood House, 1975